ravis, aren't you g *ommy good-night, too?"*

tle Mandy looked innocently from him to her ther.

Elizabeth started, and her big brown eyes got even bigger as Travis slowly approached her bed. "Look," she muttered, "you don't have to—"

"Mommy, you need to be kissed good-night," Mandy insisted. "It'll make you feel better. Travis made me feel better when he gave me a kiss."

"Purely medicinal," Travis agreed.

"Medicinal?" Mandy struggled with the word.

Travis didn't take his gaze off Elizabeth's face. Color rose steadily in her cheeks. "It means doing something for healing purposes," he explained. "Like taking medicine."

He rested his hands on Elizabeth's shoulders. Her sweet breath fanned his face. His stomach tightened in anticipation.

"And," he drawled, "I do my best work under pressure."

Dear Reader,

Welcome to Silhouette **Special Edition**...welcome to romance. Our New Year's resolution is to continue bringing you romantic, emotional stories you'll be sure to love!

And this month we're sure fulfilling that promise as Marie Ferrarella returns with our THAT SPECIAL WOMAN! title for January, *Husband: Some Assembly Required*. Dr. Shawna Saunders has trouble resisting the irresistible charms of Murphy Pendleton!

THIS TIME, FOREVER, a wonderful new series by Andrea Edwards, begins this month with *A Ring and a Promise*. Jake O'Neill and Kate O'Malley don't believe in destiny, until a legend of ancestral passion pledged with a ring and an unfulfilled promise show them the way.

Also in January, Susan Mallery introduces the first of her two HOMETOWN HEARTBREAKERS. Was sexy Sheriff Travis Haynes the town lady-killer—or a knight in shining armor? Elizabeth Abbott finds out in *The Best Bride*. Diana Whitney brings you *The Adventurer*—the first book in THE BLACKTHORN BROTHERHOOD. Don't miss Devon Monroe's story—and his secret.

The wonders of love in 1995 continue as opposites attract in Elizabeth Lane's *Wild Wings, Wild Heart*, and Beth Henderson's *New Year's Eve* keeps the holiday spirit going.

Hope this New Year shapes up to be the best ever! Enjoy this book and all the books to come!

Sincerely,

Tara Gavin
Senior Editor

Please address questions and book requests to:
Silhouette Reader Service
U.S.: 3010 Walden Ave., P.O. Box 1325, Buffalo, NY 14269
Canadian: P.O. Box 609, Fort Erie, Ont. L2A 5X3

SUSAN MALLERY
THE BEST BRIDE

Silhouette®

SPECIAL EDITION®

Published by Silhouette Books
America's Publisher of Contemporary Romance

To my editor, Karen Taylor Richman, for believing in me
and encouraging me, for seeing the vision in my stories and
helping me achieve that vision, for being kind and generous,
and wonderful to work with. You have my respect, my
friendship and my thanks. You're the best.

 SILHOUETTE BOOKS

ISBN 0-373-09933-9

THE BEST BRIDE

Printed in U.S.A.

Books by Susan Mallery

Silhouette Special Edition

Tender Loving Care #717
More Than Friends #802
A Dad for Billie #834
Cowboy Daddy #898
*The Best Bride #933

*Hometown Heartbreakers

Silhouette Intimate Moments

Tempting Faith #554

SUSAN MALLERY

has always been an incurable romantic. Growing up, she spent long hours weaving complicated fantasies about dashing heroes and witty heroines. She was shocked to discover not everyone carried around this sort of magical world. Taking a chance, she gave up a promising career in accounting to devote herself to writing full-time. She lives in Texas with her husband—"the most wonderful man in the world. You can ask my critique group." Susan also writes historical romances under the name Susan Macias. She loves to hear from readers, and you can write to her at P.O. Box 1828, Sugar Land, TX 77487.

Travis's Bachelor Chili
(As created by Louise)

1 15 oz can kidney beans
2 15 oz cans pinto beans
1 15 oz can corn
1 large onion, diced
1 large green pepper, diced
1 lb lean ground beef or turkey, cooked and drained
2 $14\frac{1}{2}$ oz cans stewed tomatoes
1 cup water
1 cup spicy tomato salsa
1 tsp cumin
4 cups cooked white or brown rice

Drain canned beans and corn. Combine all ingredients—
except for rice—in a large pot. Bring to a boil over high
heat, then simmer for 15 minutes. Serve over rice.

Great for football Sundays, and even better the second
day for lunch!

Chapter One

The white T-bird fishtailed around the corner. It sprayed dirt and gravel up onto the left front of the patrol car parked on the side of the road.

Sheriff Travis Haynes turned the key to start the engine, then flipped on the blue lights. As he pulled out onto the highway, he debated whether or not to use the siren, then decided against it. He was about to mess up someone's long weekend by giving him a ticket; no point in adding insult to injury by using the siren. The good citizens of Glenwood had contributed enough money to buy a car equipped with a siren that could wake the dead. But that didn't necessarily mean they wanted him to use it on *them*.

He stepped on the gas until he was behind the white car, then checked his speed. He gave a low whistle and looked at the car ahead. He could see a mass of brown hair through the rear window, but little else. The lady was going somewhere in a hurry. He followed behind and waited.

It took her another two minutes to notice him. She glanced in her mirror, saw the flashing lights, did a double take, then immediately put on her blinker and pulled to the side of the road. Travis slowed and parked behind her. He shut off the engine, reached for his Stetson and ticket book, then got out and walked leisurely toward the car. His cowboy boots crunched on the gravel. He noticed the California license plate tags were current.

"Afternoon," he said, when he walked up to the open window. He glanced down at the woman and got a brief impression of big brown eyes in a heart-shaped face. She looked a little pale under her tan. A lot of people were nervous when they were stopped by an officer. He gave her a friendly smile. "You were going pretty fast there."

"I—I know," she said, softly, averting her gaze and staring out the front window. "I'm sorry."

She gripped the steering wheel tightly. He looked past her to the young girl in the passenger seat. The child looked more frightened than her mother. She clutched a worn brown teddy bear to her chest and stared at him with wide blue eyes. Her mouth trembled as if she were fighting tears. About five or six, he thought, giving her a quick wink.

Travis returned his attention to the woman. She wore her hair pulled up in a ponytail on top of her head. The ends fell back almost to her shoulders. It was a warm September afternoon. She was dressed in a red tank top and white shorts. He tried not to notice her legs. "I'm going to need to see your driver's license and registration, ma'am," he said politely.

"What? Oh, of course."

She bent over to grab her purse from the floor on the passenger's side. He thought he heard a gasp, as if she were in pain, but before he could be sure, she fumbled with her wallet and pulled out the small identification. As she handed it to him, it slipped out of her fingers and fluttered toward the ground. He caught it before it touched the dirt.

"I'm sorry," she murmured. Her mouth pulled into a straight line and dark emotion flickered in her eyes.

Immediately his instincts went on alert. Something wasn't right. She was too scared or too upset for someone getting a ticket. He glanced down at the license. Elizabeth Abbott. Age twenty-eight. Five-six. The address listed her as living in Los Angeles.

"You're a long way from home," he said, looking from her to the license and back.

"We just moved here," she said.

He took the registration next and saw the car was in her name.

"So what's the story?" he asked, flipping open his ticket book.

"Excuse me?"

"Why were you speeding?"

Her eyebrows drew together. "I don't understand."

"You're in Glenwood, ma'am, and we have a tradition here. If you can tell me a story I haven't heard before, I have to let you go."

Her mouth curved up slightly. It made her look pretty. He had a feeling she would be hell on wheels if she let go enough to really smile. "You're kidding?"

"No, ma'am." He adjusted his Stetson.

"Have you *ever* let anyone go?"

He thought for a minute, then grinned. "I stopped Miss Murietta several years ago. She was hurrying home to watch the last episode of *Dallas* on TV."

"And you let her off the hook?"

He shrugged. "I hadn't heard that excuse before. So what's yours? I've been in the sheriff's department almost twelve years, so it'll have to be good."

Elizabeth Abbott stared up at him and started to laugh. She stopped suddenly, drew in a deep breath and seemed to fall toward the steering wheel. She caught herself and clutched her midsection.

"Mommy?" The little girl beside her sounded frantic. "Mommy?"

"I'm fine," Elizabeth said, glancing at her.

But Travis could see she wasn't fine. He realized the look in her eyes wasn't fear, it was pain. He saw it in the lines around her mouth and the way she paled even more under her tan.

"What's wrong?" he asked, stuffing his ticket book into his back pocket.

"Nothing," she said. "Just a stomachache. It won't go away. I was going to a walk-in clinic to see if they could—" She gasped and nearly doubled over. The seat belt held her in place.

Travis opened the car door and crouched beside her. "You pregnant?" he asked. He reached for her wrist and found her pulse. It was rapid. Her skin felt cold and clammy to the touch.

"No, why?"

"Miscarriage."

"I'm not pregnant." She leaned her head back against the seat rest. "Give me a minute. I'll be fine."

Her daughter stared up at her. He could see the worry and the fear in her blue eyes and his heart went out to the little girl.

"Mommy, don't be sick."

"I'm fine." She touched her child's cheek.

Travis leaned in and unlatched the seat belt.

"What are you doing?" Elizabeth asked.

"Taking you to the hospital."

"That's not necessary. Really, I'll just drive to the clinic and—" She drew in a deep breath and held it. Her eyes closed and her jaw tightened.

"That's it," he said, reaching one arm under her legs, the other behind her back. Before she could protest, he slid her out and carried her toward his car.

She clung to him and shivered. "I don't mean to be any trouble."

"No trouble. Part of the job."

"You carry a lot of women in your line of work?"

Her muscles felt tight and perspiration clung to her forehead and upper lip. She must be in a lot of pain, but she was trying to keep it all together. He winked. "It's been a good week for me."

When they reached his car, Travis lowered her feet to the ground and opened the door to the back seat. He started to pick her up again, but she shook her head and bent over to slide in. He returned to the lady's car and slipped into the driver's seat. The little girl was hunched against the door, staring at him. Tears rolled down her face.

"What's your name, honey?" he asked softly.

"Mandy."

"How old are you?"

She hiccuped and clutched the bear to her chest. "Six."

"I'm going to take your mom to the hospital, and they're going to make her feel better. I'd like you come with me. Okay?"

She nodded slowly.

He gave her his best smile, then collected Elizabeth's purse. After shoving her keys, license and registration into his pocket, he unhooked Mandy's seat belt and helped her out of the car. He rolled up the windows and locked the doors, then led her to the sheriff's vehicle.

Her tears stopped momentarily as she stared at the array of switches and listened to the crackling of the radio. "You ever been inside a patrol car before?" he asked.

She shook her head.

"You'll like it. I promise." That earned him a sniff. He settled her quickly beside him, then glanced back at Elizabeth. She lay across the seat, her knees pulled up to her chest, breathing rapidly.

"How you doing?" he asked.

"Hanging in there," she said, her voice tight with strain.

"I'm going to use the siren," he said, starting the engine and switching it on. Instantly a piercing wail filled the car. Travis checked his mirror, then pulled out onto the road.

Traffic was light and they were at the hospital in less than fifteen minutes. Two minutes after that, Elizabeth had been wheeled away on a gurney and he was filling out paperwork at the circular counter near the emergency entrance. Mandy stood beside him, crying.

She didn't make a sound, but he could swear he heard every one of those tears rolling down her cheeks. Her pain made it tough to concentrate. Poor kid. She was scared to death.

He bent over and picked her up, setting her on the counter next to him. They were almost at eye level. A headband adorned with cartoon characters held her blond hair off her round face. The same collection of animals, in a rainbow of colors, covered her T-shirt. She wore denim shorts and scuffed sandals. Except for the tears, she looked like just any other six-year-old.

"When did you and your mom move here?" he asked.

She clutched the tattered teddy bear closer. "Yesterday," she said, gulping for air.

"Yesterday?" There went his hope they might have made friends in town. "Do you have any family here?"

She shook her head and sniffed again.

He reached over the counter to a box of tissues beside the phone. The receptionist was also a nurse, and she had disappeared into the room with Elizabeth. Mandy wiped her face and tried to blow her nose. It didn't work. He took a couple of tissues and held them over her face.

"Blow," he ordered, wondering how many times he'd done this during summer T-ball practice. There were always a lot of tears as the kids skinned knees and elbows...and lost games.

"Where's your daddy?"

Her blue eyes filled again. "He's gone."

Gone meaning dead? Or divorced? "Where does he live now?" Travis asked.

"I don't know. He doesn't see us anymore. Mommy said he had to go away because he's big. She said he's never coming b-back." Her voice trembled.

He gave her a reassuring smile. Big? That didn't make any sense. Elizabeth Abbott must be divorced. He glanced down at the hospital forms. She had an insurance card in her wallet, so he copied that information. "Where do you live?" he asked, then realized that if they'd just moved here, Mandy wouldn't know her address yet.

"By the ducks."

"The duck pond?"

She nodded vigorously, her tears momentarily forgot ten. "It's pretty. I have a big bed all to myself. Just like Mommy. And there's little soaps in the bath." She smiled. She had a dimple in each cheek and he could see she was going to grow up to be a heartbreaker.

He pictured the buildings around the duck pond in the center of town and remembered there was a small motel on the corner. So much for having an address here.

"What about your grandmother and grandfather? Do you know where they are?"

"They live far away."

Before he could think of any more questions, the receptionist came bustling back into the room. "Appendix," she said, pulling her stethoscope from around her neck and placing it in the right hip pocket of her nurse's uniform. "Caught it in time." She looked at Mandy. "Your mommy is going to have an operation. Do you know what that means?"

Mandy looked scared again. "No."

"The doctor is going to make her sleep for a little bit while he makes her feel better. There's an infection inside and he's going to take it out. But she'll be fine."

Mandy didn't looked reassured. She bit her lower lip hard and tears filled her eyes. Travis felt like he'd taken a sucker punch to the gut. Apparently the kid didn't know a soul in town, and if the grandparents weren't local, finding them could take days. He didn't even know if Abbott was Elizabeth's maiden or married name.

He held out his arm, offering Mandy a hug, but letting her decide. She threw herself against him with the desperation of a drowning man clutching a raft. Her slight body shook with the tremors of her sobs. She smelled of sun and grass and little girl. So damn small to be facing this alone.

"Hush," he murmured, stroking her hair. "I'm right here and everything's going to be fine."

It was nearly seven in the evening before Travis was able to take Mandy in to see her mother. The nurse had informed him children weren't allowed on the ward, but he'd ignored her and marched past, carrying Mandy in his arms. He was the sheriff. What were they going to do? Arrest him?

He should have gone off-duty at four-thirty, but he couldn't leave the kid on her own, and he didn't want to take her to the local child services office before she'd seen her mother. It didn't much matter, he thought as he walked down the hospital hallway. He hadn't made any plans for the weekend.

Although Glenwood was far enough off the beaten track not to get much tourist trade even over Labor Day weekend, the last celebration of summer usually kept him and his deputies busy. There were fights at the park as too much beer was consumed, and the teenagers would get involved in illegal drag races down by the lake. Come Monday afternoon, the small jail would be filled with red-faced citizens who would work off their sentences doing community service.

The last door at the end of the hallway stood partially open. Travis knocked once and entered. He'd already warned Mandy that her mother would be hooked up to tubes, but it wasn't as frightening as he'd feared. Elizabeth had an IV in each arm, but her color was good. Medium brown hair fanned out over the white pillow. The pale hospital gown set off her tan. For someone who had just had emergency surgery, she didn't look half-bad. Hospital smells filled the room: antiseptic and pine-scented cleanser.

"We can only stay a minute," he reminded Mandy in a quiet voice.

"I know. Is she sleeping?"

"Not anymore," came the groggy response. Elizabeth opened her eyes and looked at him. She blinked. "Do I know you?"

"We haven't been officially introduced," he said, walking closer and setting Mandy on the ground. Before the little girl could jump onto the bed, he laid a hand on her shoulder. "Stand next to your mommy, but don't bump against anything. I'm Travis Haynes. I stopped you for speeding."

"That's right." Elizabeth looked away from him and smiled at her daughter. He remembered when he'd stopped her he'd thought if she ever really smiled it would be a killer, and he'd been right. Even fresh from surgery, the lady was a looker.

"Hi, sweets," she said. "It's good to see you."

"Oh, Mommy." Mandy stood as close to the bed as she could without actually touching it. She clutched her bear to her with one hand and with the other stroked her mother's arm. "The nurse said you had something bad inside, but it's gone now."

"I feel much better." Elizabeth touched Mandy's hair and her face, then raised herself up on one elbow. She grimaced. Travis moved closer. She looked up at him. "I'm trying to get a hug here."

He picked up Mandy and held her close to her mother. They clung to each other for a second. He could see the fierceness of Elizabeth Abbott's love for her child in the way she squeezed her eyes tight and he heard it in her murmured words of encouragement.

"I'm fine," she promised. "Everything is going to work out."

He set Mandy on the ground and pulled a chair close to the bed. He sat down and pulled Mandy onto his lap. If Elizabeth was surprised by his daughter's acceptance of him, she didn't show it. But in the past couple of hours, he and the little girl had become friends.

Elizabeth settled back on the bed. She pushed a button and raised the head up until she was half reclining. "So you're the sheriff."

"That's me. I've just been voted in for another term."

Her brown eyes met and held his. The dark pain was gone and the lines around her mouth had relaxed. "Did I pass?" she asked.

"Pass what?"

She smiled. "Did I have a story you hadn't heard before? I mean how many people speed because they have appendicitis?"

"It's a first," he said, stretching his legs out in front of him. "I'm a man of my word. You won't be getting a ticket from me."

Mandy shifted against his chest and yawned. It had been a long afternoon and evening for her. They'd gone to the cafeteria about six o'clock, but the kid hadn't been able to eat much. She'd fretted about her mother and beat him at checkers while they waited. Her slight weight reminded him of his oldest nephew. Drew would play video games in Travis's arms until he fell asleep and then have to be carried to bed.

"Thank you for looking after her," Elizabeth said. "You didn't have to stay and baby-sit."

"It was easy." He glanced down and watched Mandy's eyes close. "I filled out most of the forms for the hospital, but they're going to have a few questions. Do you want me to call your ex?"

She paled visibly. "What? Why?"

"To take care of Mandy until you're better."

"No!" She sounded upset. She raised her arm and stared at the IV taped in place on the back of her hand. "No." Her voice was calmer now, as if she had herself under control. "I'm not, that is, I wasn't ever married. There's no ex-husband."

"All right," he said, even though her claim made no sense. Mandy had talked about her father. Travis reminded himself this was the nineties and women didn't have to get married to have babies. He looked closely at Elizabeth. Somehow she didn't strike him as the type to have a child on her own. Still, she must have; Mandy was proof. Why would anyone lie about something like that? "Any next of kin nearby?"

She shook her head. "My parents live in Florida. Right now, however, they're cruising somewhere in the Orient. I can't..." She trailed off. "I can't call them. What am I going to do?" She shifted and winced. "I have to—"

"Shh." He pointed at the sleeping child. "You don't have to do anything tonight," he said softly. "You've just had emergency surgery and I'm not even supposed to be visiting. I thought this might be a problem, so I've already called and spoken with a friend of mine. Her name is Rebecca Chambers and she runs the local child services office. It's a county facility, but a great place."

"Rebecca?"

"Rebecca Chambers. She's the director. There are only about twenty kids there. It's on the other side of town, near the school. I've spent some time there volunteering. Mandy will be fine."

Elizabeth stared up at him. Her good humor had faded, and she looked tired and drawn. "You want to put my daughter in a home?" She blinked frantically, but tears spilled over onto her cheeks.

"Hey," he said, standing up and depositing a sleeping Mandy in the chair. He hovered awkwardly by the bed. "Don't cry. It's just for a couple of days. If you want me to call someone, I will. Just give me a name."

"I'm sorry," she whispered. "Everything is falling apart. It was going so well and now I don't know what to do or where to turn. I— There's no one to call." She looked up at him. "Can't she stay here, with me?"

"In the hospital? No. They didn't even want her to visit you, let alone spend the night. You're in no position to take care of her, Elizabeth. I know the home sounds bad, but it's not."

"You're right. I don't have another choice." She covered her face with her hands. "It just makes me feel like I'm an awful mother. It's not the place I'm worried about, I've been there. I'm going to work there." She wiped her cheeks with her fingers. "I'm Rebecca's new assistant. I moved us here to take the job. I'm supposed to start Tuesday. What's she going to think about me? I'm dumping my kid on her doorstep, and I'm going to miss my first day of work."

The sobs began in earnest. He hesitated about five seconds, then perched on the edge of the bed. Careful not to tangle the IV lines, he patted her shoulder. She clutched at his arm, all the while muttering how stupid she must look to him. The sheet slipped to her waist. He tried not to stare, but couldn't help noticing the shape of her breasts under her hospital gown.

Travis told himself he was at best behaving unethically, and at the worst acting like a pervert. He had no business noticing Elizabeth's body. She'd just had surgery for God's sake. But he did notice, and admire, all the while calling himself names.

"I'm sure Rebecca will understand," he said. "It's not as if you planned this."

"I know, but Mandy will be there all alone. I wish—"

"Do all the women in your family leak this much?"

"What?" She blinked and looked up at him. Her dark lashes stood up in spikes, her nose was red and her cheeks blotchy. She was a mess. It brought out his knight-in-shining-armor side and he resisted getting involved. He knew what would happen then. Better for both of them if he just backed off.

"Between you and Mandy, I think we could have floated a ship today."

She smiled wanly. "Don't make me laugh. It hurts."

"Okay, then I won't tell you the one about the parrot with no legs."

"How did he stay on his perch?"

Travis stood up and winked. "You'll just have to wait until you get better to find out." He glanced at his watch. "I'm going to take Mandy over to stay with Rebecca. I'll call you in the morning and make sure you're doing all right, then I'll bring Mandy back here in the afternoon."

"Why are you being so nice to me?"

"Just doing my duty, ma'am." He gave a mock salute and picked up the sleeping child. "I'll leave my number with the nurse."

"Thank you for everything," she said, pulling the sheet up and smiling at him. "If Mandy wakes up, tell her I love her."

"You can tell her yourself when you see her tomorrow."

Chapter Two

"What do you mean chicken pox?" Travis asked. He stared down at Rebecca, seated behind her desk in her office at the local child services facility.

"I mean I have eight children in various stages of chicken pox, and the other twelve have been exposed. Sorry, Travis. If you'd explained why you were coming by, I would have told you what was going on and saved you the trip. I thought you were just going to mooch dinner. I know that when you're between women you hang out with me. I thought this was one of those rare weekends." Her brown eyes looked more amused than apologetic.

"But Mandy—"

"But Mandy doesn't know if she's had chicken pox, do you, honey?" Rebecca smiled at the little girl.

Mandy shook her head and tugged on Travis's pants. "Travis?"

"Hmm?" He didn't look down at her. Now what was he supposed to do? He couldn't just leave her in the street. "Rebecca, you're not helping."

"Travis?" Mandy tugged again.

"What?"

"Do I have to stay here?"

She looked up, her head bent way back, her wide blue eyes gazing at him with absolute trust. He felt as if he were torturing Bambi.

"Why don't I make a few calls," Rebecca said, coming to his rescue. She flicked her dark hair over her shoulder and reached for the phone. "There's a shelter about twenty miles from here. I'll see if they have room." She picked up the receiver.

"Travis?" Mandy tugged again.

"Yes?"

"I want my mommy."

Travis crouched down in front of her. "She's in the hospital. She needs to sleep tonight and get better."

Mandy held her teddy so tightly, he worried she might squish the stuffing out the side. She leaned close and whispered. "I don't know that lady. I don't want to stay here. I want my mommy."

He'd spent enough time with kids her age to recognize the quiver in her voice. Tears would come next and after that, he would feel like a heel and— He stood up and jammed his hands in his pockets.

"You think I should take her home with me?" he asked, already knowing the answer.

"It would be best for her. Elizabeth isn't going to need a sick kid on her hands, just as she's getting out of the hospital herself." Rebecca rose and walked around the desk. She wore a floral print jumper over a white T-shirt. With her long curly hair and conservative style of dressing, she looked like a Sunday school teacher. Travis suspected it was a facade and that deep inside, she had the wild streak of the best kind of a sinner.

When she'd moved to Glenwood six months ago to take over as director of the county facility, he'd asked her out. His big seduction scene had ended up failing badly. They were, he'd realized within the first ten minutes, destined to be good friends. Rebecca had promised to leave his reputation as a heartbreaker intact and not tell the world his kisses had left her cold. Travis stared at her big brown eyes and sighed. He felt mild affection for Rebecca and nothing else. He must be getting old and slowing down.

"You're the only friend Mandy has," Rebecca said. "If I could take her home with me, I would. But my staff is exhausted, and I'm staying here tonight. Anyway, you have Louise."

He thought of his housekeeper. Today was her day off but he knew if he called she would come over to help and show off her latest craft project. At least she wasn't knitting anymore. He already had two drawers filled with ugly, ill-fitting sweaters and socks she'd made for him.

"I suppose that might work. But I don't know anything about children," Travis muttered, trying to ignore Mandy tugging on him again.

"Your nephews stay with you."

"Travis," Mandy said.

"That's different."

"How?" Rebecca asked.

"Travis?"

"They're family. And boys." He looked down. Those blue eyes were killing him. "What?"

"I want to stay with you."

"You're the only person she knows in town. Come on, be a hero. It's what you're best at."

He glared at Rebecca. "Thanks."

Undaunted, she smiled. "Let me get you some supplies." She disappeared down the hall.

"Why me?" he asked no one in particular.

"Travis? Are you mad at me?"

"Mandy, no." He swept Mandy up in his arms and gave her a hug. She wrapped her spindly legs around his waist. "I'm not mad. We'll have fun. I'll read you a story tonight, okay?"

She nodded. "And Mr. Bear," she said, holding out the tattered animal.

"And Mr. Bear."

Rebecca returned with a small cloth bag. "I've packed a nightgown, some underwear and a shorts set for tomorrow." She handed Travis the bag, then smiled at Mandy. "Do you want a pink toothbrush or a purple one?" She had both in her hand.

The little girl stared for a second, then pointed shyly. "Pink."

"You got it." Rebecca dropped that one in the bag and walked over to the door. "I'll be here, so call me if there's any trouble. It's only one night."

"Like you care," he grumbled.

"Stop it. You'll have a great time. Think of it as father training. For when you have your own kids."

"Not my style. Haynes men don't make good parents." It was a familiar argument between the two of them. The problem was Rebecca hadn't figured out he wasn't kidding.

She shook her head. "Let me know what happens. And tell Elizabeth not to worry about coming into work until she's completely healed. I won't be giving her job to anyone else."

"Yeah, I will." He shifted Mandy so that she was supported by one arm, then handed her the bag and dug in his pocket for his keys. "Say goodbye, Mandy."

"By." Now that she was getting her way, she smiled broadly. "Can we have the siren on?" she asked as they stepped out of the building and walked toward the sheriff's car in the parking lot.

"No."

She pouted and rested her head on his shoulder.

"Don't give me that look," he said. "I can't use the siren when it's not an emergency."

She thought for a minute. "I gotta go."

His heart sank. "Now?"

She nodded. "It's a 'mergency."

Elizabeth raised the hospital bed and stared out the window. From where she was lying, she could see the corner of the small parking lot and a plot of grass with a Chinese maple in the center. It was early Saturday morning and she'd seen only a handful of cars enter the hospital grounds.

Everything was going to be fine. She'd recited the phrase over and over, hoping by saying it enough she would start to believe it was true. But panic threatened, just below the surface of her carefully constructed facade.

She was scared. There was no getting around the lump in her throat and the cold hard knot in her stomach, just next to the tender incision the doctors had made yesterday. She wasn't frightened for herself. The surgery had gone well, and she was healing nicely, according to the doctor who had visited early that morning. She had medical insurance, so the unexpected stay in the hospital wasn't going to deplete her savings.

The lump in her throat got bigger and her eyes burned from unshed tears. She blinked them away and prayed that her daughter hadn't been too scared last night, alone in a strange place. Had they let her sleep with her bear? Had she had any bad dreams? There were, on average, twenty children at the county facility. Had Mandy gotten lost among all the other kids? Who would have been there to hold her if she cried?

Logically, Elizabeth knew she hadn't had another choice as far as her daughter was concerned. Having her spend the night in the county home had made sense. She would be fed and warm and have a bed to sleep in. But knowing her only child had been put there, like a stray puppy rounded up by the pound, made her feel like the worst kind of parent. Mothers were supposed to do better for their children. Of course, mothers were also supposed to know what they were doing when they picked out fathers—and look at how that had turned out.

She reached over to the black phone on the small metal nightstand and dialed the number she'd gotten from directory assistance. For the second time in fifteen minutes, she heard a busy signal. From what she remembered from her tour during her interview a month ago, the county facility only had one line. She hung up the receiver. She would keep trying until she got through. She wanted to check on Mandy and reassure her daughter that everything was going to be fine—even though she didn't know how.

Elizabeth forced herself to hold on to her control. She couldn't afford to give into the fear. Not now. If she started questioning herself, she might never stop. Six months ago her world had come crashing in on her. She'd managed to collect the pieces and assemble them into a life, but the structure was fragile, and this emergency was enough to send the whole thing crumbling again. The logistics of her condition whirled around in her head. How was she going to take care of Mandy when she was supposed to stay off her feet for a week and not drive for three weeks? What about feeding her, and registering her for school, buying her new shoes, and a hundred other things she'd planned to do over the long holiday weekend? What about taking her out to watch the ducks and playing tag and—

The sound of footsteps in the hallway caught her attention. She glanced over at her partially closed door and watched as it was pushed open. Sheriff Travis Haynes entered the room and smiled at her. She stared at him, surprise and a tiny spurt of pleasure temporarily hiding her worries. He'd told her he would come by today and visit, but she hadn't expected him to. He'd done too much already. Still, except for Rebecca and Mandy, he was the only other person she knew in Glenwood, and she couldn't help being pleased to see him.

Gratitude, she told herself firmly, trying to find the reason for the sudden surge of good spirits. Gratitude and nothing else.

"Hi," she said, managing a shaky smile. She pulled the sheet up to her shoulders and self-consciously touched the straggly ends of her hair. They hadn't let her have a shower yet, and she felt grungy. She'd planned to insist on getting cleaned up later that morning. She hadn't expected visitors so early.

"Hi, yourself." Travis crossed the room in three long strides and pulled a plastic chair close to the bed. "May I?"

"Please."

His khaki, short-sleeved uniform looked freshly pressed. A badge and a name tag had been pinned above the left breast pocket. He stood about six feet tall, with dark curly hair and a trimmed mustache that outlined his upper lip. He was the kind of man who, as her aunt Amanda used to say, made a woman get a crick in her neck just watching him stroll by.

As he settled himself in the chair, he tossed his beige Stetson across the bed. It sailed through the air and landed dead center on the table in front of the window.

"Neat trick," she said, trying to ignore the way his brown eyes twinkled when he looked at her. "You have to practice much?"

"Every day. I sit in my office, tossing my hat across the room. It impresses the ladies." He had a smooth, low voice, like liquid chocolate.

"Really?"

"Aren't you impressed, darlin'?"

Some, but she wasn't about to admit it. Once she'd let a man charm her and impress her and seduce her. Never again, she reminded herself. She'd learned a hard lesson from Sam Proctor. "I didn't expect you to visit," she said. "I'm sure you have other things you should be doing."

"You're the most important item on my agenda," he said, leaning back in the chair and resting one ankle on the opposite knee. The movement emphasized the muscles in his thighs.

She looked away. "Oh?"

"How are you feeling?"

"A little sore, but better than I was. The doctor says I'm healing nicely." She shifted in the hospital bed. "They gave me something to make me sleep, and that helped. I never got to thank you yesterday."

"Just doing my job."

She waved at the IV still attached to her hand. "They said that if I'd waited another couple of hours, the appendix might have burst. If I'd gone to the walk-in medical clinic like I'd planned, I might have gotten to the hospital too late."

"So it all worked out. You'll be released tomorrow."

"That's what they told me." She glanced at him sitting in the white plastic chair. He looked tanned and handsome and disgustingly healthy, while her insides felt as if a herd of buffalo had trampled through them.

"Where are you going to go when they release you?" he asked.

"Back to the motel." It wasn't a great solution, but it was the best one she'd been able to think of. Where else *could* she go?

"And then?"

"And then I'll get better and go to work. That is, if I still have a job. I need to call Rebecca and tell her what happened." She forced herself to meet his gaze, and prayed her expression looked as calm and confident as she'd made herself sound. She didn't want to foist her troubles on anyone, especially not this handsome stranger. One rescue per weekend was quite enough.

He folded his arms over his chest. His shirt stretched tightly across his broad shoulders. He had a solid look about him. He was the kind of man who could physically work for hours without tiring. He looked dependable. She shook her head. Looks could be deceiving.

Then he smiled. She told herself not to notice, that he was obviously an accomplished ladies' man, but that didn't stop her rather battered insides from responding favorably to the flash of white teeth.

"I have good news, bad news and good news," he said. "Which do you want first?"

She panicked. "Is Mandy—"

He cut her off. "She's fine. That's the first good news. The bad news is there's an outbreak of chicken pox at the children's home. I didn't know if Mandy'd had chicken pox, so I couldn't leave her there last night. Rebecca figured the last thing you'd need in your condition is a sick kid."

Elizabeth frowned. "If she's not at the home, where is she?"

"Downstairs, watching a clown make balloon animals." He shrugged. "They were having a party and she wanted to see what was going on. I thought you and I should talk first anyway."

"So where did Mandy spend the night?"

"With me. I called my housekeeper, and she took care of the basics of bathing and dressing. But I fed her breakfast." He looked sheepish and proud all at once.

"You?" Why on earth would he volunteer to take home her daughter? "Chicken pox? I can't believe this is all happening. Mandy hasn't had them yet. Thank God she wasn't exposed to them. I don't know what to say except thank you." She had a sudden thought. "I hope it wasn't too inconvenient for your wife."

"I'm not married."

She told herself she wasn't pleased by that fact. It was just a piece of information. It didn't *mean* anything. The last thing she needed in her life was a man. "I don't know how to repay you for all you've done."

"I'm responsible for the welfare of the people of this town," he said, and grinned again. "You *are* our newest citizen."

"You're very kind." She relaxed. Mandy was safe. Nothing else mattered.

The slow, sexy grin faded. "You're going to need help when they release you. Tell me who to call, Elizabeth."

She turned her head and stared out the window. "There's no one to call. I told you, my parents are on a cruise in the Orient. They're probably halfway between Australia and Hong Kong right now."

She didn't bother mentioning that she deliberately hadn't paid attention to her parents' travel plans. She didn't even know the name of the ship or the cruise line. In the past six months, she'd cut herself off from her family. She couldn't bear to tell them the ugly, disgusting truth about her life. She couldn't bear to see the shock and the shame in their eyes and to relive it all over again. She just wanted to forget everything. And she'd been on her way to doing just that. If only she hadn't had to have surgery.

"Then a friend from Los Angeles."

"No." All her friends knew what had happened. There'd been no way to keep it a secret. She hadn't been able to face them, and had quickly cut all personal ties. There was no one left to call. What about tonight? Where would Mandy sleep?

"Sheriff Haynes..."

"Travis."

"Travis," she said and paused. "I have no family, other than my parents. I know this is an imposition, but would you or your housekeeper be willing to keep Mandy tonight? I'd gladly pay you." Her hands curled into fists. She hated asking, but what choice did she have?

"I'll keep her and I don't want your money. But that only takes care of today. What happens tomorrow?"

Tomorrow she would handle whatever she had to. She turned toward him. "I really appreciate your concern, but it's not necessary. I'll be fine. In the morning, I'll get a cab. You do have cabs in Glenwood?"

"One or two."

"Good. Then I'll get a cab, collect my daughter from you and take her back to the motel. We'll be fine."

He stood up and walked over to the window. The view from the back—she caught her breath—well, it was just as good as the view from the front, she thought, staring at his tight, high rear end. The pants of his uniform fit snugly at his hips, then fell loosely over his muscled thighs. A black leather belt with snapped compartments hugged his narrow waist. His dark hair fell precisely to his collar, but didn't touch the starched material.

It was the anesthetic, she told herself. And the fact that she'd spent the last year living like a nun. It was the tension and the strain. It was the season, or the time of month, but it was certainly not the man. She wouldn't let it be.

"I have a couple of problems with your plan," he said, keeping his back to her.

"It's not your business." She allowed her temper to flare and the heat of anger to burn away the other kind of warmth threatening her composure.

"First," he said, ignoring her statement, "you're supposed to stay off your feet for a week. How do you propose to feed and take care of Mandy?"

"I'll—" She hadn't solved that yet, but she would. She would get through it the same as she'd gotten through her other problems. One day, one step at a time. "I'll think of something."

"You're not supposed to drive for three weeks," he continued.

"How do you know?"

"I asked the nurse."

"If the town has a cab service, I don't have to drive."

"Then there's your job." He turned toward her and rested one hip on the windowsill. "Which you still have."

"What?" She started to sit upright but the pain from the incision stopped her. She leaned back and stared at him. "You talked to Rebecca about my job?"

"I explained the situation when I took Mandy over to her. She says to take all the time you need to heal. Your job will be waiting when you're ready."

"Thank you," she murmured as relief filled her.

He was going to make her cry. After breaking down yesterday, she'd sworn not to cry again, but she could feel the tears forming. Maybe it was all going to work out. She'd been so afraid her life would never be normal again. Six months ago, when the police had shown up at her door, her world had collapsed. Slowly, so slowly, she was getting it back together. They were going to make it. They had to.

Before she could ask him what else Rebecca had said, the door pushed open and an attractive nurse came into the room with Mandy in tow. "We do not allow children in this ward," she said sternly, then grinned. "So I'm bringing her in here to get her out from underfoot."

Mandy held her bear in one hand and clutched a balloon giraffe in the other. There was chocolate icing on her cheek and she was dressed in a cute pink-and-white shorts outfit that Elizabeth had never seen before.

"Mommy!" When the nurse let her go, the little girl rushed toward her. Travis walked over and lifted her until she was sitting on the bed.

"Travis Haynes, I might have known I'd find you here with one of our prettiest patients," the nurse said as she paused by the door.

"You know me, Pam. I can't resist a female in distress."

Pam laughed, then looked at Elizabeth. "You watch out for this one. He's our resident heartbreaker."

"I'll be careful," Elizabeth said, knowing she wasn't ever going to get involved with any man, let alone one as charming and good-looking as Travis.

"You've got fifteen minutes," Pam said. "Then my supervisor gets back and Mandy will have to leave."

Elizabeth nodded and the woman shut the door.

"I missed you, Mommy," Mandy said, reclaiming her attention.

"I missed you, too." Elizabeth held out her arms.

Mandy dropped the bear and the balloon animal, and slipped next to her to snuggle close. Despite the tangle of IV's and the pressure on her incision as she leaned toward her daughter, Elizabeth wrapped her arms around her and held on, wishing she never had to let go. Mandy's warm body felt small and fragile cuddling against her, and so very familiar. Elizabeth stroked her head, then bent down and kissed her cheek.

"How are you doing, sweets?" she asked softly.

"There was a clown and he made me this." She picked up her giraffe. The rubber squeaked as she held it and she laughed. Bright blue eyes met her own. Sam's eyes, she thought with regret. Mandy had her smile and her nose, but her eyes and the rest of her coloring was all Sam's. It made it hard to forget her daughter's father. But forget him, she would. She'd promised herself.

Mandy laughed and tossed the balloon animal in the air, then wiggled to sit back and look up at her. "I had a cupcake."

"So I see." She wiped at the frosting. "Sheriff Haynes said you spent the night at his house."

Mandy nodded vigorously and grinned. "Louise made us another dinner. Then we had doughnuts for dessert." She sounded faintly scandalized, but quite delighted. "She gave me a bath but he read me a story. About nines and their end."

Elizabeth looked up at Travis who had returned to his perch on the windowsill. "Nines and their end?"

He cleared his throat. "You sort of had to be there. The San Francisco 49ers are looking for a decent tight end. I don't have any children's books in the house, so I read the sports page."

She grinned. "Whatever works."

"And we played with trains," Mandy said.

"I keep them for my nephews," Travis added helpfully.

"And I got a new nightgown with a bunny on the front from that nice lady, Becca."

"Rebecca?"

She nodded. "And a pink toothbrush."

Elizabeth brushed the blond hair out of her daughter's eyes. "Sounds like you had a full evening. Did you sleep all right?"

Mandy nodded. "I had one bad dream, but I hugged Mr. Bear and told him what had happened, and he said he'd take care of me until you were all better. Are you all better, Mommy?"

Elizabeth swallowed hard. She'd never loved anyone as much as she loved this little girl. She squeezed her. "Almost, honey. The doctor is going to let me go home tomorrow morning."

"Are we going to our house? The one with the bunnies?"

When she had accepted the job, Elizabeth had rented a house. While she'd stood in the kitchen and looked out at the backyard, she'd seen three rabbits scampering across the yard. She'd told Mandy about them and her daughter was very anxious to make their acquaintance. "No. We can't move in there until October first. That's about three more weeks."

"So where are we going tomorrow?"

Elizabeth could feel Travis's gaze on her. He'd asked the same question. She still didn't have a decent answer. "We'll be fine."

"Okay." Mandy picked up her bear and slid off the bed. "Travis said we could go to the movies tonight, Mommy. He said we could have popcorn and hot dogs and candy." Her body quivered with excitement. "And if I'm really good, I can stay up past my bedtime."

Travis cleared his throat. "She wasn't supposed to tell you that last part."

"I appreciate you doing this for me," Elizabeth said, wondering how it had all gotten out of hand. "She's my responsibility and I—"

Travis pushed to his feet and held out one hand to stop her. "You're not in L.A. anymore. Glenwood is a small town, Elizabeth Abbott, and we take care of our own. As of Thursday night, you're one of us. I'm on duty today, so I'm going to take Mandy with me to the station. We're right across from the park. I'll see that she gets exercise and decent food and is in bed by nine. My housekeeper promised to come by and make sure I'm doing it all correctly."

"Why are you doing this?"

"Because I don't have any plans for the weekend and I've always been a sucker for a pair of beautiful blue eyes."

Elizabeth felt a rush of disappointment that her own eyes were brown. She wanted to believe him, believe that it was just about people helping each other. The way he said it, she was almost willing to buy into the myth of small towns. But she'd believed before, had trusted before, and that trust had been betrayed.

"I hate to impose," she said.

"You don't have a choice," he answered. "What else are you going to do with her?"

She glanced down at the IV needle taped to her hand. She didn't have an answer to that one, either. "Thank you. Again."

She looked up at him. Humor danced in his eyes, humor and a little bit of compassion. As long as it didn't change to pity, she could survive. And somehow, she would pay him back.

He retrieved his hat and settled it on his head; then he held out his hand to Mandy. The little girl collected her giraffe and tucked it next to her bear. She grinned at her mother and slipped her hand in his. "By, Mommy."

"By, honey."

Elizabeth watched her daughter act so trustingly with this stranger. Maybe Mandy hadn't been scarred by the experience as badly as she'd feared. Maybe Mandy was going to be fine.

Travis paused by the door and looked at her. The Stetson hid his eyes from view, but she saw the quick smile flash under his black mustache. Her heart fluttered foolishly. The man was handsome as sin.

"I'll call before the movie," he said. "So you can talk with Mandy."

"I'd like that."

"Rest," he commanded. "The nurse said you'll be released around ten in the morning. I'll be here around nine-thirty."

"You don't have to stay," she said quickly. "But I appreciate you dropping Mandy off."

"I'm not dropping her off," he said. "Unless you can come up with something better than that motel, Elizabeth, you're coming home with me."

Chapter Three

Travis left Mandy at the sheriff's office in the center of Glenwood and walked past his patrol car to Elizabeth's white car parked on the street. The T-bird started instantly. He shifted into gear and checked the mirrors before pulling out and heading for the motel.

Within ten minutes, he stood inside the small rented room, staring at the suitcases stacked in the corner and at the personal items scattered around. A pair of high heels poked out from under the bed. A yellow blouse rested over the back of a chair. The faint scent of perfume lingered in the air. He sniffed appreciatively. He missed having a woman living with him.

His wife had left both him and Glenwood three years ago, returning to town only long enough to sign the divorce papers and wish him well with his life. He didn't resent her or the split. He should have known better than to marry. Haynes men didn't make good husbands or fathers. He came from a long line of men who failed at marriage. But he'd wanted to prove his father, brothers and uncles wrong, so he'd married the pretty, dark-haired woman he'd met in college. She'd been shy but quick-witted—and hot as hell in bed. All the ingredients had been there. Still the marriage had fizzled and he'd learned his lesson firsthand. Haynes men made great cops, but lousy family men.

Travis placed an open suitcase on the bed. He folded Mandy's nightgown and picked up her toys. In the bath-room, an open cosmetic bag sat next to the sink. He col-lected the compacts, tubes and brushes on the counter and placed them into the bag, stopping long enough to pick up a bottle of perfume and sniff the cap. He would have thought Elizabeth Abbott to be the floral type, but the aroma was spicy. Not overpowering, just intriguing. He dropped the bottle in with the other cosmetics.

After checking the shower and behind the door for clothes, he returned to the bedroom and packed up the re-maining items. A white cotton nightgown had been care-lessly tossed over a dresser. He folded it carefully, noticing the row of tiny buttons up the front and the lace ruffle around the neck and arms.

He could see Elizabeth in something like this. It would fall about midcalf on her. Not the least bit sexy; the cotton wasn't see-through. And yet—

He brushed his thumb over the soft cloth. There were always plenty of women around him. Just because he wasn't good husband material didn't mean he wasn't a great date and an accomplished flirt. But he'd *liked* living with a woman. He missed the day-to-day familiarities, the verbal shorthand, the slow, sensual sex that could take hours. There'd been no need to hurry; he and Julie were supposed to have had a lifetime.

"Getting soft, Haynes," he muttered, then shoved the nightgown into the suitcase.

He opened drawers and pulled out clothes, ignoring the feel of the lacy panties and bras, quickly filling the luggage. When everything was packed, he loaded the trunk of the car and paid the motel bill. Then he headed for the hospital.

He didn't know what he was going to say when he saw her. If she'd made other plans, he would drive her to where she was going and be done with her. If she hadn't, she was coming home with him. There was no way in hell he was going to let her and Mandy tough it out in that tiny motel for the next three weeks. Tough it out, hell. They would *starve*.

As Travis walked down the hospital corridor he wondered which it would be. He'd left her sputtering yesterday when he'd made his announcement that he intended to take her to his place. Last night, when he'd called to let Mandy talk to her mother, Elizabeth had been coolly insistent that she was not his problem. Louise had told him to use the famous Haynes charm, but he hadn't felt right about sweet-talking Elizabeth into anything.

He reached her door and pushed it open. She sat on the edge of the bed, dressed in the same shorts and tank top she'd been wearing Friday. Her hair was freshly washed and hanging loose about her shoulders in a mass of shining brown waves. A wisp of bangs reached almost to her eyebrows.

She was trying to pull on socks and didn't see him in the doorway. She bent down to slip on her socks, but she only got halfway there before grunting in pain and straightening. She raised her left foot toward her right knee, but that action caused her to clutch her side.

"Of course you'd rather rip out your stitches than ask for help," he said from his place in the doorway. He pushed back his Stetson and walked into the room.

She looked up and stared at him. Faint color stained her cheeks. "I'm not leaving with you," she said flatly.

"Fine. Where are you going?"

"Back to the motel." Fire flashed in her brown eyes. "I've already called for a cab."

He walked forward slowly, stopping when he was in front of her. Even sitting on the hospital bed, she had to tip her head back to meet his gaze.

"Not while I'm around," he said, folding his arms over his chest. "This isn't Los Angeles, Elizabeth. It's a small town, and it's Labor Day weekend. Most of the businesses are closed, including the restaurants. How are you going to feed Mandy? There's no kitchen in your motel room. Is she registered for school?"

Elizabeth slowly shook her head.

"Who's going to do that? Who's going to walk her to her class on the first day? Even if you find take-out places to deliver food, do you have the cash to pay for it, or are you going to have Mandy go to the bank to get more money?"

"Stop it," she said softly. "Just stop it."

Defeat darkened her eyes and made her shoulders slump forward. He felt like a heel, but there was more at stake here than her pride.

"You've got to think of Mandy," he said, perching next to her on the bed.

"She's all I have thought of. I've lain in this bed thinking about nothing else." She brushed her bangs off her forehead. "I just wanted to make a fresh start."

"You have. So things aren't going exactly as you planned them. It could be worse."

"Yeah?" She turned her head to look at him. "How?"

He grinned. "It could be raining."

A smile twitched at the corner of her mouth. "I happen to like rain."

"Sit back," he said, jerking his head toward the pillows.

"Why?"

He leaned forward until his face was inches from hers. He was close enough to see three faint freckles on her nose, close enough to inhale the scent of her body. It wasn't that spicy perfume, but it was still mighty appealing. Close enough to see the rise and fall of her breasts under her red tank top. Close enough to study the shape of her full mouth and feel the stirrings in his body. Women of all ages, shapes and sizes got his attention, but when the lady in question came in a package this tempting, it was hard to think about anything else.

It was part of his job, he told himself. He would have taken her in if she'd been a fifty-year-old man with grandkids. Yeah, he would have taken her in, but it wouldn't have been nearly as much fun.

"Do it," he growled.

She scrambled away from him and leaned against the pillows, drawing her legs up onto the bed. He grabbed one ankle and set her heel on his thigh. She started to pull away. He clamped down.

"You are the most stubborn woman I have ever met," he said, slipping the sock over her foot.

She had small feet, and her toenails were polished a bright pink, he noticed as he slid on her athletic shoe and tightened the laces. Trim ankles and a nice tan. He thought briefly about tan lines, where they would start and end and what color her pale breasts would be, then he told himself he was on duty and to can the sexual interest.

He put that foot down on the bed and grabbed the other one. When he pulled the sock over her instep, his thumb brushed against her skin. She jumped and giggled. He looked up. "Ticklish?"

"Very." Her smile faded. "Thank you for everything."

He studied her for a moment. "I live in a big old house on the edge of town. Six bedrooms. I'm restoring it. There's a yard and a playroom and a lock on the bedroom door. I'll charge you twenty bucks a night if it makes you feel better.

When you can move around, you can cook me dinner on the nights my housekeeper doesn't work, because I'm damn tired of frozen dinners zapped in my microwave. If you still feel guilty, you can even do my laundry. Louise will be thrilled. In three weeks, when you can drive, you can move into your own place and we'll part friends. Deal?"

She searched his face as if trying to see what he got out of the offer. He wanted to tell her it was just his job, but he knew deep in his heart he would be lying. He would have made the offer if she'd been old and bald and male, but he wouldn't have wanted her to say yes so badly. It was, he realized with a touch of chagrin, his way of playing house. He would never have a family of his own, so for three weeks, he could pretend.

"It's not that I don't trust you," she said slowly, "it's just that—"

"You don't trust me."

She stared down at her hands. "I'm sorry. It's not personal."

"You don't have a choice, darlin'. I'm the best of a bad situation. Where else are you going to go?"

She bit her lower lip, then looked at him. The raw pain in her eyes made him straighten. It wasn't about physical discomfort, he thought, wanting to turn away, but unable to tear his gaze from hers. It was about some secret in her past. She'd said she'd come to Glenwood to make a fresh beginning. He understood that. Lots of people left places to start over. But she'd left something mean and ugly behind. Something big enough to make her not trust anyone. A man. He wondered what the bastard had done to her.

She nodded once. "If it wasn't for Mandy, I'd say no, but you're right. I don't have a choice. She's the most important part of my life. I accept your offer." She held out her hand, then drew it back. "But I won't do your laundry."

He laughed. "Deal." They shook hands. He finished putting on her other shoe, then stood up. "I'll tell the nurse you're ready to go."

Elizabeth watched him leave. In his cowboy boots and Stetson hat, he looked more like a cow town lawman than the sheriff in a sleepy California town. She wanted to trust him. Desperately. She sat up straight and shifted to the edge of the bed. It wasn't possible. She would never trust any man again. Worse, she would never trust herself.

Travis was right. He *was* her best choice. Right now her options were extremely limited. But when she could drive and move into her rented house, she would pay him what she owed him and disappear from his life.

She heard conversation in the hall. Travis came in, followed by a nurse pushing a wheelchair.

"All set?" he asked.

"Yes." She stood up and stepped toward the wheelchair. When she was settled, he put the small bag containing her personal belongings on her lap and pushed her out of the room.

She was surprised to see the T-bird parked in front of the hospital. "This is my car."

"I know. Did you want to go home in the patrol car? You're just like your daughter. She's always trying to trick me into using the siren."

She laughed. "I don't need a siren. I'm just surprised. I was afraid my car was still parked on the side of the road."

He set the brake on the wheelchair and opened the passenger door. "I had it moved to the sheriff's station. Not that we get much car theft up here."

She stood up slowly. He offered his hand and she took it. His fingers felt warm and strong as he guided her toward the car.

"Watch your head, darlin'," he said, wrapping his other arm around her waist and easing her down.

The incision pulled slightly and she winced. "I'm fine," she said, before he could ask. She looked up at his eyes and the thick, dark lashes framing them. For a heartbeat, his gaze dropped to her mouth. She had a fleeting thought that he was going to kiss her, and her body tensed in anticipation. Then he stepped back and the feeling disappeared, leaving her surprisingly disappointed.

What was wrong with her? she asked herself as Travis gave the nurse the wheelchair, then came around to the driver's side of the car. She wasn't interested in him or in any man. Dear God, hadn't she learned the biggest lesson of all?

Travis didn't glance at her as he slid inside. She wondered if he'd seen the expectation in her face. Embarrassment filled her. She slumped in the seat and closed her eyes.

Something warm brushed across her breasts. She jumped and her eyes flew open.

"Seat belt," Travis said, pulling the belt down and locking it into place.

She stared at him and her heart fluttered foolishly. He'd simply bumped her when he'd grabbed for the restraining device. *Why me?* she wondered and sighed.

"I thought we'd go straight to the house," he said, tossing his Stetson to the back seat. "I want to get you settled. Mandy is at the park with Kyle."

"Kyle?"

He started the engine and pulled out of the parking lot. "One of my deputies and my youngest brother. She's already twisted him around her little finger."

"How do you know?"

Travis shot her a grin. "When he left the office, he turned on his siren. Something tells me that was Mandy's doing."

"She can be stubborn."

"I guess she gets that from her mother."

She glanced at him out of the corner of her eye, but he was staring at the road. She relaxed in the seat and watched as he drove through the small town. As they neared the park, traffic became heavy. She saw families walking together. Her stomach clenched, not from the surgery, but from envy and regret. She and Mandy should have been part of a family like that. It had all been taken away from them. Stolen. She stared out the window and willed the tears away. No. Not stolen. They'd never had it in the first place. It had all been a lie.

As they passed the duck pond, she saw the motel. "Wait, I have to get my things."

"Already done," he said, not bothering to stop. "I went there this morning and checked you out. Your suitcases are in the trunk."

She didn't know whether to thank him or yell at him for invading her personal space.

"Before you get huffy and start hollering at me," he said, as if he could read her mind, "I knew you would want your things with you even if you'd made other plans. So I didn't *assume* you would take me up on my offer."

It took too much energy to get angry, so she simply leaned back in the seat and went along for the ride. He'd been right. She couldn't have made it work at the motel. They passed a sheriff's car parked on the side of the road by the park. Elizabeth looked around but she didn't see Mandy.

"When will Kyle bring her back?" she asked.

"I'll bring her home about four-thirty. There's a parade today, and a big barbecue. Games for the kids. I thought she might enjoy it and you need the rest. I'm going to have to drop you off then head back to the park myself. Have to make an appearance. Between Kyle and myself, we'll keep an eye on Mandy. Louise is off until Monday so you should have plenty of peace and quiet."

He entered a tree-lined residential area. Elizabeth recognized it from her house hunting. He drove around the high school and along a narrow two-lane road she'd never been on before. The houses got larger and farther apart from each other on oversize lots.

"You mentioned Kyle was your youngest brother," she said. "How many are there?"

"Four, counting me. Craig is the oldest, then me, then Jordan and then Kyle."

"So Kyle is a deputy. Are you all cops?"

"It's a family tradition. My dad used to be the sheriff in Glenwood. All his brothers are in police work. Jordan is the only rebel. He's a fire fighter up in Sacramento."

"A real black sheep."

Travis grinned. "We give him a hard time about it. Yup, the Haynes family grows boys and cops. Not a girl in the last four generations. What about you?"

"I'm an only child."

"Too bad."

"Why? It's all I know. My parents were older when I was born and they only wanted one child."

"They got a pretty one."

Elizabeth chuckled. This man could charm milk out of a snake. She would do well to remember talk was cheap. But she had to admit Travis Haynes had a certain amount of style to recommend him, and his heart was in the right place. She resisted glancing at his firm body so close to hers in the confines of the car. From what she had seen, everything else was in the right place, too. But the last thing she needed was to get involved with a heartbreaker. Her heart hadn't recovered from what Sam had done.

They pulled off the road and onto a long driveway. Maple trees and oaks grew on either side of the path. Up ahead she saw a peaked roof, and more trees. Then the path curved around and they drove up into a clearing and parked in front of a beautiful three-story house.

He'd told her he was restoring an old house, but he hadn't said it was a mansion. Big windows opened up onto a wide front lawn. A porch wrapped around the front. The columns holding up the porch covering had been painted white, as was all the trim. The rest of the building was dove gray, soft and light in the morning sunshine.

"You could get lost in there," she said, staring at the masterpiece.

"I did, the first couple of days. Stay in that seat and don't even think about moving."

He got out of the car and came around to her side. He opened the door, then helped her to her feet. Before she could take a step, he bent over and slid one arm behind her back and the other under her thighs.

"What are you doing?" she asked even as he lifted her against his chest. Elizabeth grabbed his shoulders to maintain her balance.

"And here I thought you were smarter than that." He started toward the house.

Her face bumped against his shoulder, and she could smell his masculine scent. He'd shaved only a couple of hours before, so his neck was smooth. She fought the urge to nestle against him. "Travis, put me down. I can walk."

He ignored her. There were four steps up to the porch. He climbed those easily and headed for the front door. She held on, ignoring the way her right breast flattened against his chest and the heated strength of his body. She was wearing shorts so the arm under her legs touched bare skin. Each of his fingers seemed to be leaving a warm imprint on her flesh. She thought about struggling, but her side hurt and she was tired of fighting. Instead, she gave herself up to the feeling of being safe and protected.

When he opened the front door and stepped inside, she stared at the beautiful interior and caught her breath. He had told the truth when he'd said he was restoring the house. Several of the walls had been stripped but not painted or papered. There wasn't a rug on the wooden floor, and she could see the pile of tools next to the front door.

But none of that mattered. He released his arm and she slid to the ground. Instead of moving away from him, she leaned against him and looked around. A crystal chandelier hung in the foyer. The cut glass caught the sunlight and diffused it into a hundred tiny rainbows. The long staircase swept up to the second story where it split and circled around both sides. Arched doorways led to high-beamed rooms. A giant fireplace filled one wall of the parlor to her left, while on the right, a study with floor-to-ceiling bookshelves held sheet-covered furniture.

"Wow." She looked at him. "You live here?"

He shrugged. "Yeah."

"All by yourself?"

"I do now. I was married when I bought the place. Some people have a baby to try and save their marriage. Julie and I bought this house." The humor left his brown eyes.

"I'm sorry."

He shrugged. "Don't be. There were no hard feelings. Sometimes it doesn't work out. Julie and I kept bumping into each other on the curves. Hell, it was no one's fault. Cops don't make good husbands and neither do Haynes men. I had no business trying."

She was about to ask why when he collected her in his arms again and started down the hallway next to the stairs.

"I'm going to put you in here," he said, using his shoulder to push open a door. "There's an attached bathroom. It's small, but I didn't think you'd want to hassle with the stairs."

Even though she hadn't moved much since leaving the hospital, her side was already aching. "You're right."

A double bed stood next to a window looking out on the side garden where roses had grown into a tangled disarray of blossoms. A single nightstand and a long dresser took up the rest of the space in the room. There was a half-open door and she could see through to a bathroom.

"This will be perfect," she said.

"Mandy's been sleeping upstairs." He set her on her feet. "She can stay there, or I can dig up a cot for her in here. It would be a little crowded, but—"

"Don't worry about it. I'm sure Mandy is happy where she is."

"I'll go get your luggage." He disappeared back the way they'd come.

Elizabeth settled on the bed and touched her healing incision. Just three days ago she'd arrived in Glenwood, hoping to make a fresh start. Many things hadn't worked out the way she'd planned, but they were getting better. She could feel it. She had to get on with her life. It was the only way to put the past behind her.

Travis looked at the empty plate on the table, then at Elizabeth. "Are you done?"

She laughed and patted her stomach. "Yes, thanks. It was wonderful. Here you had me believe you didn't know how to cook."

"I'm okay with omelets," he said, and carried the plates over to the counter. "And I know my way around a barbecue, but other than that, it's just me and the microwave."

"I can make French toast," Mandy announced proudly from her place opposite her mother.

"I know, darlin'. You made it for me this morning."

"How long did it take you to clean up the mess?" Elizabeth asked.

Travis rinsed the dishes and put them in the dishwasher. "About an hour."

She looked at him and smiled. "Amazing, isn't it?"

"I found eggshells everywhere."

"He ate four pieces," Mandy said.

"Good," Elizabeth said, but he could see she was more tired than enthused. There were dark circles under her eyes, and her smile wasn't as bright as it had been that morning when he'd brought her to the house.

He wiped his hands and turned toward the table. The kitchen had been the first room he'd remodeled. That had been before Julie had left. She'd picked out the cream tiles edged in blue flowers, and she'd been the one to insist on bleached oak cabinets. He'd wanted a more traditional kitchen but he had to admit her taste had been better than his. The rectangular room was bright and airy, despite an overabundance of storage and the large subzero refrigerator and six-burner range.

"Mandy, let's put your mama to bed. Then you can help me clean up."

"But it's early yet," Elizabeth said.

"You're dead on your feet."

"I can't be. After you left, I had a nap. I've only been up for—" she glanced at her watch "—three hours." She punctuated her observation with a yawn.

Mandy laughed. "You're tired, Mommy."

"I guess I am." Elizabeth braced her arms on the table and slowly pushed herself to her feet. Travis moved closer, but she waved him off. "I made it to the kitchen under my own power, I think I can make it back."

"Have it your way."

She took small steps. Mandy dogged her heels, and he brought up the rear, ready to jump to the rescue in case she slipped. Her nap wasn't the only thing she'd done while he was gone all afternoon. She'd also showered and changed clothes.

The shorts and tank top had been replaced by a loose-fitting summer dress. It dipped low in front and back and, as he had served his famous vegetable omelet, he got a flash of cleavage. He hadn't seen where the tan ended and her pale skin began, but the peek had more than stirred his interest. He'd spent most of dinner giving himself a stern talking-to.

Elizabeth was his guest. Despite his claim to want to be paid for the room, he would no more take her money than he would hurt Mandy. He was simply temporary shelter and the only friend she had in town. He couldn't take advantage of her, or the situation. It wasn't right. If he wanted a woman, there were plenty in town to oblige him. He'd never once had a problem finding company.

As she turned down the hallway, the last rays of sun caught the thick braid hanging down to her shoulder blades. Her hair gleamed with rich color, brown and gold with a hint of red, so different from Mandy's pale blond hair. Had Elizabeth's hair once been that color, turning darker with age, or had Mandy inherited her hair color from her father?

They reached the bedroom. Elizabeth sank onto the bed and smiled at her daughter. "I'm going to rest here for a few minutes before I get ready to sleep. Why don't you kiss me good-night now and then go help Travis in the kitchen."

Mandy reached up and kissed her cheek. "I love you, Mommy."

"I love you, too, honey."

"I'm glad you're not in that old hospital anymore. Tomorrow can you come upstairs and look at my room?"

"We'll see." Elizabeth stroked her daughter's head, then glanced at Travis. "Thanks for everything. I really appreciate it."

"Just being neighborly," he said from his place in the doorway.

"Hardly, but I do appreciate everything." She motioned to the room, and then smiled at her daughter. "I don't know what I would have done—"

He cut her off. "All you should worry about now is getting better. Leave the rest of it alone. Come on, Mandy. Your mother needs to sleep." He held out his hand.

Mandy looked from him to her mother. "But, Travis, aren't you going to kiss Mommy good-night, too?"

Chapter Four

Elizabeth looked up at him, obviously startled. Her big eyes got bigger and her lips parted slightly with surprise. But she hadn't flinched.

He pushed off the door frame and slowly approached the bed. Her gaze never left his. "I do my best work under pressure," he drawled.

"I'll bet," Elizabeth muttered, then looked away. "Look, you don't have to—"

"Mommy, you need to be kissed good-night," Mandy said, and bounced on the bed. "It'll make you feel better. Travis made me feel better when he gave me a kiss. I didn't have even one bad dream last night."

"Simply medicinal," he said.

"What's mecidinal?" Mandy asked, struggling with the strange word.

He didn't take his gaze off Elizabeth's face. Color steadily climbed her cheeks. She glanced at him, at Mandy, at her fingers twisting together in her lap. He approached the bed and bent over.

"It means doing something for medical purposes," he said. "Like taking medicine."

He rested his hands on her shoulders. Their eyes met. Mandy asked another question, but he couldn't hear all the words. Elizabeth's irises were a pure brown, almost chestnut colored. Her sweet breath fanned his face. His stomach tightened in anticipation, which, he told himself, was stupid. She'd just had major surgery, her six-year-old daughter sat inches away. He was simply going to give her a quick peck on the cheek. So what was the big deal?

But he didn't kiss her cheek. He moved his head to the left side of her face, but at the last minute veered back and brushed his mouth against hers.

He'd expected some kind of attraction. He was a healthy single male, and she was damned good-looking. But he hadn't expected to get third-degree burns from the heat.

The contact, lasting no more than one or two seconds, seared his mouth and sent flames of need racing through his body. Instinctively, his hands tightened on her shoulders. Her arms reached up toward him. He felt them whisper by his sides then fall back. He wanted to haul her to her feet and pull her firmly against him. He wanted to feel her body pressing along his, thighs brushing, hips rotating, chest to breast in exquisite delight.

"Don't you feel better, Mommy?" Mandy asked.

He raised his head. Elizabeth's eyes were wide and unfocused as if she, too, had felt the conflagration. She swallowed and looked away. But not before he'd seen the answering desire in her gaze.

"Much," she answered, her voice low and husky. She cleared her throat. "I do feel better. Thank you."

Travis stared down at her. Who was this woman and what had brought her to Glenwood? Why was there no one, no man, for her to call in her time of trouble? He took a step back and fought a grin. Not that he minded the fact that she was single and in his house. If anything, their kiss had shown him the next three weeks could be very interesting. But why was she alone?

"Come on, Mandy," he said, holding out his hand. "Let's let your mom get some rest. I rented a movie for us to watch."

"Okay." Mandy jumped off the bed and gripped his fingers. "Night, Mommy."

"Night, sweetie," she said, and smiled at her little girl. Her gaze raised to the middle of his chest and stopped. "Good night, Travis. Thank you for...everything."

Yeah, he couldn't stop thinking about their kiss either, he thought. "Get some rest." He led Mandy from the room and closed the door behind them.

A large sofa with a matching chair in soft ivory leather sat in front of an oversize television. Mandy released him and ran over to the VCR. Expertly she pulled the rented tape from its protective cover and inserted it in the machine. Her chatter made him smile, but he had trouble concentrating on her words. He couldn't stop thinking about Elizabeth Abbott. He was sure there was a logical explanation for everything that was going on, but some sixth sense whispered there was a mystery.

As he sat on the sofa and Mandy climbed onto his lap, he mentally listed what he knew about Elizabeth and her daughter. It wasn't much. He was too good a lawman to let anything that intriguing go unsolved. If Elizabeth wouldn't cooperate and answer some questions, he was going to have to find out on his own.

Elizabeth got coffee going before her exhaustion and the pain in her side forced her to retreat to the kitchen table. She sank into one of the bleached oak chairs. She'd hoped the doctor had been kidding when he'd told her to stay off her feet for a week. Apparently not. He'd reminded her that despite all the improvements in medical technology, the fact was she'd had her tummy cut open, through all the muscles. There were multiple layers of tissues to heal. She hadn't realized how much she used those muscles until she tried to move around and they reminded her they weren't working well. She pressed her hand against her side and shifted on the chair. Maybe she would just sit here for a while.

She drew in a deep breath and inhaled the scent of the brewing coffee. At least she'd accomplished something. She smiled. Maybe later, when she'd gathered her strength, she would get wild and attempt toast.

"What are you smiling about, darlin'?"

That voice. It made her think of something warm and rich and decadent slowly slipping through her fingers. It made her think of liquid satin on bare skin. It made her think of last night and their brief kiss. She turned to look at him.

Travis stood in the doorway with his arms folded over his chest. Her breath caught in her throat. She'd never seen him out of uniform before. Her gaze traveled from his scuffed black cowboy boots up the long, lean length of his legs. Worn jeans, faded with lines of white radiating out from the seams by his hips and crotch, clung with the familiarity of an old lover. A red polo shirt stretched across his chest and shoulders, emphasizing his muscles. He looked powerful, but more than that he made her think of a dependable man, a hard worker. His watch was black, some sports kind with a couple of buttons. He didn't wear any rings or other jewelry. Except for the glint in his dark brown eyes and his teasing smile, there wasn't anything flashy about him.

Solid, she thought. That's the word she'd been looking for. Travis Haynes was a solid man.

He took a step into the kitchen. His gaze moved over her face, pausing on her mouth long enough for the tingling to start in her toes and work its way up. Last night she'd lain awake in the dark reliving the brief touch of his lips on hers. It had been nothing significant. A teasing kiss instigated by her daughter. So why did she wonder what it would be like to be held in those powerful arms and pulled hard against that solid chest? Why was her heart beating faster and her breasts tightening in anticipation? Nothing had happened and nothing was going to happen. It couldn't. She knew better than to get involved.

"You didn't answer my question," he said, strolling over to check the coffee. The pot had stopped sputtering. He opened the cupboard above the machine and pulled out two mugs.

"I don't remember what I was smiling about." Her voice sounded completely normal, she thought with some relief.

"How do you take it?"

"With milk, please."

He stirred her coffee and handed her the mug, then took the seat opposite her. "How did you sleep?"

"Great. I feel better."

"You're supposed to be staying off your feet."

"I know. I just wanted some coffee, and I didn't know what time you got up."

She felt a little awkward talking about the intimate details of living together. She barely knew Travis. She tilted her head toward the table, then glanced up at him through her lashes. She liked the way his hair curled slightly around his ears, and the trimmed mustache outlining his upper lip. Last night she'd felt the faint tickle of his mustache against her skin. She wondered what that soft, groomed hair would feel like—

The back door opened, cutting off her dangerous train of thought.

"Yoo-hoo, Travis, are you up?" a loud female voice called.

He grinned. "If I wasn't, Louise, I would be now."

A woman entered the kitchen. She was in her mid to late forties with short blond hair and a figure that could only be described as an hourglass. Her pants were a bright lime green color, her short-sleeved blouse a blend of greens, yellows and oranges. A wide gold belt emphasized her small waist, while a trio of silver chains dipped toward her generous bosom. Dark eye shadow and lots of mascara highlighted her blue eyes. Her red lipstick clashed with everything, but somehow looked all right.

"You must be Elizabeth," Louise said, moving forward and holding out her hand. "Your daughter is the sweetest little girl." She smiled and her eyes got a faraway look. "Maybe I should have had children." She paused. "No, I think Alfred is more than enough trouble, don't you?"

"Alfred?" Elizabeth asked as they shook hands. "Your husband?"

Louise laughed. "No, my dog. Hi, I'm Louise."

Elizabeth didn't know whether to be embarrassed or laugh back. She settled on smiling weakly. Louise bent over and gave Travis a kiss on the cheek, then moved to the refrigerator and started pulling out food.

"Louise is my housekeeper," Travis said.

"I figured that."

"She works here three days a week—"

"But I'm willing to come in more while you're getting better, Elizabeth," Louise said, cutting Travis off. "When I heard what happened, well, I just had to rush over and do whatever I could to help." She set a pitcher of orange juice on the counter. "Maybe you would like to work on some crafts while you're recovering. I'm thinking of doing something with clay."

"Absolutely not," Travis said. "There will be no clay in this house."

Louise mumbled something under her breath about men being pinheads.

Travis leaned forward and lowered his voice. "Louise is going through a stage right now."

The chesty blonde glared at him. "I can hear every word you're staying and this is not a stage. I'm exploring my art."

"She's driving me crazy. She makes things and gives them to me."

"It's a sign of affection, but if you'd rather I didn't, then fine." She slammed the refrigerator door shut and turned her back on them.

"I have this drawer full of sweaters and socks."

Elizabeth stared at him. "Why is that a problem?"

"They're not—" he glanced from her to Louise and back "—normal. Most of the socks have no heel. The sweaters aren't anatomically correct."

Louise walked over to the table and grinned. "I'll admit I didn't quite get the hang of knitting. I never could figure out parts of the patterns, but some of the wool was real lovely." She held two eggs in her right hand. "How would you like them cooked?"

Elizabeth blinked several times. "Scrambled?"

"Fine." She glanced at Travis. "I know what you want, but the way you've talked about me this morning, I'm of a mind to let you go hungry."

"Your threats don't scare me." As Louise passed him, he reached out and patted her rear end affectionately.

"Don't you try your wild ways on me, Travis Haynes," she said, giving him a mock glare. "I'm old enough to be your very young and attractive aunt."

Elizabeth couldn't help it. She started laughing. Even the sharp pains in her side couldn't stop her from chuckling.

"Mommy."

Mandy entered the room. She was washed and dressed in a pretty blue dress with tiny white flowers. She came over to her and held out her arms for a hug. Elizabeth pulled her close.

"Are you ready for your first day of school?" she asked. Travis was going to walk Mandy to the elementary school and register her.

Mandy nodded. "Travis helped me pick out this dress to wear. Did we choose the right one?"

"Of course, Mandy. You look perfect."

"I have ribbons." She held them out. "Will you put them in my hair?"

"Sure."

Elizabeth turned and Mandy slipped between her legs. When the girl saw Louise, she squealed with excitement. "Louise, you found us."

Louise looked at her. "Morning, baby girl. What do you mean I found you?"

"Travis said you were lost."

Elizabeth glanced at him. He'd taken a sip of coffee just as Mandy spoke and now he started to choke. Louise came over and pounded him on the back several times while he coughed.

Louise gave her a quick wink. "He probably said I was trying to find myself."

The next thud on his back sounded a little harder. He turned to her and held up his hand. "That's enough," he said, his voice raspy and faint. "I'm fine."

Elizabeth wasn't sure, but she thought she saw a flush of color on Travis's cheeks. She bit back her laughter and concentrated on Mandy's hair. When the braid was secured with the length of blue ribbon, Mandy pulled out a chair and climbed onto the seat. As Louise fixed breakfast, Many chatted with Travis and Louise about what Mr. Bear had told her in the night. Louise slid a plate in front of the girl, containing a waffle shaped like a popular cartoon mouse. Cut strawberries formed a bright collar at the bottom of the waffle. A glass of milk completed the meal.

Elizabeth looked up at the older woman. "Thank you for making that."

Louise shrugged. "It's nothing. The first day of school should be special for a little girl. And Alfred was never impressed with my waffles."

Elizabeth wanted to ask if Louise really did feed her dog waffles, but she didn't dare. As the smells of eggs, bacon and coffee mingled in the kitchen, she leaned back in her chair and savored her feeling of relief. She and Mandy were going to make it. In three weeks she would start her new job and move into her own place. In the meantime, they were safe here.

She glanced at Travis and found him staring at her. His gaze dropped briefly to her mouth. The sensation of being touched was so real, she wanted to touch him back. The attraction flickering just below the surface fanned to life.

He was her salvation and her greatest problem. This, this mindless reaction to him, had to stop. She knew better than to get involved with a man, any man. But he was even worse than most. She knew what his easy ways and quick, tempting smile meant. She'd already been seduced by one charmer and those results had been more awful than she could ever have imagined. The only decent thing to come out of her relationship with Sam Proctor had been Mandy—and that had been an accident.

Louise served them breakfast, then poured more coffee. Elizabeth hesitated before picking up her fork.

"Dig in," Travis said. "Louise is a great cook."

"I don't doubt that, it's just..."

He leaned across the bleached oak table and laid his hand on top of hers. Heat flooded her fingers, warming her blood and making its way up her arm. She told herself to ignore it, and him, but she couldn't seem to look away from his dark gaze.

"It's just nothing," he said. "Everything is going to be all right. I'll make it all right. I'm the sheriff. I can do anything."

"I believe you," she said and was rewarded with a smile. She *did* believe him. That was the problem.

She picked up her fork. It was only for a few weeks, she reminded herself. She just had to stay strong and resist the powerful charm of Travis Haynes. She could do it, she had to. Her life depended on it.

Elizabeth sat in the family room and stared at the television. The screen was blank. She picked up the remote control, then tossed it down. She didn't want to watch television; she wanted to be with her daughter on her first day of school.

She swallowed against the lump in her throat, but the pressure didn't go away. Her eyes burned and she wanted to scream at the unfairness of it all. Little Mandy had gone off with Travis an hour ago. She'd waved and smiled, and promised to make her mom something pretty in class.

"I should have been with her," Elizabeth said softly, fighting the frustration. She touched her side, feeling the bandage under her shorts and panties. There was no way she could have made it from here to the school and back. It took all her strength to walk from the kitchen to the family room. But she'd so wanted to see Mandy's classroom and meet her teacher. Her daughter would only enter the first grade once and she'd missed it. What kind of mother did that make her? It wasn't enough she'd taken Mandy away from everything she knew in the world, but now the girl was going to a strange school, escorted by a strange man. It wasn't fair.

"Television is generally more interesting when you turn it on," Louise said.

Elizabeth looked up at her. The other woman stood in the doorway to the family room. She had a mug of coffee in each hand. "I wasn't really planning on watching," she said.

"Would you like some company?"

Elizabeth nodded. "That would be nice, if you have the time."

Louise handed her one of the mugs and plopped down at the opposite end of the butter-soft leather sofa. "I've got plenty of time. That boy hasn't even furnished most of the rooms in this monstrosity. There's not that much cleaning to do. I suspect he hires me so that he can have a taste of someone else's cooking and a friendly face to come home to a couple of days a week."

"Are you saying Travis is lonely?"

"Could be."

Louise fluffed up her bangs with her fingers. Elizabeth noticed she painted her long nails a bright red and had thin stripes of gold dotted on the tips.

"So what do you think of him?" Louise asked.

That was certainly subtle, Elizabeth thought, fighting a grin. "He seems very nice."

Louise's eyes narrowed. "Now I don't think any of the Haynes boys would appreciate being called 'nice.' Ladies' men, maybe. Irresistible, certainly. But nice?" She shook her head and smiled. "You'd better keep that opinion to yourself."

"I guess I'll have to." She took a sip from her mug. "Travis mentioned he has three brothers."

"That's right, and his daddy is one of five." She leaned her head back against the leather sofa. Her expression got soft and dreamy. "That means there are nine Haynes men walking around on this earth tempting women with their wicked ways. When I was in high school, Earl—that's Travis's father—came to speak to my class about drinking and driving. I don't remember a word he said, but I do remember how handsome he looked in his uniform. When he smiled, I about melted in my seat." She straightened and shrugged. "I was barely seventeen, and my boyfriend and I had just broken up. Earl Haynes looked mighty good. Of course he was a much older man."

"Of course," Elizabeth murmured. Louise was certainly a little left of center, but Elizabeth found herself liking the other woman.

"And his uncles. Hell-raisers all of them. I don't think they were ever faithful longer than a minute. Heaven help the women who tried to tame 'em. Of course the Haynes men did give this town something to talk about. Then when Earl went ahead and had four more boys of his own, there was even more talk. Do you know there hasn't been a girl born to the Haynes family in four generations?"

"Travis mentioned that."

Louise laughed. "Travis is the most easygoing of the four boys. Not like Jordan. That one's always been a mystery. But Travis knows what he wants and gets it." She winked. "Maybe he'll decide he wants you."

Elizabeth shook her head. "I'm not interested in a relationship. Certainly not with a man like him. The last thing I need is some Don Juan upsetting my life."

"Oh, you can't believe everything you hear about him. He's not exactly the heartbreaker everyone says. Despite what he thinks, he's nothing like his daddy." Louise grew serious. "You can trust me on that one, honey. I know for a fact."

It didn't matter how much of Travis's reputation was real and how much hype. Enough of what Louise had said was true for Travis Haynes to be trouble.

Sam had been a charmer, too. His easy smile and quick wit had seduced her in a matter of hours. Of course she'd been a willing participant. And young. Far too young for a man like him. She'd never had a clue as to what was going on. She'd known the relationship was in trouble, but even that hadn't prepared her for the police showing up at her doorstep in the predawn hours of morning. If she lived to be a hundred, she would never forget the feeling of horror when the Los Angeles Police Department officers had taken Sam away. Thank God Mandy had slept through it all.

Louise leaned forward and patted her leg. "You feeling better?"

"What?"

"I thought you might be a little down, what with missing Mandy's first day at school. You feel better now?"

Elizabeth looked at Louise, with her bright makeup and dangling earrings. The left one was a teapot, the right, a cup and saucer. "You probably don't want to hear this any more than Travis, but I think you're nice, too."

Louise gave her hand a squeeze and rose to her feet. "Just don't let word get out. I have my own reputation to keep up. Now I'm going to get to work on lunch. I heard Travis's truck in the driveway. He can tell you all about Mandy's classroom. Don't worry, honey. You'll get to see it soon enough."

She left the room and passed Travis in the doorway. Elizabeth half turned to face him. "How did it go?" she asked.

He studied her for several seconds. There was an odd look in his eyes, as if he'd never seen her before.

"Travis, is something wrong?"

"No. Everything went fine. Mandy loved her teacher and when I left, it looked like she'd already started making friends."

Elizabeth sagged back in the sofa. Some of the tension left her body. Maybe, just maybe, she hadn't destroyed her daughter's life.

"These might help," he said as he walked toward her. He held out several instant photos.

"You took pictures?"

"I thought they might make you feel like you'd been there."

She smiled up at him. "That was so thoughtful."

She took the photos and looked through them. The first showed Mandy smiling in front of the school. There were three shots of the classroom and one of Mandy with her teacher. The little girl was laughing at something the woman had said. Elizabeth felt tears forming in her eyes. She blinked them away.

"This is wonderful. I don't know how to thank you."

Travis shifted his weight from one foot to the other. "It's nothing special. I didn't even think of the idea. Craig does it for his kids. He says it's fun to look back later. You're not going to cry, are you?"

She sniffed. "No." She touched one finger to the smooth flat surface, as if she could touch Mandy's warm cheek. Her daughter's smile made her own lips curve up in response. "She *does* look happy, doesn't she? And the teacher looks nice. Did you talk to her?"

"I know her."

There was something about the way he said the words. "Oh?"

"I sort of, you know." He shoved his hands into his jeans pockets. "We dated for a while."

"Ah. Is she—" Elizabeth paused, then found the correct word. "Is she nice?" She had to bite her lip to keep from smiling.

Travis was obviously uncomfortable with the conversation. "Yeah, she's really great. With kids, I mean."

"I'm sure Mandy will like her."

"Most of the kids do."

He pulled his hands out of his pockets and walked over to the window. The bright light outside lighted his tall, muscular body. He was very handsome, with his dark hair and eyes. Elizabeth could see why he'd acquired his reputation. If his brothers were half as good-looking, then it's no wonder the town found the family a great source of gossip.

"Tell me about your ex-husband," he said.

She felt as if he'd thrown a bucket of cold water in her face. Every muscle in her body tensed. She had to put the photos down when she realized she was mangling them. She folded her hands in her lap and forced herself to relax.

"I don't have an ex-husband. I told you, I was never married." She could feel the heat of her flush climbing from the scoop neck of her T-shirt, up to her face. It had been six months, yet she was still embarrassed to remember what had happened. Would this ever get easier?

"You're sure?"

"I would hardly forget being married."

He walked to the sofa and braced his hands against the tall back. "The reason I ask is because when I registered Mandy for school, she got confused about her last name. When I first asked, she said it was Proctor. I reminded her that your last name is Abbott. She said that was her last name, too. So which is it, Elizabeth?"

He was still handsome as sin, but the friendly, teasing man who had shared breakfast with her had disappeared. In his place was a probing stranger. For the first time she saw the dark side of him. No doubt he made an excellent sheriff.

But she couldn't tell him the truth. It was too awful, too embarrassing, too unbelievable. She had trouble believing it had happened, and she'd lived through it. Besides, she didn't want to see that pitying look in his eyes. She didn't want to know he thought of her as less, or stupid. No, the truth was her own secret, one she would never share. She could, however, tell him part of the truth.

She raised her hand to flick her hair back over her shoulder. "Proctor is Mandy's father's last name. She used it for a while, but now she's using my name."

"I see." He drew his eyebrows together. "You mentioned you had rented a house here in town."

What did that have to do with anything? She nodded slowly. "I can take possession on October first."

"Is your furniture in storage?"

"Why are you asking me this?"

He moved around the sofa until he was standing in front of her. She had to tilt her head back to meet his eyes. She wished he was wearing his Stetson so she didn't have to see the cold black swirling through his irises.

"Is it?"

"No. I don't have any furniture. I left it all behind in L.A. I didn't want to move it. Travis, why are you acting like this? Why are you asking all these questions?"

"So you have no furniture, Mandy has very few toys. In fact, all your possessions can fit in the trunk of your car." He wasn't asking a question.

Her heart pounded in her chest. She wanted to stand up and stare him in the eye, but the tension was making her side ache too much. She could only sit on the edge of the sofa and fight the fear.

"Travis—"

He cut her off with a wave of his hand. "I want the truth, Elizabeth. Did you kidnap Mandy?"

Chapter Five

She couldn't have looked more stunned if he'd slapped her. All the color left her face and her lips parted, but she couldn't—or didn't—speak.

Travis noted her reactions, the cynical lawman side of him wondering if she was the genuine article or a very good actress. The male part of him, that part of his being that had reacted to her presence in his life, wanted to believe. He wanted her to be just a single mom looking for something better for herself and her kid.

It shouldn't matter, he told himself. He wasn't going to get involved. It would be better for his hormonal state if she was some kind of criminal. After his marriage had collapsed he'd acknowledged the futility of ignoring the truth. As long as he had Haynes blood flowing through his veins he didn't have a prayer of having a decent long-lasting relationship. So he shouldn't mind if everything about Elizabeth Abbott-Proctor, or whatever her name was, turned out to be a lie.

Except he knew it was too late. He couldn't get involved with her, but that didn't stop him from liking her. And Mandy. The kid had him wrapped around her finger. This morning—

Can it, he ordered himself. He couldn't afford to think about how great it had been to take Mandy to her first day of school. So what if her trusting smile had given him a lump in his throat? Marriage, a wife and kids weren't for him. He didn't have whatever mysterious something it took to be a decent husband and father. He had to focus on Elizabeth and the mystery in her life. He might not be good domestic material, but he was a damn fine sheriff.

Elizabeth glanced up at him, then turned away. "It's a very effective technique," she said, her voice low and strained. "Glaring at people like that, I'm sure most of your prisoners crack under the pressure."

Only then did he realize how long he'd been staring at her. But he didn't look away. "Just tell me the truth. I'd have to be blind not to see there's some kind of mystery in your life."

She stood up slowly. Her mouth twisted, but he sensed it was from the strain on her incision rather than fear. When she was standing, she squared her shoulders and looked up at him. Emotional and physical pain darkened her wide eyes. All the color had faded from her cheeks, leaving her pale and drawn. He could see the beginning of tiny lines around her eyes.

Her long hair fanned out over her shoulders. He wanted to touch that hair, touch her and pull her close. He wanted to ease her pain and promise it was going to be all right. But he couldn't. He didn't know how it was going to be.

"I don't know whether to be furious or grateful," she said, and stepped away from him.

He knew she was too weak from the surgery to run, but instinctively his body tensed as he prepared to grab her if she went too far. He needn't have worried. She circled behind the sofa and leaned against the back.

"There's no mystery, Travis," she said softly. She studied the leather couch and traced a line of stitching back and forth with her finger. "I'm not and never have been married. Sam Proctor is Mandy's father. Our relationship—" She hesitated, then drew in a deep breath and looked at him. "Our relationship doesn't exist anymore. Sam is out of our lives. I came up here to make a fresh start. I left behind everything Sam had given me, including the clothes and toys and furniture. I only brought what is mine and Mandy's. Sam signed custody of Mandy over to me. I didn't have time to open a bank account and get a safety-deposit box, so I have the papers with me. I would be happy to show you her birth certificate and anything else you'd like to see."

"I don't need to see the papers."

"But you don't believe me."

"I didn't say that."

He didn't have to. They both knew she'd been lying. Oh, not about Mandy. He did believe that. It almost made sense, the leaving everything behind part. It seemed like an expensive, impulsive gesture, but nothing about women surprised him.

She'd only lied once. When she'd told him there was no mystery in her life. There was a damn big one and he was no closer to figuring it out. She'd said she'd never married. He almost believed that. So what did that mean? That she'd shacked up with some guy and had his baby?

He studied her. With her hair loose around her face, she looked younger than twenty-eight. Had she gotten involved with a married man? He didn't want to believe that of her. It reminded him too much of his father and the older man's string of young women. Earl Haynes had gotten a kick out of seducing the innocents, making them believe he was going to leave his wife and family. He'd never left them, at least not permanently. His way of justifying his life-style had been waking up in his own bed every morning. Every time Travis had heard his mother and father fighting about his father's infidelities, Earl had glossed over his behavior by saying he always woke up in his bed. What more could a woman want?

Travis had been there once, when it had happened. A woman in her early twenties had been in town visiting family. They'd met in the hardware store. Within fifteen minutes, Earl'd had the woman eating out of his hand and leaving the hardware store to get a drink. Travis had run away as fast as he could. He'd only been fourteen at the time, but he'd known what was happening. He hadn't made it home before he'd had to stop and throw up in the bushes. He'd cried then for all he'd never had, cried for the loss of a father who was like other dads. A father who cared more about his wife and his sons than other women. It had been the last time he'd shed tears.

"Stop staring at me," Elizabeth said, and spun away. The quick movement caused her to gasp and clutch her side.

He moved toward her, but didn't touch her.

"I'm not going to faint or anything," she said, straightening. "I just wish you'd stop looking at me like I... Jeez, I don't know. I haven't committed a crime, okay? Isn't that enough for you?"

Anger radiated out from her, and that more than anything caused him to trust the feeling in his gut that said she told him the truth.

"I guess it has to be."

"I didn't ask to come here with you and I'll be happy to leave." She started for the door. "If Louise can't give me a lift back to the motel, then I'll call a cab."

He caught her in one stride and gently took her arm. "I don't want you to leave."

"I don't believe you." She pulled her arm free and glared up at him. "You keep staring at me as if I've just made off with the family silver. I haven't done anything wrong. None of this is my fault."

It was the fact that she didn't cry that finally convinced him. He could see the strength it took to hold on to her control. Her mouth quivered from the effort and perspiration dotted her forehead.

Maybe the guy had beaten her, he thought suddenly. Maybe her ex-boyfriend had been one of those sick types who got off on hitting women and children. He glanced at her bare arms, but there were no telltale marks. Of course she could have been on her own for several weeks.

Dammit, what the hell was her story?

She took another step and seemed to stumble. He caught her up in his arms and carried her to the sofa. She clung to him for a moment. He ignored the way her curvy body felt against his chest, the long length of her legs and the soft pressure of her breasts against his shirt. When he set her on the sofa, she immediately tried to slide away. The movement caused her to clutch at her side and glare at him.

The anger in her gaze made him smile. Her temper he could handle.

"You're overreacting," he said mildly.

Her mouth dropped open. "*I'm* overreacting? Wait a minute. You're the one accusing of me of who knows what. Maybe it would be better if I just—"

"No." He settled next to her on the couch and touched her cheek with the back of his hand. She jerked her head away, but there was no fear in her eyes. Relief flooded him. If she'd been beaten on a regular basis, she would have been terrified. Instead she reacted with completely understandable indignation.

"Don't touch me, or try to sweet-talk me," she said. "You accused me of kidnapping my daughter."

"Given the little that you've told me, would you have thought any differently?"

"I—" She drew in a deep breath and brushed her hair out of her face. "I suppose not. But you didn't have to be such a cop about it."

"Just doing my job."

She nodded slowly. "I understand."

"So you're not going to make a run for it?"

"To the best of my knowledge I haven't committed a felony."

He winked. "Sometimes the misdemeanors can be even more interesting."

She smiled. "Oh, please. Don't get me started. I don't even want to know what you're talking about." Her smile faded. "I really haven't done anything wrong, Travis."

He hesitated and then said, "I know."

She held out her hand. "Friends?"

She wanted to shake on it. As Travis took her warm fingers in his, he glanced at her full mouth and wondered if it would taste even sweeter if he kissed her without a six-year-old audience to censor the moment. Better to shake hands, he told himself. Safer. For both of them.

"Friends," he said and released her. Only then did he remember he still hadn't solved the mystery.

Elizabeth hobbled over to the table and gratefully sank into the seat. She was breathing heavily and all she'd done was assemble the ingredients to make cupcakes.

"From a mix," she said, disgusted with her weakened condition. She grabbed the package and ripped it open. The effort necessary to raise the box to dump it in the bowl made her incision ache.

She leaned back in the chair and took a deep breath. Thank God she wasn't trying to make it on her own in that small motel room. She and Mandy would have starved.

The line of thinking was a mistake, she acknowledged, as thinking of not being in the motel made her remember how she'd been rescued by the very handsome, the very inquisitive Sheriff Travis Haynes. Which made her think of this morning and what had happened between them.

He was not a man she wanted to cross. Despite the wicked charm and sinful good looks, he was intimidating when he was angry. All his questions had made her nervous, but he'd never once stumbled close to the truth. Of course, why should he? It wasn't the first thing anyone thought of. Things like that only happened in the tabloids. That's where she belonged. Right between the cover story on the aliens abducting the residents of a local pig farm and the woman giving birth to the four-legged child.

She felt guilty, too, knowing that Travis had given her the benefit of the doubt, trusting her when she hadn't told him the whole truth. She picked up an egg and held it. Was it so wrong not to want him to know? She *hadn't* done anything wrong, had committed no crime, save the one of being too young and too trusting. Okay, she'd been a fool. But was that illegal?

"Just what is it you think you're doing?"

Elizabeth jumped guiltily at the sound of the voice. Louise stood in the doorway to the kitchen. She planted her hands on her curvy hips and stared.

"I'm, ah, making cupcakes for Mandy."

Louise shook her head. "And you look like such a bright girl, too." She walked over and grabbed the egg from Elizabeth's hand. "The doctor told you to stay in bed for a week."

"I know, it's just—"

"A week is seven days. This is day two. If I have to tie you up, I will, but won't that be hard to explain to the neighbors?"

Elizabeth grinned and held up her hands in defeat. "I give. Just don't make me laugh. It hurts too much. If I promise to be good, can I at least sit here for a little while?"

Louise looked stern. "For a few minutes. Then I want you to go lie down until Mandy gets home."

"Yes, ma'am."

Louise took the seat next to her and finished pouring in the mix. "I remember when I was little my mama used to make cupcakes for me."

"Mandy loves them."

"So do I." The older woman smiled. "I haven't baked anything in ages. I wonder if Alfred would like some cake with his dinner." She thought for a minute. "No, he's still trying to lose weight." She leaned forward. "Alfred is a beagle and they tend to get a little heavy when they age."

Elizabeth hoped Louise was only kidding about making a cake for her dog, but she wasn't completely sure and she didn't want to ask.

Louise stirred in the other ingredients, then started pouring the batter into the cupcake pan. "So, I heard you and Travis fighting. You want to talk about it?"

"You aren't one to beat around the bush, are you?"

Louise shrugged. "I'm pretty straightforward," she admitted. "It would probably be easier if I'd just learn to keep my mouth shut. Maybe I'll get it eventually. But you seem like a real nice lady. Mandy is the sweetest little girl and I've found you can usually judge a mother by her children. Travis Haynes is one of my favorite people on earth. Why, if I was five or six years younger, I might just risk my heart on him." She paused, then shook her head. "On second thought, I'll leave the Haynes boys to the rest of you. I've already had my heart broken once by that family."

It was too much information to absorb, Elizabeth thought, not knowing whether to laugh, cry, be insulted or flattered.

"He's a good man," Louise said, carrying the full cup-cake pans over to the oven and sliding them inside.

"Who?"

"Travis."

"I know that."

"He was just doing his job, asking all those questions, I mean." Louise poured herself a cup of coffee. When she held up the pot, Elizabeth shook her head. "Of course any woman would know you're that girl's mother through and through. She's got your smile. Her daddy must be some kind of looker."

"He is," Elizabeth said. Sam certainly was good-looking. Not nearly as handsome as Travis, but attractive enough to make any woman look twice. She'd been so caught up by his face and body, the charm and easy smile, she'd never thought to question anything except her good fortune. Imagine little Elizabeth Abbott catching someone like Sam. Only, she hadn't exactly caught him.

"So, you still mad at Travis?"

"No. I understand that he had questions." But she wasn't willing to give him all his answers. Still she couldn't blame him for asking. She'd expected him to wonder what her story was, but she hadn't expected him to come up with kidnapping!

"I'm glad." Louise sipped her coffee, then glanced at the clock over the stove. "Looks like it's time for me to leave. Travis and Mandy should be back in an hour or so. You're not going to get out of control and start vacuuming, are you?"

"I promise I'll behave."

Louise set down her cup. She picked up her purse from the counter, then crossed to the table, bent over and gave Elizabeth a hug. "I'm here if you want to talk," she said. "I might not have any answers, but I'm a great listener."

Elizabeth hugged her back. The other woman's perfume was a clingy Oriental scent that somehow suited her perfectly. Louise stepped back and waved, then left the kitchen. The back door banged shut behind her and the kitchen was silent.

Elizabeth stared around the empty room, wishing the digital clock would tick so there would be some sound. She was completely and totally alone. She wasn't afraid to be on her own. It was the questions that came to her, making her wonder if she'd made the right decisions for herself, and more importantly, for Mandy. Had she had other options and not realized it? Would she ever know how many clues she'd missed? She'd been worse than a fool.

The timer on the oven clicked down another minute. She thought about Louise who had offered to be a friend. Elizabeth knew that she needed to make some friends. She desperately needed someone to talk to and have fun with. Louise was a little offbeat, but that didn't matter. The reason Elizabeth couldn't reach out to her was because of herself, not because of the other woman. She couldn't dare be friends with anyone. She would always have to hold some part of herself back, be it from Louise or Travis.

Thank God he hadn't guessed the truth. She leaned back in the chair and sighed. Every time she thought she'd put it all behind her, something happened to remind her again.

She tried to think about nothing more complicated than whether or not she had the strength to frost the cupcakes. In the end, she decided she didn't and pulled the muffin pans from the oven and left them to cool. She lay down on her bed and closed her eyes, but she couldn't escape her past even there. So she tried thinking about other things. About the kiss.

Her eyes flew open. Not that. But now that she'd remembered it, she found it hard to forget the soft brush of his lips on hers yesterday. Today, when he'd sat next to her on the sofa and they'd shaken hands, for a moment she'd thought he might kiss her. Softly, tenderly, holding her close in those strong arms.

He carried her so easily, but that was an impersonal gesture made to aid an invalid. She wanted to be held close by a man who needed to hold a woman. She wanted to know if Travis could make her feel safe and secure in his embrace, if he could loan her a little of his strength and confidence. Foolish dreams. She hadn't answered all his questions. They both knew that. He might believe that she hadn't broken any laws, but she'd seen the look in his eyes. He was reserving judgment on her until he knew the truth. Imagine what he would think of her then.

The back door opened and she heard Mandy's laughter as she came into the kitchen.

"Mommy, Mommy, where are you?"

"In here," she called, sitting up slowly and leaning against the headboard.

Mandy flew into the room. She had several papers in one hand and her bear in the other.

"How was your first day of school?" Elizabeth asked, holding out her arms.

Her daughter scrambled onto the bed and threw herself into her embrace. Elizabeth held her close. Even the pain in her side didn't matter, she thought, as she stroked her daughter's hair.

Mandy leaned back and knelt on the bed. "I had fun."

"Did you?"

Mandy nodded. "Miss Brickman says we're going to learn to read."

Elizabeth touched Mandy's paint-smudged cheek. Her dress was wrinkled, her ribbons loose and coming undone, but there was a bright glow of happiness in her child's eyes that made her heart lighten. Maybe she had made the right decision after all.

"You already know how to read."

"I know." Mandy grinned. "She said she'd help me learn better. And we're going to do counting, too. Here." She thrust out her papers. "I did these."

Elizabeth looked at the drawing of what she was pretty sure was supposed to be this large house, a sheet with Mandy's name painstakingly spelled out in a childish scrawl, and a note from Miss Brickman outlining the homework schedule for the first half of the year.

"You're supposed to sign this one," Mandy said, pointing at the note from the teacher. "We're going to have homework, just like the big kids." She sounded delighted. Elizabeth wondered how long that would last.

"Someone's been busy."

She looked up and saw Travis standing in the doorway. He held a tray containing a plate with several chocolate cupcakes and two glasses of milk.

Mandy's blue eyes got big. "Mommy, you made cupcakes for me."

"I thought you weren't supposed to get out of bed," Travis said.

"Louise did all the work."

"Why don't I believe that?"

"Don't ask me, because she did."

"Sure." He put the tray down on her nightstand, then pulled Mandy off the bed. "Maybe you should change into play clothes before you get crumbs all over that dress. What do you think?"

Mandy looked at her mother, who nodded, then sighed. "Okay, but don't eat all the cupcakes before I get back."

"We won't," Elizabeth said and watched her daughter scamper out of the room. She glanced at the cupcakes and saw they'd been iced. "Thank you," she said. "I meant to get back to that, but I must have dozed off."

"Hey, I opened a can. How hard could it be?" He perched on the edge of the bed. "You're not overdoing it, are you?"

Exhaustion overwhelmed her with all the subtlety of being hit by a large truck. She tried to smile, but suddenly she was too tired. "Maybe just a little."

He leaned forward. For a second she thought he was going to kiss her. She found out she had just enough energy left to get excited by the thought, then was disappointed when all he did was lay his hand against her forehead.

"No fever," he said, "but you should stay in bed for the rest of the day. The last thing you need is to land yourself back in the hospital."

"I know." She picked at the bed cover, then looked at him. He'd shaved that morning, but the shadowy darkness of his beard highlighted his strong jaw. He had dark eyes framed by thick lashes. A firm mouth that was threatening to curve into a smile. Nothing in his expression reminded her of the questions he'd asked that morning. Yet that conversation sat in the room like a rather large intrusive elephant.

"I'm sorry," she said.

His expression hardened, and his mouth pulled into a straight line. "You don't have to apologize."

"I *want* to. You've been very kind to me."

"This is a full-service community."

She chuckled, then clutched her side. "Travis, don't make me laugh. It still hurts."

"Okay, I'll be serious."

He leaned closer, bracing one hand on the far side of her body. She wanted to reach up and pull him close. She settled on inhaling the scent of his body. He smelled like a fall day, with a hint of musk thrown in for temptation.

"Tell me your secret," he said softly.

When she'd first met Sam she'd thought she'd loved him with her whole heart and soul. He only had to look at her to make her want to be with him, next to him, touched by him. She'd learned later that her feelings for Sam Proctor were more about the newness of a physical relationship than anything else. But it had already been too late. She'd committed the ultimate foolish act and fallen in love with him.

Nothing about Sam's practiced charm had prepared her for Travis's lethal combination of strength and concern. It would be so easy to lean on those shoulders she admired, to tell him everything. But to what end? Once he knew the truth— She couldn't even bear to think about it.

"I can't." She met his gaze and held it.

"You won't."

"Yes. I won't. Please don't ask me again. I don't want to have to lie to you. I haven't done anything illegal. It's a silly little secret, but it's mine to keep. If telling you everything about my past is the price for staying, then I have to leave."

He studied her a long time. His gaze swept over her face, stopping at her mouth before dipping to her throat and returning. He reached up and touched her cheek, much as she'd touched Mandy's. But his caress was anything but maternal. Her stomach tightened and her breasts tingled in response.

Before she could say anything, or think about touching him back, he reached down for the comforter folded up at the foot of the bed. He pulled it over her and smoothed it in place. Then he leaned down and brushed his lips against her forehead.

"Go to sleep, darlin'," he said, and stood up.

She watched him leave the room and close the door quietly behind him. Her eyes burned with unshed tears. It would be so easy to let Travis into her world, she thought sadly. So easy to try to believe again. If she had the strength and the words, she would explain that it wasn't so much about him. Sure, she couldn't risk trusting a man again, but worse, she couldn't trust herself.

Chapter Six

"You're nervous," Travis said, taking off his Stetson and sending it across the family room. It landed neatly in the center of a writing desk on the left side of the window.

Elizabeth sank into the leather sofa and rolled her eyes. "Number one, if you keep doing that hat toss trick to impress me, I'm immune."

"Liar," he said as he crossed the room.

His khaki uniform, slightly wrinkled from his day at work, made his shoulders look broader and his legs longer. His wide black belt emphasized his trim waist. And yes, she had been lying. The nightly toss of the Stetson got her heart racing as if she'd just climbed three flights of stairs.

He settled on the sofa and grinned. "What's number two?"

"Number two is I have nothing to be nervous about."

"Double liar." He leaned closer, resting his weight on his elbow. His perfectly trimmed mustache outlined the teasing curve of his mouth. "I've made tougher women than you swoon with my cowboy hat, and while there's no reason to be nervous about having dinner with Rebecca, you are. I can see it in your eyes."

She opened her mouth to deny his statement, then closed it. He was right; she *was* nervous. "Okay, just a little."

He sat up straight, then leaned over and patted her bare leg. "Don't be. Rebecca's a sweetheart." He kept his warm hand on her knee. She told herself she should move away, but she liked it when he touched her.

She raised her eyebrows. "Do you realize that every time a female citizen of Glenwood is mentioned, you've dated her?"

"Only if they're between twenty-five and forty."

She reached behind her for one of the throw pillows and batted his hand away. "What's wrong with you?"

"I'm one of the Haynes boys. What else am I supposed to do?"

She'd been in Travis's house for six days. Louise had filled her head with enough stories to tell her what being a "Haynes boy" meant. "Settle down with one woman. Try monogamy for a change. There is something to be said for quality rather than quantity."

His good humor faded quickly. "I tried that, remember?"

"Oh." She did recall him mentioning a divorce. "Sorry." She was silent for a moment. "So what happened?"

He turned his head until he was looking at her. The lines around his eyes crinkled when he smiled. "You've been hanging around with Louise a little too much, don't you think? You could have been a bit more subtle with that question."

"Probably," she admitted shamelessly. "So what happened? Or don't you want to talk about it?"

"There's nothing to say. It just didn't work. I'm sure some of it was her fault, but I have to take most of the blame." He held his hands out in front of him, palms up. "It's a little difficult to get past who I am."

"So that's why you know Rebecca is a sweetheart?"

"Want to know a secret?"

She wasn't sure she did, but Travis was difficult enough to resist most of the time, and now, when he was rumpled and just tired enough to let his guard down, he was impossible to refuse.

"Sure."

He slid closer to her. Her body tensed. Her incision had healed quite a bit, although it still hurt if she moved around too much. She wanted to pull back, but there was nowhere to go except off the sofa. Six days with Travis had taught her two important things. The first was that being in his presence made her very aware of her body, his body and the potential those two bodies had together. She told herself it was just hormones, and being lonely and afraid that brought on that thinking. The second thing she learned was that even if she was ever foolish enough to get involved with a man again. Travis Haynes was absolutely the worst one she could pick. He and his brothers had reputations for being lady-killers and heartbreakers. Louise had told her story after story about the female conquests made and cast aside. Elizabeth had to admit that in most of the stories, Travis had been honest, caring and had at least tried to make the relationship work. But the reality was he made Sam Proctor look like an amateur when it came to seducing women.

He leaned over so he could whisper in her ear. His chin rested on her shoulder, pushing aside the thin strap of her tank top. Stubble grazed her suddenly sensitized skin, making her muscles jump and her toes curl against the thick carpet.

"Rebecca is my greatest failure."

"What?"

She made the mistake of turning to look at him. He hadn't pulled back and their faces were inches apart. Breath mingled with the heady scent of his warm body. She clutched her fingers tightly together to prevent herself from reaching out toward him and touching his arm, his chest, anything she could get her hands on.

"Shortly after we met, I took her out on a date. It was supposed to be this great seduction. I had everything planned."

The pain in her midsection wasn't from the surgery, she realized, chagrined. It was envy, pure and simple. She prayed he couldn't see it in her eyes.

"I picked her up at seven-thirty. By eight-ten I figured out I'd made a large error in judgment."

"Which was?"

"Chemistry. It was all wrong."

She stared at him, at his dark eyes that suddenly seemed to be flickering with the most intriguing fire.

"What was wrong with it?" she asked, barely able to disconnect from the flames enough to follow the conversation.

"There wasn't any between us. Rebecca and me. We were destined to be good friends. But it's a secret. What would people say if they knew the truth? After all, the Haynes charm is supposed to be all-powerful."

It was working just fine on her, she thought as she lowered her gaze to his mouth. So close. She licked her lips. Three, maybe four inches separated them. The longing inside of her grew. She wanted to know what it would be like to be kissed, really kissed, by him.

She closed her eyes and forced herself to turn away. Why was she doing this to herself? Hadn't Sam taught her anything?

"Everybody needs friends, Travis. Rebecca seems very nice."

"Oh, she is."

He stood up and stretched like a powerful cat taking a moment's rest from stalking the mouse. That was *her* destiny: Elizabeth Abbott-rodent. She giggled.

"What's so funny?" he asked.

"Nothing. I'm pleased that you and Rebecca are friends. Now I get the chance to spend some time with her before I start my job." She smiled brightly, trying to banish the lingering lethargy and leftover passion, not to mention the image of herself with whiskers and a tail. "She's going to bring some paperwork by for me, to help fill the days." She pointed at the television. "I can only read so much, and TV is quickly losing its appeal."

"Just so you don't overdo it."

She gave him a mock salute. "Yes, Sheriff. I'll be careful. And I'll keep your secret."

"It's just as well it didn't work out," he said, walking over and picking up his Stetson. "I have two women in my life already. Even I couldn't handle a third."

"Two women?"

Her heart seemed to falter slightly. He was dating *two* women? She told herself the sudden dullness she felt was exhaustion. She'd probably done too much when she'd gone to the grocery store with Louise that morning. She could feel her smile fading and did her best to keep it in place. She didn't want Travis to know she was even slightly attracted to him. In fact she wasn't at all. He had two women. Good for him. She wished him well.

He paused by the doorway and looked back. "Although I have to say, of the two of you, Mandy is definitely my weakness. I guess it's those blue eyes of hers."

Elizabeth's mouth dropped open. She stared at him. The teasing glint in his eyes told her she'd been had.

She picked up the pillow beside her and tossed it at him.

He easily ducked out of the way. "Gotcha," he said and stepped into the hallway. Before she could finish fuming, he poked his head back into the room. His mouth straightened and those flames were still flickering in his dark eyes.

"For what it's worth, Elizabeth," he said slowly, never taking his gaze from hers, "the feeling is mutual."

With that, he left. She heard his footsteps as he walked down the hall, then made his way up the stairs.

Trouble. This was all very big trouble. She was willing to admit there was some kind of chemical reaction between her and Travis. Sometimes she worried that the heat between them was going to set the house on fire. But it didn't have to mean anything. It *couldn't* mean anything. She wasn't ready to get involved. She might never be ready for a real relationship. Even if she was willing to take a chance, it wouldn't be on Travis Haynes. The man was a walking, breathing heartbreaker. And she'd had enough heartbreak to last a lifetime. What woman would willingly give herself to someone who was destined to leave her for the next conquest?

She stood up and walked toward her room. Although she was healing, her side still gave her a little trouble. Travis had offered to move her to an upstairs bedroom so that she could be closer to Mandy, but she preferred to stay where she was. Her daughter was safe and happy in this big house, and Elizabeth wanted as much distance between her and Travis as possible. Just because she knew she would never get involved with Travis didn't mean she'd figured out a way to tell her body to get over its physical attraction to him.

She undressed then stepped under the warm spray of the shower. There was still over an hour until Rebecca was due to arrive, but everything took Elizabeth longer since the surgery. She was getting her strength back, but not as quickly as she'd hoped. The doctor hadn't been kidding about the recovery time needed. Her trip to the market with Louise had wiped her out for the entire day. She'd had to take a three-hour nap. But it had been worth it to get outside for the first time since the surgery.

As Elizabeth washed her hair, she wondered about Louise. The older woman had mentioned she was divorced. Elizabeth wanted to ask what had happened. For the most part Louise was funny and outgoing, but at the mention of her marriage, she'd gone all quiet. What made it all the more curious was her suspicion that Travis knew exactly what had happened. A couple of things Louise had said hinted at that. But Elizabeth wouldn't be asking anyone for the story. As much as she'd tried to hold herself back, knowing there were secrets she could never share, she and Louise were becoming friends. If Louise wanted her to know the truth, she would tell Elizabeth herself. If not . . . well, she certainly understood the need to keep some things private.

After drying off, she applied a little mascara and blush, then started blow-drying her hair. It still hurt to hold the dryer up for very long, so the process was slow. As she rested, she thought about Rebecca and hoped her new boss remembered to bring over some work for her to do. She would like to get a head start on her job so that when she went back full-time, she would know what was going on.

Elizabeth clicked the dryer back on and held it in one hand while fanning out her hair with the other. What must Rebecca think about her living arrangement? What must the whole town think? She was a virtual stranger, living with a single man, in his house. Was there talk? She shook her head and continued drying. Of course there was talk. She was living with Travis Haynes. One of *the* Haynes. A man with a reputation for women and trouble.

Elizabeth chuckled. That made Travis sound like a guy in a black leather jacket from some sixties B-movie. He certainly wasn't a troublemaker, although she wouldn't mind seeing him in a black leather jacket.

She put down the dryer and picked up a brush. The small bathroom was still steamy from her shower so her damp hair curled up toward her shoulders. She smoothed it with the brush, then slipped on a rose-and-green fabric-covered headband.

Despite his rather wicked reputation, she had to admit he wasn't at all what she'd thought he would be. Sam had left her alone so much, she'd practically raised Mandy on her own. She was used to making all the decisions and handling the responsibilities. She hated to admit it, but it felt kind of nice to have someone else making some of the choices. She even liked living with Travis. He was fun and easygoing. He made her laugh. Better than that, he helped her forget her past.

Her rose sundress had a sweetheart neckline and elastic ribbing in the back to hold it up. The skinny straps were more show than to secure the bodice. She pulled the dress down over her strapless bra and closed the side zipper. After slipping on a pair of high-heeled sandals, she stepped out into the hall.

She could hear a cartoon video playing in the family room. Mandy was excited at the thought of company at dinner, but even more thrilled that she was being allowed to watch her favorite show twice tonight. Elizabeth smiled. Life was certainly simple for a six-year-old.

She turned toward the kitchen to check on the dinner that Louise had made and left warming. A sound on the stairs caught her attention. She looked up and saw Travis.

He'd showered, as well. His hair was still damp, his face freshly shaved. She liked the clean look of his cheeks and jaw, but missed the darkening shadow of his afternoon stubble. He wore a long-sleeved white shirt rolled up to the elbows, and gray trousers. It wasn't all that different from jeans or his sheriff's uniform, but that didn't stop her heart from beating a little faster or her breath from catching in her throat.

She waited until he reached the first floor, then she looked him up and down. "Very nice," she said, struggling to keep her voice sounding normal. "Are you sure Mandy and I won't be in the way?"

"I told you, Rebecca is just a good friend."

"But it's Friday night. Shouldn't you be out on a date? You don't have to stay in to keep us company."

His dark eyes drifted over her face before dipping down to the bodice of her dress. She hadn't thought it was all that low-cut before, but she had the sudden urge to check to see exactly how much cleavage showed. His gaze left her feeling shivery and her knees threatening to buckle. Maybe the dress was a mistake.

"I didn't cancel a date to stay in with you, Elizabeth, so quit worrying about it. I want to spend time with you and Mandy, and I haven't had Rebecca over for a while."

He headed toward the front parlor. She followed, feeling that he was just being polite.

"But I don't want you to think that—"

He turned so quickly, she almost ran into him. As it was she stopped a scant inch from his tall, broad body and had to crane her neck back to see his face.

"I don't think anything," he said. His eyes darkened to the color of black velvet before brightening with a fire she didn't dare identify. "Except that you look very beautiful."

She blushed. Elizabeth wanted to put her hand on her cheek to make sure, but she knew the sensation of heat on her face could only mean one thing. "I— You—" She swallowed. "Thanks, but you don't have to say that. I mean, I'm just a paying guest here."

"Hardly that." He moved away to a stereo set on the floor in the corner. Wires disappeared into the walls. Louise had mentioned that he'd put speakers in the whole house. While he flipped through his CD's, she walked around the large empty room.

"This is going to be a beautiful place when it's finished," she said.

"I hope so. It's taking longer than I'd thought." He slipped a couple of CD's into the machine, then rotated the table to insert three more. "So what about you, Elizabeth? Why don't you have some guy from L.A. pounding down my door?"

"Me?" She laughed. "I haven't had a date in years." Seven years to be exact, she remembered. Her last date had been with Sam. That's when she'd told him she was pregnant with Mandy and had foolishly assumed they would do the right thing and get married. It was hard to believe her life had ever been that simple.

She touched the bare walls of the cavernous room, then looked up at the high ceiling. The basic structure of the house was lovely. Nothing like the cramped place she and Sam had rented. She'd wanted to buy a house, but he hadn't. She remembered the fights they'd had about that, and about having another child—she'd wanted four. That had changed, as well. She'd realized that with Sam gone so much, more children would be difficult. She'd practically lived as a single mother. She'd had such high hopes for the relationship, but the truth was it had been in trouble for the past two years. She'd been on the verge of leaving Sam when the police had arrived to take him away. What irony, she thought, stopping by the window and staring out into the night. She'd been wrestling with her commitment to Mandy's father, wondering if leaving was the right thing, or just the easiest solution to her unhappiness. She hadn't known that in a matter of days the question would be decided for her.

The soft sounds of classical music filled the room. Elizabeth turned and looked but she couldn't see the speakers. Travis stood up and brushed off his hands.

"Pretty impressive, huh?"

She nodded. "A regular seduction factory."

He grimaced. "Hardly. You might want to keep in mind that Louise does have a tendency to exaggerate things."

"Oh? You haven't seduced every female in a fifty-mile radius?"

He moved closer. "Nah. Now if she'd said a thirty-mile radius, that would be different."

"Oh, Travis, we are a pair, aren't we? You can't decide how many women you want, and I never want to get involved again."

"Is that why you haven't had a date in years?"

He asked the question so casually, she almost answered it. Almost. She nearly blurted out, "No, it's because I was married." But she caught herself in time.

"I was involved with Mandy's father. Call me a prude, but I've always believed in one relationship at a time."

"Me, too."

She stared at him in disbelief.

He put his hands on his hips. "Okay, what has she been telling you?"

"Nothing."

He raised his dark eyebrows. "She had to have said something for you to assume that I've never been committed to one woman at a time."

"Are you?"

"Yes. I believe in monogamy."

"For everybody, or do you exclude yourself?"

"Elizabeth!"

She shrugged. "I'm just asking. You have to admit you have this reputation in town. I heard it from the nurse, Louise—even Mandy mentioned something about it. You've dated her teacher, my boss. What am I supposed to think? That you're in training to be a monk?"

He grinned. The curve of his mouth and the flash of white teeth had her smiling in response. Realistically, she should be angry at him in the name of femalehood or something. But the truth was she liked Travis. Despite his obvious flaws, he was a good and kind man. At least he kept his socks picked up.

"I am involved with one woman at a time, Elizabeth Abbott." His voice got lower and more seductive. She felt herself falling under his spell and she couldn't summon the energy to care. "That woman gets my complete attention, the total sum of my energy and focus for as long as the relationship lasts."

His gaze never left hers. His hands stayed on his hips. So why did she feel as if he were physically touching her all over? Her skin grew heated, her fingers curled into her palms. How could he do that with just a look and his voice?

"Oh."

With that he left the parlor and stepped into the hall. Before she realized she'd been abandoned, he was back with a bouquet of flowers.

"These are for you, darlin'," he said.

That woman gets my complete attention. She stared from the flowers to him and back. No. He couldn't mean anything by them, could he?

"Why?" she asked, almost afraid to hear his answer. What if he wanted her? What if he didn't?

"It's been a week since your surgery. I thought you might be feeling a little lost." He thrust the flowers at her and she was forced to take them. "You can lose that panicked expression. I'm not out to seduce you."

"You're not?" She wasn't sure if she was relieved or disappointed.

He shook his head. "Not while you're under my protection."

Which might mean she would have to watch herself when she wasn't under his protection, or it might be a polite way of saying he wasn't interested in her at all. Stop thinking about it, she ordered herself. *She* was the one not interested, remember? She was the one sworn to never get involved.

She lowered her head and sniffed the bouquet of flowers. The colorful blooms smelled rich and sinful, not like those long-stemmed roses Sam had often brought her after he'd been gone for several weeks. She'd never had the heart to tell him she didn't like those roses. They were so straight and scentless, almost mutated versions of natural flowers.

She touched the cheerful pink petal of a carnation. "Thank you." She turned toward him and smiled. "They're beautiful." He was close enough to touch. She reached out and placed her hand on his forearm. "This is probably going to make you cringe, but I think you're very nice."

The second to the last thing she expected was him to say, "I'm glad." The last thing she expected him to do was step closer and wrap his arms around her waist. She almost dropped the flowers before gripping them in her right hand. Emotionally she was too stunned to pull back; physically, she was too intrigued. Sam had been tall—maybe an inch or so taller than Travis—but Travis was powerful and strong. She could feel the muscles in his arms where they pressed against her side. She could see the strength in his shoulders.

And his eyes. She would like to stare into his brown eyes forever, warmed by the fire flickering there. Her gaze dropped to his mouth. He wasn't smiling. She was glad. She would have hated him to find this moment funny. She didn't think it was at all amusing. If anything, she was fighting the burning at the back of her eyes. She didn't know why she wanted to cry. Maybe it was because in his arms she felt safe and secure. She hadn't felt that way since she was a young girl, not much older than Mandy.

He pulled her close, until her thigh brushed against his and her breasts flattened against his chest. She reached up and placed her free hand on his shoulder. He was going to kiss her. For the first time since he touched her, she remembered she was supposed to be fighting this. Travis wasn't for her. But she needed him to kiss her. She needed to forget, even for just a moment. She sensed that once his lips touched hers, she wouldn't be able to think about anything else.

He didn't disappoint her. He breathed her name, then lowered his mouth to hers. Soft and hard and prickly and hot. She absorbed the sensations of his lips brushing back and forth on hers, the fire that flared between them. Her eyes drifted shut. Questions of right and wrong, her place in his house, Sam, her future and Mandy all faded, silenced by the powerful force of pleasure. He didn't assault her or press for more. He simply held her close and moved his mouth slowly, so slowly until she knew every millimeter of his lips.

She wrapped both her arms around his neck, carefully holding on to the flowers. But that was her only conscious thought. Everything else she simply felt. The hard chest flattening her breasts, the stroking of his hands up and down on her back, the shivers as his fingers grazed the bare skin by her shoulder. Her position pulled her incision, but not enough to matter.

He moved his head slightly so he could brush his lips against her jaw, then her ear. She arched her head back, liking the gentle caresses, the absence of pressure. Her blood flowed faster, hotter, fueled by the slow assault. His warm breath tickled, sending goose bumps rippling down to her toes.

He nibbled on her earlobe. She caught her breath, then whispered his name. With her free hand, she touched his still-damp hair, liking the way the smooth strands felt against her fingers.

He read her perfectly. When she grew impatient with his gentle teasing on her jaw and throat, he returned to her mouth. He didn't ask or hint, he simply opened his mouth on hers. As if she had no will, her lips parted to admit him.

Like his previous caresses, he moved slowly, tenderly, tracing her lips, touching the damp, sensitive inside, touching the edge of her teeth before stroking her tongue with his.

One small flicker was like the first faint flash of lightning. He moved against her again, touching, retreating, touching, circling, touching, tasting. The storm moved closer and closer. She felt the vibration of the thunder, the echoing of his heartbeat, matching the rapid cadence of her own. She saw the flash of light behind her closed eyelids.

Her body sought his, pressing harder to absorb his strength. Against her belly, she felt the hardness of his desire. Between her thighs an answering need flowered, leaving her warm and waiting. Her breasts tightened in anticipation. His hands moved lower, down her back, over the curve of her hip to cup her derriere in his large hands. He didn't pull her up against him; instead he squeezed gently, lovingly.

She reveled in the feel of being next to him. Every move was slow, not calculated as she might have thought, but savored. As if he had nothing more important in his life than this moment. As if he'd spent the whole day thinking about kissing her.

He wasn't as tall as Sam, but he was broader and she liked the way his size made her feel protected. Foolish needs, she thought, knowing that she was on her own. But for these few minutes it was enough to hold and be held, tempt and be tempted.

He sucked on her lower lip, the delicious sensations forcing all thoughts from her mind. He kissed her harder now, hungrily, the passion building between them. It was all she could do to stay upright and not sag completely against him. Her fingers had trouble holding on to the bouquet of flowers. His scent and warmth filled her body until she wanted him to be a part of her. He seemed to sense her need, moving even closer, tightening his arms around her as if he were as hungry for love as she.

Love. The word echoed in her brain, the cold reality of its meaning doused her passion and she pulled back. She wasn't hungry for love. She couldn't afford to be. Passion, maybe. Sex—well, it had been a while, so probably. But not love. Never love.

She stared at the open V of his white shirt and watched his chest rise and fall in a rapid cadence that matched her own. Not love. Never love. Love makes you blind. You can't trust it. Ever. She'd learned that lesson the hard way. She'd loved Sam with all her heart, and he had betrayed everything she'd held sacred and special. There had been a hundred clues, but she'd missed them all.

Travis was just like Sam. He was a womanizer, a smooth-talking charmer who made a hobby of breaking hearts. So what if he claimed to practice monogamy? That was part of the trappings of his disguise. She knew what he really was.

She realized they'd been standing there, breathing heavily for several seconds. She half expected him to say something, apologize. But he didn't.

The worst part of it was that her body still tingled from the power of their kisses. Her breasts ached, her thighs felt trembly and weak, and her blood hummed with a powerful need that even the most rational of arguments couldn't quench.

She swallowed thickly, then forced herself to look up at him. The fire in his eyes burned hotter than she'd ever seen it. His mouth was still damp from her passionate kisses. She wanted to look down but didn't dare. She couldn't bear to see the proof of his need. She would think about how he would feel next to her, inside of her. It had been over a year since she'd made love, but some chilling little voice at the back of her head whispered this wasn't all about simply doing without. It was more about the man in front of her than the need within her body, and that thought scared her to death.

"I'm sorry," she said, her voice shaking. "We shouldn't have done that. It's better if it doesn't get out of hand."

He smiled then, a slow, lazy, satisfied and very male smile. The skin on the back of her neck tingled and her breasts swelled painfully.

"What do you mean—'it'?" he asked.

"You know. Our relationship."

The smile turned into a grin. "I didn't know we had a relationship."

His amusement fueled her temper. "You're right," she snapped. "We don't have a relationship, and I would prefer to keep it that way." She turned and started to walk away.

He caught up with her instantly and touched her arm. She wanted to pull back, really she did, but she couldn't. It felt too good to have him touch her. A bright danger sign flashed before her eyes, but she had a bad feeling it was already too late.

"Don't be upset," he said, his thumb stroking her forearm.

"I'm not."

He arched his eyebrows. Yeah, well she'd never been a very good liar. So what else was new?

"It was just a kiss, Elizabeth."

She pulled free of his hand and continued walking down the hall. When she had turned the corner and was out of sight of the parlor, she raised the bouquet to her face and smelled the sweet flowers. Then she touched her free hand to her still-trembling lips. It had felt like a whole lot more than just a kiss to her.

Chapter Seven

"And then there was the time the blood bank brought one of those mobile trucks. You know the kind. They stay for a few days and take donations." Rebecca paused long enough to finish setting the silverware, then looked up and laughed. "He dated both nurses."

"You're kidding?" Elizabeth asked. "Both. So much for monogamy, Travis," she called, glancing back at him over her shoulder.

"I *was* monogamous. The first one didn't work out, and her friend wanted to comfort me," he said from his seat on the floor at the edge of the big dining room. It was one of the few rooms he'd actually bothered to furnish. The rosewood table and hutch had once belonged to his mother. She'd left it behind, along with everything else when she'd left him and his brothers. Their father hadn't wanted the set. Both Jordan and Kyle lived in apartments. Craig had told him to take it because his three boys would destroy the beautiful pieces in a matter of days.

"Travis, it's your turn to move," Mandy said impatiently. "Hurry, 'cuz I'm winning."

"I'm hurrying," he told the little girl. He rolled the dice and counted out the squares with his marker. Mandy crowed when he landed on a chute that carried him almost to the bottom of the board. "Guess you're going to win, huh?"

She nodded vigorously, her blond braids bouncing on her shoulders. She grinned. "Mommy, I'm winning. Come see."

Elizabeth turned in her chair and looked down at the game. "Very good, sweetie." She gave him a quick glance. A tiny spot of color stained each cheek, but she didn't turn away.

Travis was glad. He'd barely had time to recover from his obvious and somewhat painful reaction to their kiss when Rebecca had arrived for dinner. So far he hadn't had the chance to make sure Elizabeth was all right. He told himself he hadn't meant to kiss her, but he knew he was lying. He'd been thinking about it ever since her first night here, when he'd briefly touched her lips with his. He'd wanted to know if the heat between them was real or imagined. The still-burning scars reminded him the heat was plenty real. Their kiss had only made him want more.

Which was, he acknowledged, an obvious problem. He didn't want to get involved with Elizabeth for several reasons. Not only was she a guest in his house, but he knew better than to risk it all with someone like her. She was the kind of woman who believed in commitment and forever. He didn't know how to do that. If he was honest with himself, he didn't have what other men had to make something special last. Four generations of failed relationships couldn't be argued with.

But the kiss had been tempting. He only wished he'd had a chance to ask Elizabeth if everything was okay. But Rebecca and Mandy were in the room. If that wasn't bad enough, his friend was taking perverse delight in telling Elizabeth a string of stories about his supposed conquests with women.

"What about that trick roper you dated?" Rebecca asked.

Elizabeth's eyes widened. "A trick roper. I don't think I want to hear about that one."

Travis shook his head. "That happened about six years ago. Long before you'd even heard of Glenwood," he said, turning to Rebecca. "You're repeating gossip."

"I know. Isn't it terrific?" She walked over and patted his shoulder. "I love this guy. He is the ultimate male weapon against women. One look and they go weak in the knees."

He rolled the dice and moved three places. Mandy rolled and won the game. She laughed with delight, then leaned forward and gave him a big hug. He held her close. Funny how both Abbott women got to him. Elizabeth made him want dangerous things, while Mandy made him feel a fierce need to protect her. And a longing to be more. He would give his soul to be a decent father to some kid. She planted a wet kiss on his cheek. Deep in his chest, he felt a sharp stab of pain piercing his heart.

"You're the best, Travis," Mandy said.

"I rest my case." Rebecca headed for the kitchen.

Mandy scrambled off his lap and followed "Becca," as she called the other woman. He glanced up at Elizabeth still sitting in her seat watching him.

"I took each of the nurses out once," he said, wondering why he was defending himself. She wouldn't believe him. No one ever did. "I don't think I even kissed the second one good-night."

"Sure." She smiled.

"The trick roper was an old friend. I'd known her in college. You know people make up a lot of stories about me and my brothers. They think we get a lot more—'' He hesitated, searching for a polite word.

"Action?" she offered helpfully.

"It wouldn't have been my choice."

God, she was beautiful. The skinny straps of her rose sundress showed off her tanned shoulders. The long line of her neck made him remember how she'd tasted when he'd kissed her there. Her mouth was perfect, pulling into a wide smile. It was her eyes that always got to him, though. There was a wariness in her expression that seemed out of place. Was it that Sam guy who had made her cautious? What had happened in her life? What was the big secret? Hell, a man could go crazy thinking about it.

He rose to his feet and took the chair next to hers. "A lot of people assume my brothers and I get a lot more action than we do. Part reputation, part circumstances."

She tucked a loose strand of hair behind her small ear. "Are you trying to make me feel sorry for you?"

"No, I'm trying to make sure we're still friends."

"I would think you have so many women in your life that one more wouldn't matter."

He leaned close to her, stopping only when their arms brushed. He was pleased that she didn't move away. "I'm not talking about women in general. I'm talking about you. Friends?"

She glanced at the tablecloth. He couldn't see her expression, so he sweated it out. He hated that it mattered what she thought.

"I'm not a jerk, Elizabeth. I'm not what everybody says."

"I know." She bit her lower lip. "You're a nice guy."

He winced.

"You are!"

"Great."

"You want to shake on it again?"

He'd rather kiss on it, but hey, he would take what he could. Her hand felt small and delicate in his, but it was her smile that just about knocked him from his chair. She grinned up at him then leaned forward.

"So tell me the real story about the trick roper."

They had barely sat down to dinner when the doorbell rang. Travis threw his napkin on the table. "I'll get it," he said, rising to his feet.

He walked to the front door and pulled it open. He grinned. "Austin, come in."

Austin Lucas strolled into the hallway and paused. He sniffed the air. "I smell dinner."

"You hungry? Louise left plenty."

His friend shrugged. "I wouldn't say—"

"Travis, who is it?" Rebecca called.

Austin raised his dark eyebrows. "Sorry. I didn't know you had company."

"It's not what you think." Travis grabbed his friend's arm and steered him toward the dining room. Austin let himself be pulled along, but Travis knew his heart wasn't in it. Austin didn't go out of his way to be sociable.

"Look who I found on the doorstep," he said. Elizabeth and Mandy both looked up expectantly. Rebecca rose to her feet and smiled, even though she couldn't see who was behind Travis. He stepped to one side and let Austin precede him into the room.

He raised his arm to Austin's shoulder, as much to show affection as to keep the other man from bolting. Austin didn't do crowds.

"Austin Lucas, this is Elizabeth Abbott and her daughter, Mandy. They're staying here while Elizabeth recovers from a bout with appendicitis. Next to my brothers, Austin is my oldest friend in Glenwood."

Elizabeth stood up and held out her hand. Travis watched her sharply, waiting for the inevitable reaction. She said hello and smiled at him, but that was it. Interesting, he thought.

"And you've already met Rebecca," he said.

Rebecca nodded several times. "The committee meeting on town support for the home. You were there." She paused. Her brown eyes widened. "I mean, everyone was there, weren't they? All the people in the town." She paused. "Not all of them, of course, but a good many. Not just you." Color flared on her cheeks. She smiled tightly. "Good to see you. Again. Here, that is." She reached for her water glass. Her fingers slipped and she knocked it over on the table. "Oh, no. I'll just—" She motioned helplessly toward the rapidly spreading pool of water. "I'll get a cloth."

"I'll help," Elizabeth said and followed her into the kitchen.

"What's gotten into her?" Travis asked no one in particular; then he glanced at his friend.

"Don't look at me. This is only the second time I've met the lady. She was a lot like this at the meeting, too. She must have dropped her pen a hundred times." He shrugged.

Elizabeth came back alone with a couple of dishcloths. She mopped up the spill. Travis waited, but Rebecca never reappeared.

"Have a seat," Travis said.

Austin shook his head. "I just came by to tell you that I'll be here for the football game."

"Great. But really, there's plenty of food."

"You're having dinner with two beautiful women. I don't want to get in the way."

"You wouldn't be." Travis meant it. In the past several minutes, Elizabeth hadn't even given Austin a second glance. Good news because his friend's reputation with women rivaled that of any of the Haynes brothers. Austin topped Travis by at least three inches. He'd been described as handsome as the devil himself. Between his self-made fortune, his solitary ways and the gold hoop earring Travis and his brothers never tired of teasing him about, he drew women like a shell game drew suckers. So Elizabeth was somehow immune to the infamous Lucas charm. Too bad he couldn't say the same about Rebecca.

"Mister?"

Travis glanced down and saw Mandy was tugging on the sleeve of Austin's shirt.

"What?" Austin asked.

"I'm beautiful, too. Mommy said so."

Austin drew back his head and laughed. "You're right, Mandy. You are very beautiful. I'm sorry I didn't include you."

The little girl dimpled, obviously charmed.

"Tell me, Mr. Lucas, how long have you lived in Glenwood?" Elizabeth asked.

Austin looked at her. "It's Austin, and I've lived here since junior high school."

She folded her arms over her chest. The action pushed her full breasts up slightly. Travis remembered the feel of them against his chest. His mouth grew dry.

She smiled slowly. With her long hair curling over her almost-bare shoulders and the rose-colored dress outlining her feminine curves, he knew he didn't have the power to resist what she offered. Fortunately for him, she wasn't doing any offering. The last thing he wanted to do was hurt Elizabeth.

"I was wondering. I've heard all these stories about Travis and his women. Are the stories true?"

Austin glanced at him. Devilment twinkled in his pale gray eyes. "Every word, ma'am. Gospel."

Travis jerked his thumb toward the door. "Get out of here, you traitor." He followed Austin down the hall toward the front door, all the while accompanied by the sound of Elizabeth's laughter.

"I'll get you for this," he said as Austin got into his car.

"I'm scared." Austin gave him a salute. "Enjoy the ladies." He pulled his car door shut and started the engine.

When Travis returned to the dining room, Rebecca had come out of the kitchen.

"Oh, is he gone?" she asked, twisting her hands together. "I hate it when that happens."

Elizabeth glanced at the other woman. "What exactly happened?"

Rebecca sank into her chair and buried her face in her hands. "I can't be around that man without turning into a klutz. I have a master's degree, I got good grades in school. I run the entire child services department for the county." She looked up at Travis. "I do a good job, don't I?"

"The best." He had to fight back a grin.

"Don't you dare laugh, Travis," she said. "I'm a pathetic creature. Every time I'm around that man, I fall apart. I drop things." She grimaced at the tablecloth. "Or spill them. I can't finish my sentences. I've only met him three times, but it's getting worse." She sighed. "Maybe I should move."

Elizabeth giggled. Rebecca turned toward her. "This is not funny."

"I'm sorry." Elizabeth bit her lower lip, then burst out laughing. "You have a crush on him."

"I know. It's awful."

Travis reached over and rested his hand on Rebecca's shoulder. "Be careful, kid. Austin has broken more hearts than my brothers and I put together. He's not into relationships except for the convenient kind."

She looked up at him and smiled. She was dressed in a floral print dress that floated around her body. The garment was loose enough not to even hint at curves below. With her long hair, minimal makeup and flat shoes, she looked like everyone's stereotypical idea of a librarian. Or a Sunday school teacher. The innocence lurking in her gaze had been one of the reasons nothing had happened between them. He didn't want that on his already-full conscience.

"I know that," Rebecca said. "There's just something about him."

"He's dangerous."

"Yeah, kinda like you."

He and Rebecca sat on the front porch swing while Elizabeth put Mandy to bed. He could hear the sounds of Mandy's laughter floating out of the upstairs window. He liked the domesticity of their arrangement. If he couldn't have the real thing, this was a damn close second best.

"Elizabeth seems very nice," Rebecca said, pushing off the porch with her foot and causing the swing to rock.

"Uh-huh."

"That's what I like best about our friendship," she said, poking him in the side. "Your articulate statements."

He didn't bother responding. Rebecca had something to say, but he wasn't going to make it any easier for her.

"You're a fool if you let her get away."

He didn't answer.

"I know you probably think it's too soon to know if she's the one or not, but you two look right together. She's bright, funny, great with her daughter and—"

"Shut up." He softened the words by resting his arm on the back of Rebecca's shoulders and pulled her next to him.

"But—"

"No, Rebecca. I can't do this. I'm not a fool if I let her go, I'm a fool if I try again. You're right. Elizabeth is great. Mandy's irresistible, but so what? I come from a long line of failures in the relationship department. None of my uncles, or my brothers have been able to make it work. Neither could I."

"Maybe Julie wasn't the right one for you."

"Maybe I should quit trying to be something I'm not."

She looked up at him. The porch light illuminated her pale skin and the concern in her eyes. She was as slender and fragile as a porcelain figurine, and just as beautiful. He'd held her close, even kissed her once. And felt nothing. Damn. Why did Elizabeth Abbott have to be the one to make him crazy? It would have been easier to try again with Rebecca. He told himself it was because they were friends, but he knew better. It would have been easier with Rebecca because with her he didn't have as much to lose.

"You don't have to be like them," she said, snuggling closer. There was a slight chill in the air. He welcomed the decrease in temperature. Maybe it would cool his desire. "You're your own person. Blaze a new path. Start a new tradition in the Haynes dynasty."

"If it looks like a duck and walks like a duck and sounds like a duck, it's probably a duck. No point in trying to be something else."

She grinned. "What are you saying?"

He chuckled. "That I'm a duck."

"Well, go ahead and be one if it makes you happy."

The trouble was it didn't make him one bit happy. He wanted more. That was the hell of it. He couldn't be like his father, going from woman to woman. None of his brothers were. They all wanted to make a relationship work and settle down with one woman. Like them, he wanted to get married, have a herd of children and wake up in the same bed for the next fifty years. What right did he have to try for something that was doomed to failure?

"But maybe Julie *wasn't* the one for you."

"She was the perfect wife. A guy couldn't ask for more."

"Maybe you didn't love her."

Interesting thought. He was beginning to think he didn't know what love was.

"Travis!"

He stood up when he heard Elizabeth call his name. "Be right back."

Rebecca rose and stretched. "I'll come with you. I want to say good-night to Elizabeth and then leave. I have a lot of work tomorrow."

She stood on her tiptoes and kissed his cheek. He waited, hoping for some reaction. Some hint of desire. Nothing. Not even the tiniest spark. She could have been his sister.

"Hang in there," she said.

"I will." He opened the front door for her to go in first.

Elizabeth watched Rebecca and Travis enter the hallway. They looked good together. Both tall and attractive. Rebecca said something, and Travis laughed. How easily they spent time together. Elizabeth fought down a feeling of envy. After the first year it had never been easy with Sam. He'd been charming, of course, but he'd never let her inside and never shared his feelings. Now, of course, she knew why. But then she'd always wondered what was wrong with her. Why wasn't she enough to keep her man happy?

Travis looked up at her.

"Mandy wants to say good-night to you," she said.

"Sure." He climbed the stairs two at a time and went into Mandy's room. Rebecca followed more slowly.

Elizabeth wanted to ask what they'd been talking about outside. She'd heard the creak of the swing. It had been an intimate sound. Elizabeth told herself she wasn't jealous. Why should she be? She wasn't interested in Travis. At least not romantically. She resisted the impulse to touch her nose to see if it was growing.

Tonight she was going to have to have a long talk with herself. She couldn't afford to get involved with anyone, and certainly not him. He would sweep her up in passion, muddle her thinking, pleasure her body and then leave her for the next one on the list. Which almost made it easier. If Travis wasn't such a flirt, she would have a more difficult decision. She would have to face trusting her judgment about a man. She shook her head. Never again. She was done making those kinds of mistakes.

Rebecca reached the landing. "I'm glad we got to spend some time together."

"Thanks for bringing me the work. I'll get started on it in the morning."

"Oh, please take your time." Rebecca frowned. "I don't want to be responsible for you not getting better. You don't have to do any of it if you don't feel up to it." Her frown turned into a smile. "Heaven knows the paperwork has waited for months now. A couple more weeks isn't going to matter."

"I'm desperate for something to do during the day. Between Louise and Travis, I barely have to move around at all. I'm looking forward to getting back to work."

"Your desk is waiting for you." Rebecca nodded toward Mandy's room. "Now you take care of yourself and that hunk in there. He needs some looking after."

Elizabeth rolled her eyes. "After all the stories I've heard, looking after is the one thing he doesn't need more of."

Rebecca sobered. "Maybe I shouldn't have passed on all those stories about Travis. He really is a nice man. Don't judge him too harshly."

"I don't judge him at all. He's been great to me and Mandy, but he's not my type."

"Too bad. He's not mine, either." Rebecca stared off in the distance for a moment. "There must be someone brave enough to take on this particular Haynes boy. I haven't known Travis for all that long, but I know him well enough to know it would be worth the trouble." She touched Elizabeth's forearm briefly. "Get better, but don't push yourself. The piles of paper aren't going anywhere. Good night."

She started down the stairs. Elizabeth moved to follow her but Rebecca stopped her with a raised hand.

"I'll find my own way out. You'd just have to climb the stairs again to tuck in your daughter. I'll talk to you soon."

"By."

Elizabeth watched as her boss left. When the front door closed, she stared at it for several minutes. Rebecca was great. She was looking forward to working for her. It would be nice to have some new friends in her life. Except—

She shook her head and turned toward Mandy's room. Except for the secrets she had to keep. They made it hard to open up. There was always a barrier between herself and anyone she wanted in her life. She knew she should put it behind her, but she couldn't. What would Louise and Rebecca think if they knew the truth? Worse, what would Travis think? She didn't want to even imagine that moment. He would know what a fool she'd been. He would blame her, as she blamed herself, for not figuring it out, for not getting the clues. There must have been hundreds.

Stop thinking about it, she told herself. But it was hard to forget what was keeping her from the life she really wanted. Tonight's dinner had reminded her how much she liked having people in her life. Being with everyone had taunted her with the vision of what she'd once imagined her life with Sam to be like. She'd thought they would be a family together; she'd been wrong.

Brushing aside the unpleasant thoughts, she moved toward Mandy's room. As she entered the room she saw Travis sitting on the edge of the bed holding Mandy in his arms. They both had their backs to her.

"Sometimes I miss my daddy," Mandy said.

"I know, honey," Travis answered.

Elizabeth felt as if someone had stabbed her in the heart. Mandy had adjusted so well to all the changes that sometimes she allowed herself to forget how this must be upsetting her daughter. Of course she missed her father.

She wanted to go to Mandy and comfort her, but Travis seemed to be doing a fine job. Besides, it was her fault the girl didn't have a father anymore. She'd been the one to demand Sam sign custody of their child over to her. She clutched the door frame. Sam hadn't given her any trouble. He'd signed the papers, then passed them to her. His blue eyes had spoken his silent apology as the prison guards had led him away. That quiet apology hadn't been enough.

Elizabeth knew this was hard on Mandy, but it was better this way. Sam had never really loved either of them. She'd finally figured out it had all been a game to him.

"How come your hugs make me feel better?" Mandy asked, settling back on her bed.

"They're magic hugs." Travis bent over and kissed her cheek. When he straightened, he saw Elizabeth standing just inside the room. "Hi. We were discussing her father."

"I heard," she said. Elizabeth addressed Mandy. "Were you feeling sad?"

"A little." Her little girl looked up at her with Sam's eyes. "Travis gave me a magic hug and I'm better now."

"Aren't you lucky." Elizabeth picked up her stuffed teddy and placed him next to her. "Are you ready to go to sleep?"

Mandy nodded.

"I love you, sweetie."

"I love you, too, Mommy."

Elizabeth fussed with the covers for as long as she could, knowing she didn't want to turn around and face Travis. What must he be thinking about her? Every time they came to some kind of agreement, something was there to remind him about the mysteries in her life. She knew he was curious. She just prayed he would stop asking her questions she couldn't answer.

Travis was waiting for her in the hallway. Without saying a word, he placed his hand on the small of her back and led her down the stairs. When they reached the foyer she was about to say good-night, but he opened the front door.

"Come outside," he said. "It's a beautiful night."

She hesitated. It would be better for both of them if she went to her room—alone. The two of them sitting in the dark could get into a lot of trouble. Their kiss this afternoon had proved that, and it had still been daylight. But the cool night beckoned. She was tired from her long day, but not in pain.

"I won't bite," he promised.

How could she resist him? "If you're sure," she said, and stepped out onto the porch.

The light beside the front door cast a soft glow down the steps. The swing was to her left, but she felt that would be tempting fate too much, so she sat on the top step and pulled her full skirt over her knees to her ankles. Travis settled next to her. The night air was full of sounds: crickets, the soft buzz of invisible flying wings, the hoot-hoot of an owl. She inhaled the smells. Damp earth from a brief afternoon shower, the last lingering sweetness of the roses by the porch rail and the hint of woodsmoke from some faraway fireplace.

A quarter moon hung just above the horizon. This was a different sky than she was used to. The lights of Los Angeles washed out most of the stars, but up here she could see the twinkling lights of the constellations.

Travis sat close enough for them to touch. Shoulder to thigh. She should probably pull away, but he was warm and familiar, her only anchor in her new world.

"You want to talk about Mandy's father?" he asked. He'd lowered his voice, but it still sounded loud in the quiet evening. "I assume you heard what she said."

"Most of it." She folded her arms on top of her knees and rested her chin on them. "I can't."

"How about your father?"

"What?"

She glanced sideways at him. He smiled at her. In the soft light, he looked like a chiseled statue. His hair and mustache were the color of midnight, his skin a polished bronze. If it wasn't for the warmth of his arm brushing her and the heat seeping through her dress from hip and thigh, she would have wondered if he was real. She'd escaped her past and had somehow stumbled upon this man. Was fate being kind or playing the most horrible joke on her?

"I'm changing the subject. Tell me about your family. Did you grow up in L.A.?"

"In the area. Near San Bernardino. A small town, a lot like this one. Then I went to the big bad city to go to college."

"And you're the only child."

"Yes. Mom was in her late thirties when I was born, and that was a lot less popular then. I was lonely growing up. I'd always planned on having three or four kids of my own to make up for it, but it didn't turn out that way."

"You could have them now."

"I'm not sure. Being a single mom is hard. I'm not getting married." *Again.* She almost said it, but at the last minute held back the word. Still it hung in the night like a winged creature before taking flight and disappearing into the silence. She cleared her throat. "What about you?"

Either he didn't notice that now she was the one changing the subject, or he was too kind to comment. She had a feeling it was the latter.

"Four boys, an assortment of uncles dropping by to visit. It was noisy." He shrugged. She felt the rise and fall of his shirt as it brushed against her skin. It was nice. "My dad was sheriff of Glenwood for about twenty-five years."

"Did you work for him?"

"Yeah." He chuckled. "For about a minute. He took an early retirement, but there was a month there when I was his newest deputy." He paused. When he spoke again, his voice was different. "He rode me hard."

"Did it make you angry?"

He turned to look at her. "Why do you ask?"

"You sounded . . ." She trailed off. "Bitter, I guess."

"Maybe I am. Not about the work, that was fine. Dad and his brothers were the original good ol' boys. They lived hard, drank hard, played hard. By the time I was ten, three of my four uncles were divorced. The fourth one, Bob, never bothered getting married. I knew my dad had a bunch of girlfriends, not to mention a mistress he kept in the next town." He drew in a deep breath. "This is the seedy side of the Haynes family legend. Sorry. You don't want to hear this."

She felt bad that he'd gone through that, but part of her was grateful to have something to focus on other than her own problems. She shifted until she was facing him. Her knees bumped his thighs. He leaned forward, resting his elbows on his knees and letting his hands hang loose.

"People in town think it was all good times and parties at our house," he said at last. "It wasn't. My folks fought a lot. You can imagine what my mom thought of my dad's activities." His mouth twisted into a grim smile. "He was so damn proud of himself. He had four sons and, no matter what else he did, he woke up every morning in his own bed. What a saint." He drew in a breath. "She split when Kyle was fifteen. Packed her bags and left. Not a word, or a note. We thought about looking for her, but we figured if she wanted to stay in touch, she knew where to find us."

"How old were you?"

"Twenty-one. It didn't really bother me. I'd just finished college and was about to find my own place anyway, but it hit Kyle hard. Jordan, too, but he wouldn't show it."

Elizabeth's heart squeezed painfully. Jordan wasn't the only one who didn't want to show his pain. Travis might have been older, but she had a feeling his mother's abandonment had hurt him just as much. She was torn. Part of her couldn't blame the woman for walking out on Travis's father, but she didn't understand how a mother could abandon her sons.

"So you decided to punish all women for what she'd done?" she asked.

"No. It's not like that. None of us are angry at women. Nobody has figured out how to make it work." He turned his head and looked at her. She saw the sadness in his eyes. Instinctively she reached out and rested her hand on his forearm. He didn't acknowledge the comfort, but she didn't mind. He felt warm and strong, even with all his pain. She liked to think she was giving a little back.

"Craig got married right out of college. Had three boys. But he couldn't make it work. I tried with Julie. You know what happened there. I come from a long line of ducks."

"What?"

"If it looks like a duck and walks like a— Never mind. We talked about it, my brothers and I. Watching our dad and the uncles fool around convinced us that we were all going to be faithful to the women in our lives. Wishing isn't enough, is it? Monogamy doesn't guarantee success. There's something else we all just don't get."

He stared into the night. Their backgrounds were so different, she thought. Yet here they sat together, facing their personal demons. She was glad that she and Travis could be friends. They needed each other.

"So you stay single forever?" she asked.

"There doesn't seem to be a choice."

"What about children?"

He turned on the step, shifting so his back pressed against the railing. He parted his thighs and rested his right foot on the porch, bending his knee. His other foot balanced on the bottom step. Her calves brushed against his inner thigh. It was a very intimate position. Her gaze seemed drawn to his chest, drifting lower to his trousers. She looked away before she reached dangerous territory, but their new positions made her hyperaware of his heat and scent. She clutched her arms to her chest.

"I'd like a family," he said, seemingly unaware of what he was doing to her. "But it's not in the cards for me."

"Too bad. You're wonderful with Mandy."

He brushed off her compliment with a flick of his wrist. "Speaking of Mandy, I've been thinking. There's a soccer league for the younger kids. It gives them something to do during football season. The teams are coed, but they match them up by size and skill. Sign-ups are tomorrow. I thought I could take her to the park. What do you think?"

"I think you're a sheep in wolf's clothing, Travis Haynes. All this tough talk, but underneath, you're a sweetie."

His slow, sexy grin chased the last of the shadows from his eyes. "Tell anyone, and you're dead meat."

"Tough guy, you don't scare me. Soccer will be great for Mandy. Thanks for offering to take her."

"No problem. I know the coaches. She'll have fun and make lots of friends."

She leaned forward. "Travis, you're wonderful with kids. This is a perfect example. You shouldn't dismiss that."

"The truth is, I'm a sprinter. It's easy to play daddy for a couple of hours, but it makes a big difference when the kids are yours. I know. I've seen Craig struggling."

"You keep saying that you don't have what it takes, but from everything I've seen, all the parts are in working order."

He raised his dark eyebrows. Instantly her gaze dropped to his crotch and she remembered the feel of his hardness pressing against her. She blushed and looked away. "You know what I meant."

"I prefer *my* interpretation of what you said."

She sank back against the railing. "I think it's time for me to say good-night."

"Not so fast."

He stood on the bottom step and loomed over her. His head moved lower, blocking out the night stars. His hands touched her almost-bare shoulders, making her instantly tremble. But at the last minute, she turned her face away. His mouth grazed her cheek.

"Elizabeth?"

"I can't," she whispered. She risked looking up at him. Confusion filled his brown eyes, fighting the fire there and slowly putting it out. She couldn't. For a thousand sensible reasons that all boiled down to being afraid of making the same mistake again.

If only she'd met Travis seven years ago. If only he'd been the one to steal her heart and seduce her body. But it hadn't been Travis, it had been Sam. Maybe if Sam had beat her or cheated on her, it would have been easier to get over what happened. But how was she supposed to recover from being a fool? How was she supposed to forget the lies?

Travis stepped back and held out his hand to help her up. She ignored him and rose. A pain jabbed her side as her movements pulled the incision.

"I'm sorry," she said, looking over his left shoulder. "I can't do this. I'm not what you think I am." She smiled sadly, knowing she either had to smile or cry. Already her eyes were burning. She prayed she made it to her room before she gave way.

"So it all comes back to that damn mystery," he growled. "What is so terrible?"

"Don't ask me, please. I really appreciate everything you've done. I'm very grateful."

"I don't want your gratitude."

She blinked several times, but it didn't help. One tear rolled free. She brushed it off her cheek. "It's all I have to give you, Travis. There's nothing else. Please believe me. I'm not who you think I am."

Chapter Eight

The coach blew his whistle, but none of the kids on the field paid any attention. They continued to chase the white soccer ball, screaming with excitement in the frenzy of being the first one to actually kick the ball. When the ball made a sudden left turn, Mandy was right there. She stared down at it, her expression a mixture of confusion and delight; then she kicked for all she was worth. The ball sailed into the air and landed out of bounds. Travis stood up and cheered. The coach wearily shook his head and continued to blow the whistle. Finally the dozen or so six- and seven-year-olds quieted down to listen.

For the fifth time, the coach explained the rules of the game. Each of the children nodded earnestly, then scattered in an effort to find and kick the ball. Travis chuckled. Mandy was right in the middle of the pack. With her bright red shorts and T-shirt she was easy to spot. Her blond ponytail swung with each step.

"The kid's a natural athlete," he said.

"You sound like a proud papa."

He shifted on the bleachers set up on the side of the field and turned around. A sultry brunette with legs that stretched from here to forever smiled down at him. Her cropped T-shirt and microscopic shorts left little to the imagination.

"Unless you've been hiding something, Travis, she couldn't possibly be yours."

"No, Amber. She's the daughter of a friend of mine. I brought her to the practice. I'm surprised to see you here."

"Jimmy's playing." She motioned to the field. A short dark-haired boy ran tenaciously after the ball. "You know how Karl is about sports."

He did know. Karl was one of his deputies. A former college football hero, Karl had hoped for a career in the pros. He had the heart but lacked speed. Amber had married him before the 49ers released him from his contract. Rumor had it she wasn't happy about being cheated out of her role as the professional football player's wife. Travis couldn't confirm the rumors, but the last two times he'd stopped Amber for speeding, she'd offered to pay her ticket with something other than cash. He'd refused. Even if Karl hadn't been his subordinate and a friend, Travis didn't dally with married women.

"My husband's working today," she said, moving down closer to where he was sitting. "But then you know that, don't you? Are you going to be at all the practices? They take a couple of hours, don't they?" She moved closer and smiled. "Maybe we could get a cup of coffee, or something."

It was the "something" that had him worried. "Thanks, but I don't think so, Amber. I'd rather stay with the kids."

Her perfect features twisted into a snarl. "I always knew your reputation was a lot of hype, Travis. Figures there'd be nothing hot in this crappy little town." She jumped off the bleachers and stalked away.

It was starting to make sense, he thought, remembering how distracted Karl had been lately. Amber must be making his life hell. He grimaced. Looks like the Haynes boys weren't the only ones who couldn't keep their marriages together.

He returned his attention to the field. The coach was trying to set up drills for the kids. It wasn't working. Travis thought about volunteering his services, but he was already committed to a pint-size football team. In a couple of weeks the practices would overlap.

Mandy continued to run back and forth, laughing as she tried to kick the ball. Her smile made him think of her mother.

Life wasn't fair. Amber was ready to get involved in an affair. She would understand it for what it was and not expect more of him. He hadn't had a woman in months, so he should have been tempted. But Amber didn't do a thing for him. Not to mention the fact that she was married. He shrugged. He had a bad feeling that even if Amber had been single, he wouldn't have been interested.

Elizabeth, on the other hand, could turn him on in a heartbeat. She was single but not available, and certainly not the type a man played around with. If it wasn't for that damned feeling he got when he was around her—the sense of belonging—he could put her out of his mind.

But instead of trying to not think about her, he recalled their kiss. Hot and perfect. She'd gone all soft in his arms, holding on, kissing him back. His chest still burned where her breasts had pressed against him. She'd tasted sweet and ready. God knows he'd been ready. Even thinking about it made his jeans uncomfortable. He shifted on the bench and glanced at the kids still playing. Think about something else, Haynes, he told himself.

I'm not who you think I am. Her words haunted him. What could they mean? She said she wasn't married, and he didn't think she was a liar. So what was it? Damn. He should have made her tell him. Barring that, he should have kissed her again, kissed her until neither of them cared about her mystery, or anything but the feelings they generated when they were together.

A white sheriff's car pulled up, distracting him. He stood and stretched, then walked over to the vehicle. Kyle stepped out and walked around the car.

"What's up?" Travis asked.

Kyle shook his head. "Nothing's up. I called the house and Elizabeth said you were here." Kyle grinned. "Is she as pretty as she sounds?"

"What happened to Lisa?"

Kyle leaned against the car and folded his arms over his chest. "We broke up."

"You dumped her."

"Yeah. I guess."

Travis studied his twenty-eight-year-old brother. He'd been the one hardest hit by their mother's leaving. He was six-two, lean, with the Haynes dark hair, eyes and good looks. Girls, women and old ladies loved him. He dumped them all before they could dump him.

"What happened this time?" Travis asked.

"You know, same old thing. She wasn't right. So tell me about Elizabeth. I heard from Louise that she's really pretty. And about my age."

"Don't even think about it," Travis growled.

Kyle grinned. "Jealous, old man? That's a first."

"I'm not jealous. Elizabeth is going through some things right now and she doesn't need to get involved with a Romeo like you."

Kyle leaned forward and mockingly punched him in the stomach. Travis feinted right and shot back a jab of his own.

"You've got it bad, big brother. The lady has you hogtied with *luvvvv.*"

"It's been less than two weeks. We're just . . . friends."

Kyle dropped his arms to his side. "Sell it somewhere else. I recognize the signs. You'll be parking your slippers under her bed by the end of the month."

Travis shoved his hands into his jeans front pockets. "It's not what you think, Kyle. I like her." How long had it been since he'd admitted that to himself or anyone else?

Kyle's good humor faded. His mouth pulled straight and his eyes darkened with sadness. "I guess that means you're going to stay away from her, huh?"

"I don't have much choice."

"The Haynes curse." Kyle turned and braced his forearms on the top of the marked sedan. "We're all pretty bright. You'd think we'd have figured out a way to break the thing."

"You keep trying."

"Not anymore. I'm giving up on women."

"That'll last about a minute." He looked out at the field and watched Mandy play. She saw him and waved then went back to her game. "We make a sorry group, Kyle."

"That we do. And we're contagious. Austin was probably normal before we got ahold of him."

Travis shook his head. "I don't think so. Austin had trouble before he ever got to Glenwood. Maybe the five of us should start a twelve-step program. Hi, my name is Travis, and I don't know how to make a relationship work."

Kyle pushed off the car and stepped into the street. "Let me know if it helps. Are we on for the game this Sunday?"

Kyle, Austin and whichever of his other two brothers were around usually came over to watch football in the fall. He'd canceled last week because of Elizabeth.

"Sure. She's feeling better."

"So I will get to meet her." Kyle's smile didn't reach his eyes.

"Yeah, but watch yourself."

"I will."

Travis watched his brother open his car door. Before he stepped inside, Travis called, "Wait a minute." He walked around the hood of the vehicle and hesitated. "Can you run a name for me?"

"Sure. Who?"

He shouldn't do this. If Elizabeth found out, she would be furious. Worse, she would be hurt. She'd *said* she hadn't done anything illegal, but what if she'd been lying? He didn't want to think that of her, but there was obviously something she wasn't telling him.

He pulled a pad of paper out of his back pocket and borrowed Kyle's pen. He vacillated another second, then wrote the name "Sam Proctor" down and handed Kyle the sheet.

"Call me if you find anything. And keep it under your hat."

Kyle studied the name. "No problem. See you Sunday."

Travis watched the car pull away from the curb. What would Elizabeth think when she'd found out what he'd done? What would *he* think if he learned her secret?

Mandy licked her ice-cream cone frantically, but the drips were faster. "Travis, help," she called, holding out her hand.

He grabbed two napkins and wiped her clean. By the time he was done with that hand, the other one was a mess.

"You've got to learn to eat them quicker, honey."

Mandy giggled. She had several grass stains on her shirt and shorts from the soccer practice. There was a smudge of dirt on her cheek and chocolate ice cream on her chin. She was adorable.

"I'm done." She gave him the half-finished cone, which proceeded to drip all over *his* hand.

"Great. Thanks." He licked it a couple of times, then tossed it in the plastic-lined trash container in the ice-cream shop. He wiped both their hands, then collected their packages. Mandy slid off her stool and followed him out onto the street.

"Hold this," he said, handing her one of the bags. He reached in his back pocket and pulled out the list Elizabeth had made. "Okay, we bought T-shirts."

"Three of them," Mandy said helpfully.

"Yes, three. And shoes. We got underwear."

"With pink bunnies."

"The bunnies are nice." It had been tough deciding between bunnies, a popular female cartoon figure and flowers. He'd picked out female lingerie before, but not cotton panties for a six-year-old. He hoped Elizabeth approved of the bunnies. He scanned the list. "That's it, kid. We just have to go by the post office and collect your mom's mail. Then we'll head home."

"Okay." She started down the sidewalk.

"Mandy?" he called.

"What?"

"It's that way." He pointed in the other direction.

She smiled. "Okay." The bag was light, but almost as big as she was. He reached down and took it from her.

"I didn't mean for you to carry that, sweetie. I'll take it."

"But I want to help."

He sorted through the other packages. "Here. Take this one."

"Mommy's present?" She looked in the small gift store bag and smiled. "Mommy will like it."

"I hope so." It had been an impulsive purchase. A small yellow stuffed duck. She wouldn't get the joke, but seeing it would remind him not to try to be other than he was.

Mandy walked at his side chatting about school and soccer practice. He liked the sound of her voice and her stories. He liked how she looked up at him and simply assumed he would keep her safe. She accepted him with the tacit trust of a child raised in a house full of love and security. So where was the girl's father?

Thinking of Sam Proctor sent a shiver of guilt slipping down his spine. As they crossed the street and he saw a restaurant up ahead, he had the urge to step inside and use the phone to call Kyle at the station. It would be easy enough to tell his brother to back off. Why did it matter who Sam Proctor was? But he passed the restaurant without making the call.

They reached the post office. There was a short line. Mandy stood patiently, humming softly under her breath. He glanced down at her pretty face and beautiful blue eyes. Eyes she had to have inherited from her father. He smiled at her. She grinned in return and reached for his hand. The trusting gesture twisted his heart. A stab of loneliness caught him off balance. It was going to be hell when Elizabeth and Mandy moved into their own place.

When it was their turn, he approached the counter and collected Elizabeth's mail. She was having her forwarded correspondence held until she had her own place. He resisted the temptation to flip through the stack of envelopes. Checking on Sam Proctor was one thing, reading her mail quite another.

"Ready to go home?" he asked.

She nodded. "I had the best time, Travis. I like doing things with you. My old friends did stuff with their daddies but mine was always busy. I like soccer, too."

The slightly confused speech gave him the in he'd been hoping for. As they approached the car, he dug in his front jeans pocket for his keys.

"You haven't seen your daddy in a long time, have you?"

Mandy shook her head. "Mommy said he had to go away. My daddy left because he's big."

She'd said that once before. What the hell did it mean? "Big?"

She nodded. "I heard her say that once. Mommy was on the phone. I was supposed to be in bed, but I got up for a drink of water. Mommy said Daddy was big. Then she started to cry." Mandy's mouth twisted into a frown. "I got scared and went back to my room. Mommy and Daddy fought sometimes. I could hear them." She handed him the bag then climbed into the front seat of his Bronco. As he bent over to fasten her seat belt, she glanced up at him. "It made Mommy sad when he went away. It made me sad, too."

He could see that sadness in her eyes and felt like the lowest kind of scum for questioning her. To distract her, he bent over and tickled her.

"Sad? No one is allowed to be sad in *my* car."

She twisted away and giggled. "Is it a magic car, like the magic hugs?"

"Absolutely." He handed her the mail and closed her door.

After tossing the packages on the back seat, he climbed in and started the truck. Mandy's good humor had been restored and she chatted happily. His mind reeled with curiosity.

My daddy left because he's big. Elizabeth Abbott, who are you? He signaled to turn out of the post office parking lot. Frustration welled up inside of him. He drew in a deep breath. He wasn't going to get answers anytime soon. Kyle might come up with something, or he might not. Until then, he would just have to let it go. He liked Elizabeth and found it hard to believe she was involved with anything shady. His gut trusted her, and he trusted his gut.

"Look at the pretty dog," Mandy said, pointing at a teenage boy walking a collie.

Travis stopped at a red light and turned to look. Mandy raised her hands to wave at the dog. The mail on her lap slipped off on the floor. He glanced at the light to make sure it was still red, then bent over and picked up the envelopes. He told himself not to, but he couldn't help glancing at the address. It was a suburb of Los Angeles. He looked up a line, to the addressee. His teeth clenched together. He flipped through the rest of the envelopes. Almost all of them were addressed to the same person: Elizabeth Proctor.

She'd lied.

Elizabeth wiped the kitchen counter. Again. It had been clean the last four times she'd wiped it. She was wasting time, trying to avoid the inevitable.

Travis had put up a good front through the late afternoon and even into dinner. But she knew there was something wrong. She could see it in his eyes, hear it in the way he hesitated before answering her questions. He'd held himself apart from her ever since he and Mandy had come home.

She looked around the clean kitchen, liking the way the cream-and-blue tiles complemented the bleached oak cabinets. It wasn't a traditional kitchen, but it suited her, and the house. She would miss it when she left.

She walked over to the coffeepot and poured out two cups. Sitting on the shelf above the sink was a stuffed yellow duck. The little creature seemed to smile at her, as much as a duck could smile. The gift had delighted her. Only Travis's seeming emotional distance distracted her from her pleasure. Something was wrong and she was going to find out what.

She carried the mugs carefully to the stairs and started to climb. Travis was fitting cabinets in the big bathroom off the master bedroom. Mandy had been in bed for almost an hour. Her morning on the soccer field had worn her out. She had new clothes, thanks to Travis's patience at shopping, and several new friends. Life was good for the six-year-old.

Elizabeth walked down the hallway to the last door. Like most of the rooms in the house, the master bedroom was vacant, the walls stripped of wallpaper, the hardwood floor in need of repair. But even empty and abandoned, it was a beautiful room. Bay windows overlooked the back of the property, creating an intimate sitting area. There was a stone fireplace in the corner and a huge bathroom through the doorway at the far end.

She made her way over the stacks of supplies and tools. She could hear a file rubbing against wood.

"You ready to take a break?" she called. "Or should I come back later?"

"I can take a break."

"Good." She entered the bathroom. Molding for the ceiling lay stacked in the center. Travis had told her he planned to do the master bed and bath in a Victorian style. He'd even ordered a claw-footed bathtub. Several cabinets stood around the outside of the room. Pipes stuck out from the wall.

Travis sat in the middle of the floor, an open cabinet in front of him. He looked up as she entered. Something flickered in his eyes. Not passion, not even interest. It was almost a fleeting hint of sadness, followed by a healthy dose of mistrust. She stopped dead in her tracks.

"What's wrong?" she asked.

"Nothing." He blinked and the expression was gone, replaced by one she couldn't read.

Her stomach tightened as worry made her gnaw on her lower lip. She handed him a mug of coffee. He took it and nodded his thanks, then sipped the steaming liquid. Silence stretched between them. She didn't know what to say. Apparently he didn't, either, because the room stayed quiet.

She walked over to the rolls of wallpaper and studied the rose-and-ivory pattern. She could feel Travis's gaze on her back. What had she done?

"You didn't have to stay home tonight to keep me company," she said at last, still staring at the wallpaper.

"I've been neglecting the house." He picked up his file and went to work on the cabinet.

She wanted to believe that was all it was, but she couldn't. The knot in her belly was too big to be ignored.

"Then tell me what's wrong. Are you angry with me?"

The file clinked when he dropped it to the floor. She heard him stand up and move close to her. She drew in a deep breath and turned around.

He'd set his coffee on the cabinet and stood with his arms folded over his chest. Worn black jeans hugged his strong thighs. His flannel shirt, rolled up to the elbows, had seen better days. The faded, soft fabric clung to him, highlighting his strength. When she gathered enough courage, she raised her head to look at his face. Dark eyes revealed nothing, nor did the straight set of his mouth.

"I didn't deliberately look through your mail," he said.

The knot in her stomach tightened. When he and Mandy had come back with her mail, she'd had a moment's unease. What if Travis had noticed who it was addressed to? But Mandy had proudly told her that she'd carried it all by herself. When Travis hadn't said anything, Elizabeth had assumed he hadn't looked.

"Mandy kept it on her lap. When it fell off, I picked it up. It's all addressed to Elizabeth Proctor. There's a postcard from your parents, Elizabeth. Your own parents use Sam's last name. Why did you lie?"

She expected the shame. When the hot emotion flooded her, she had to fight to keep from ducking her head. She could feel the blush creeping up her cheeks. Even in the soft light of the bathroom he would be able to see her embarrassment. But she hadn't expected to feel such sadness and regret. Travis had believed her. Despite the evidence against her, despite his questions, he'd trusted her to be who she said she was. He hadn't pressed to know her secrets. He'd been there for her, a good friend, and now that was gone.

"I'm sorry," she said slowly, gripping her mug tightly. "I didn't want anyone to know. I couldn't tell you because I knew what you would think."

"What's the problem?" he asked. His eyebrows drew together. He unfolded his arms and held out his hands, palms up. "It's no big deal. People get divorced all the time. Hell, I'm divorced. Why would you think anyone would care?"

"It's not that simple."

"What's not that simple? Did he beat you? Was he into men instead of women? Dammit, Elizabeth, tell me the truth."

She'd always known it would come to this. She should have known the secret would get out. What would Travis think of her when he knew? Would he despise her? Call her a fool? She shook her head. He couldn't say anything worse than what she'd already told herself.

"None of those things," she said at last. "Sam Proctor was already married when I met him. I didn't know, and he didn't tell me. Sam was a bigamist."

Chapter Nine

If the situation hadn't been so sad and serious, Elizabeth might have laughed. Travis couldn't have looked more shocked if she'd stripped off all her clothes and started dancing around naked. The giggle in the back of her throat cracked and threatened to become a sob. She covered her mouth with her hand and turned away.

"You're the second wife?" he asked.

"Y-yes." She cleared her throat. It didn't help. Her legs started to tremble. She clutched at a stack of boxes of tiles, but the support wasn't enough. Shame, bitter regret, pain and confusion flooded her. She didn't want to lose Travis. Not yet. She needed him to be her friend. Now everything was lost.

She stopped trying to hold on and sank to her knees. The floor was cold through her jeans, but she didn't care. She clutched her arms to her chest and fought to stay coherent.

"I didn't know," she said, not turning around to face him. She didn't want to see the disgust in his eyes. "I swear

I didn't know. I should have, of course. I was stupid. Young, naive. It was my fault for not questioning more. But I was barely out of my teens. Things like that didn't happen to girls from like me." She spoke quickly, as if by telling the tale fast he would be more likely to believe her.

"I met Sam at a lecture, at college. My parents had wanted me to stay home and go to a local junior college, but I wanted to get away. They seemed so old and out of touch with everything. I was working and going to school part-time. There was this lecture. I saw his picture. He was blond and good-looking. When he spoke, it was wonderful. The lecture was on staying motivated to achieve goals. He was very big on staying motivated." She paused to catch her breath.

"You don't have to tell me this," Travis said quietly. He was still behind her. She didn't dare turn around; she couldn't. Maybe if she explained it all correctly, he would understand. Maybe he would know that she'd tried, really tried. She hadn't meant to make such a big mistake.

"I sat in the back because I was shy." She sniffed. "Silly. I didn't have the courage to ask my questions in front of the group. There were probably two hundred people in the room. But afterward I went up to talk to him. There was a crowd, mostly women. They were older and well dressed. I was just a kid. When he spoke to me, I was enchanted. He looked at me as if I were something special. Something different. That meant a lot. When he asked me to go for coffee ... well, I couldn't refuse."

"Elizabeth, don't."

"I have to. I have to make you understand."

"I understand."

"No, you don't." She looked up at him. Shock still flared in his dark eyes. He sat on the edge of the cabinet staring down at her. His arms were folded over his chest. His body language told her he'd pulled back. The teasing man who opened his home to her was gone, replaced by a judging stranger.

"I was a late bloomer. I didn't know how to dress or act around kids my age. My parents didn't help. The clothes they bought me were inappropriate for school. Too dressed-up and conservative. I'd never had a boyfriend. Sam was ten years older than me, but very hip and sophisticated. I was overwhelmed." She looked up at him and forced herself to smile. It felt a little shaky. "You know how that is, Travis. You've knocked your share of women off their feet."

"One or two," he admitted. "But I'm not judging you."

"Yes, you are. Of course you are. Do you think I don't judge myself? I made it so easy for him." She closed her eyes remembering how eager she'd been for his kisses, his touch. She'd never been with a man before. Sam was tender, teaching her the ways between a man and a woman. She'd fallen in love in a matter of days.

"He lived in Seattle but commuted to L.A. on business a lot. I even visited him there, once, at his apartment." She opened her eyes and stared at her clenched fists. She tried to relax her fingers, but she couldn't. She was holding on to all of herself to keep from breaking down. It was overwhelming, knowing what Travis thought, what other people would think. Knowing she'd been irresponsible and foolish and gullible. Feeling horribly alone. There was no one to turn to.

"I know now that apartment must have belonged to a friend. He was already married. He has two children with his real wife. A boy and a girl. When I got pregnant, I just assumed we'd be married. He'd never said anything about a wife. I never thought to ask. He said of course we would. He loved playing the odds. It was all a game to him. His dual life was exactly the kind of challenge he thrived on. I should have known."

"Elizabeth, I don't know what to say."

"I don't blame you. I didn't know what to say, either. I lived with that man for six and a half years." She laughed, then stopped before the laugh turned into a sob. "I found out when the police knocked on my door in the middle of the night. They arrested him, right there in my living room. You know the funny part?"

He didn't answer.

"I was going to leave him and get a divorce. The marriage—the whatever we had together—had been in trouble for a while. It didn't work with his separations. Of course his already being married would have put a strain on things, too, if I'd known."

"Elizabeth—"

"No, I know what you're thinking. Any kind of moron could have figured it out. My God, in six years there should have been hundreds of clues. There were. I know there were." She couldn't look at him anymore. She stared at the loose tiles in front of her. One was plain cream with tiny flecks of rose. The other was the same cream background with rose-colored flowers in each of the corners. The bathroom was going to be beautiful when he was done. She wondered if he would let her come and look at it then, or if he wouldn't ever want to speak to her again. She couldn't blame him. Her friends had stared at her with disgust. Most had stopped calling. The ones who had continued to speak to her had made her feel worse. She hated their pity.

"I should have known. There I stood on my wedding day, so happy. I knew I would be the best bride, the best wife, the best mother. It was all a joke."

The colors on the tiles blurred. She heard a movement behind her. Travis crouched next to her and grabbed her shoulders. "Dammit, stop beating yourself up."

She stared at him, at his wavering image and only then did she realize she was crying. She raised one hand to her cheek. It was wet with tears.

"I told you," she whispered, her voice low and husky. "I warned you I wasn't who or what you thought."

"Give me a break," he said impatiently. "You made a mistake. So what? People make mistakes all the time."

"Not like this."

"Hey, this isn't half as terrible as some of things I've been imagining."

"You don't mean that."

"Elizabeth, you aren't the bad guy. You didn't do anything wrong."

"Except be stupid."

He smiled slightly. "That's not against the law."

She pulled free of his grip. "You haven't thought this through, Travis. It's not just about being stupid. I was never married. Every document I have is a lie. I won't even bother with the details of what the IRS had to say about this. We had joint property together. It's still not all straightened out. And my daughter—" Her voice started to shake. "My daughter doesn't have a father anymore. I wasn't married when she was born. Even her birth certificate is a lie. I love her more than anything, yet I might have destroyed her life. I only wanted the best for her and look what happened."

"I'm sorry."

He reached for her, but she pulled back. She leaned against the pile of tiles. "Do you know what it's like having the police show up at your door at four in the morning? Do you know what my neighbors thought or said the next day? Sam was gone about two weeks every month. I used to wonder why he didn't want to buy a house. Now I know it's because his other life would show up on the credit report. He didn't want me to go back to work, but thank God I did. When this all hit, I walked away with my daughter, my personal savings account and only what I'd paid for. I left behind everything else. I wanted to start over." The tears began to flow again. She felt her voice getting thick, but she couldn't stop. She had to explain it all. "I didn't know. I swear I didn't know."

"Hush." He reached for her and this time she didn't have the strength to resist him. After months of carrying around her guilty secret she felt cleansed, having spoken the truth at last. She knew that Travis would never be able to understand what she'd been through or look at her without feeling disgusted, but right now she couldn't deal with that.

He drew her into his embrace. He was warm and comforting, all the things her life lacked.

"Don't touch me," she said, willing herself to fight, but not able to find the strength. "I'm incompetent. I ruined my life and Mandy's, and—"

"Never," he whispered. He rested her head on his shoulder and stroked her back. "Never."

"It's true. I am. I'm—"

He silenced her with his kiss. His firm lips brushed against hers, his mustache tickled her skin. He tasted salty; then she realized it was her own tears. She clung to him, to his strength, letting herself believe that this was real. Even for just a second, it was enough. His powerful body acted as a shield from the horrors of her past. In his arms, she could forget her part in the debacle that had been her life. She could ignore how it had affected Mandy, and caused them both to be cut off from friends and family. Even her parents didn't know the truth. She couldn't face telling them.

She turned her face away, breaking the kiss. "I wish you didn't know," she said, inhaling the scent of his warm body, knowing he would soon remove his strength from her reach and she would be alone again. "I wish I didn't have to see the disgust and pity in your eyes."

He touched her chin, forcing her to look at him. "What do you see in my eyes?" he asked.

She saw the flames that had been there the last time they'd kissed. She saw compassion, and something she couldn't identify.

"You haven't had time to think it through," she said, not willing to believe it was that easy.

"Give me a little credit for knowing myself."

She didn't say anything because she knew he was wrong. In time he would get angry at her for being so young and blind. Her friends had. She'd certainly gotten angry at herself. She was used to the weight of disapproval.

He rose and pulled her to her feet. Then he bent over and picked her up in his arms. She thought about protesting, but she didn't have the energy. She wrapped her arms around his neck and savored the feeling of being safe.

He carried her down the hall into his bedroom. She'd never been in here before. There was a large sleigh bed pushed against one wall. It dwarfed this room, but would look perfect in the master suite. An antique rocker stood in one corner. He settled down on the seat. She started to struggle.

"I'm not Mandy," she said. "I don't need to be treated like a child."

"Maybe not," he said mildly, "but you need a good holding anyway and this is the best way I know to do it. Relax, Elizabeth. Everything is going to be all right. I promise."

"You can't make it all right."

"Sure I can. Even if I can't make it right forever, I can fix it now. Close your eyes. Don't think about it anymore."

He held her head against his shoulder. His other hand moved slowly up and down her back. The comforting embrace weakened her resistance. She felt the tears forming. She clutched at his shirt and gave in to the pain.

It filled her, surrounding her. All the days and nights she'd lived with her shameful secret, all the lies she'd told, willingly and unwillingly. She'd hoped for a fresh start in this small town. Nothing was the way it was supposed to have been. This shouldn't have happened to her.

Travis murmured quiet words of encouragement. Her sobs lessened. She drew in a ragged breath and turned her face toward his neck. His shirt was damp against her cheek, his legs hard beneath hers. Big strong hands held her gently, as if she were the most fragile of creatures. Something precious. She wanted to believe his embrace. She wanted to know that she was fragile and special, something of value.

"Better?" he asked when she'd been silent for several minutes.

Elizabeth nodded slowly. "Thanks for understanding. Sometimes I'm so overwhelmed by all of it. Not just what went wrong with Sam, but for everything we've lost. I wanted to give my daughter a perfect home with two loving parents."

"Mandy is fine. You have a new job, you're healing from the surgery. You're both going to make it. So what's the problem?"

She stared at his neck, studying the way his evening stubble roughened his skin. She wanted to touch him there, to see what he felt like against her fingers, but she couldn't. It wasn't right to repay his kindness with her own selfish needs.

"I can't marry again. I would never trust myself to pick the right man."

"That's a big decision to make, based on one mistake."

She sat up and glared at him. "It was a hell of a mistake. Who are you to be telling me what I should think about marriage? You've had one bad experience, and you're never getting married again."

One corner of his mouth turned up in a smile. "I'm glad you're feeling better." She tried to wiggle out of his lap, but he held her firm. "It wasn't just one experience," he said, resting his hands on her waist.

She stopped fighting and sagged against him. "Does it hurt you, too? Does it hurt to know you'll always be alone?"

"Yeah. It hurts like hell."

He reached down for her at the exact moment she raised her head toward him. Their lips met. Unlike their other kisses, there was nothing gentle this time, no soft exploration. It was hard and hot, hungry and desperate. She could feel her own pain and his pain. The hurt, the bleakness of their futures compounded one another, growing until they were both close to drowning in need.

She clung to him, to his arms and shoulders, shifting to move her body closer. His strength would be her salvation. Just for this night, just for this tiny slip of time, she would steal what she had to, give all she could so he would be saved, as well.

His mouth angled over hers, his lips parted. She welcomed him, welcomed the sensations he brought, the forgetfulness of pleasure. That is what she needed, she thought, feeling his tongue with her own, tasting him, being tasted. She needed to forget everything in her life.

He touched her face, her hair, her shoulders, her back. Whisper-light touches that barely grazed her skin. They set her on fire. She moved closer so that her side pressed against him. Her breasts ached. She wanted him to touch her there, touch her everywhere. The heat of the fire helped her forget. She could get lost in the smoke. Disappear into the flames. He made her come alive in ways she'd forgotten existed.

His hands rested on her waist, then began to move higher. Her breasts swelled, her nipples puckered inside her bra. Against her hip she felt the hard ridge of his erection. An answering wanting moistened her panties.

"Travis," she breathed in anticipation as his fingers stroked her rib cage.

He buried his face in her neck, kissing the sensitive skin under her jaw, nibbling on her earlobe, whispering her name like a prayer. His lips were warm and damp.

His hands moved higher still, at last cupping her full breasts, taking their weight into his palms. His thumbs swept across her nipples, sending sharp jolts of pleasure down to curl her bare toes. She arched against his caress, searching for more and more of his touch. But instead of assuaging her need, he moved his hands up to her shoulders, then slipped his fingers through her hair and held her head in place.

She opened her eyes and stared at him. The fire burning in his dark irises left no room for any emotion other than passion. She reveled in the need and desire that matched her own.

Never taking her eyes from him, she touched his face. Her fingers traced the straight line of his nose, the shape of his jaw. She heard the rasp of her fingertips against his stubble, and felt the smoothness of his mustache. She touched his damp mouth, tracing the shape, enjoying the heat. He parted his lips and licked the tip of her finger.

She laughed. He smiled at the sound; then his smile faded and she saw the questions forming in his eyes. Questions that quenched the fire and overpowered the need.

The loss was more than she could bear. "Don't," she whispered.

"Elizabeth, you're reacting. It's too soon."

The disappointment tasted bitter. "I thought men always wanted to get women into bed. I guess it's not true." She tried to slide off his lap, but he held her in place. She flushed. "Or it's not true with me."

He thrust his hips forward, pressing his erection hard against her. "Do you need more proof that I want you? I'm trying to keep you from having regrets in the morning."

"You're thinking about my past." It hurt to be rejected out of hand. The feeling was made worse by the fact that he was the first man she'd been attracted to, or had even kissed, since Sam. She hadn't made love for over a year. She'd never once been tempted to stray, and since she found out the truth about her marriage, she'd been too ashamed to try dating. Nothing had changed. She was still the shy little nobody. The girl who didn't understand boys or know how to attract them. The boys had grown into men, but she was just as lost as ever.

"I'm sorry I embarrassed you," she said stiffly, wishing she wasn't turning bright red.

"Damn it, Elizabeth, what do I have to do to prove to you that I'm trying to act like a gentleman?"

"Nothing at all— What are you doing?"

He placed one arm around her back and slipped the other underneath her legs. As he rose to his feet, he pulled her against his chest. He walked four steps to the bed.

"You are the most stubborn woman," he growled as he bent over and placed her on the comforter.

"Stop. You don't have to do anything. In fact, I'd rather you didn't." She started scrambling off the other side.

He grabbed both her hands in his. One he held down at the mattress, the other he drew to his crotch and placed against him. Even through his jeans he was hard and hot. He held on to her wrist and moved her palm up and down. A tremor shot through his body, and he gritted his teeth.

"Had enough?" he asked, his eyes once again burning with the fire.

"No," she said truthfully.

"Elizabeth, don't tempt me like this. You're still recovering from your surgery. You're upset about your past. I don't want you to wake up and hate my guts. I like you too much for that."

If he'd promised to love her forever, she would have never believed him. If he'd said the truth didn't matter, she would have never forgiven him for the lie. But liking her she could believe. She liked him back. He was the closest thing in the world she had to a friend. He knew the truth about her and hadn't turned his back on her. He might tomorrow. He might pity her or get angry. But for tonight he was her friend.

She reached for the first button on his jeans. "It doesn't have to mean anything. It could just be about tonight."

"Hell." He brushed her fingers away and bent down and kissed her.

He didn't wait for an invitation, but thrust inside her mouth savagely, hungrily, as if he'd been given permission to devour that which he most desired. He sucked on her lower lip, nipped her chin, then moved lower to the neck of her T-shirt. He paused long enough to slip off the offending garment and continue his journey of exploration.

His hands led the way, unfastening her bra to bare her breasts. The evening air was cool, in contrast to the heat of his mouth trailing ever closer. Damp kisses ignited her skin. His scent surrounded her, filling her with images of the man who touched her. She reached out to embrace his body, feeling the muscles in his arms and back, touching his short dark hair.

He murmured her name over and over again as if it were an incantation. His fingers reached for and found her puckered nipples, toying with them, readying them for his mouth.

He moved until he was straddling her. Their jeans slid back and forth creating friction. The bulging male part of him mated with her softer, damper center. Through the layers of clothing, she felt the promise of their joining.

Her hands fluttered against his chest and touched the buttons of his shirt. Before she could unfasten even one, he touched her right nipple with his tongue.

All rational thought fled. Her body awakened painfully to the joy of moist heat, the suckling that pulled exquisitely from her breast through her belly down to her swelling center. Her arms fell to her sides and her hands clung to the comforter. Her hips arched against him seeking the re-lease of his touch.

Her breathing increased. She'd tried not to think about making love with Travis. She hadn't been as successful as she would have liked. She'd known he would be tender and patient, qualities she'd seen in him every day. She thought she might enjoy the feel of his body close to her, on top of her, his powerful strength reminding her of her female-ness. His broad shoulders made her feel fragile—and safe. She'd known she would enjoy his attentions, but she hadn't expected to lose control.

His fingers toyed with her other breast, teasing the hardened tip with the flick of his thumb. His kiss on her deepened, then he drew back and moved his lips over her nipple. The individual hairs of his mustache swept over her sensitized skin, making her gasp and bringing her shoulders up off the bed. She reached up and grabbed his head, holding him in place. She'd never been aggressive in bed before. She'd never offered any comments on Sam's performance. He'd pleased her most of the time, and she'd been content with that. He'd occasionally asked her to be the aggressor, but she'd never had the courage to act with-out being acted upon.

But now, she had no choice in the matter. Those tiny prickling caresses made her breath catch and legs tremble. She couldn't bear for him to stop. He kept moving back and forth against her breasts, taunting her with the movement. Her hips flexed again and again, pressing harder against his arousal. She was more ready than she had ever been. So close it hurt to breathe hard, and yet he hadn't even touched her there.

When she thought she would explode or go mad, he slid down her body, trailing kisses to the waistband of her jeans. He sat up and unfastened the button and slipped the zip-per down. She had enough awareness to raise her hips to assist him.

It was only when she felt his mouth on her thigh that she realized he'd taken off her panties along with her jeans. Before she could be embarrassed, he moved his hands between her legs and urged her to part them.

She willingly availed herself to him, anticipating the skillful touch of his fingers. Something warm fanned her most secret place. A breath of air. Her eyes opened. Before she could react, his fingers drew her open and he kissed her moist, quivering center.

A thrill of pleasure shot through her. Her protest died unspoken. She'd read about this, of course, had even taken Sam into her mouth once, but he'd pushed her away telling her it was dirty. She'd wondered what it would feel like to have a man touch her so intimately. A thousand questions filled her mind. What exactly was he doing with his tongue? Did he like the taste and scent of her? Could he feel her muscle contracting as he—

Her breath caught in her throat. It was as if he knew exactly how to touch, where to touch. She relaxed back on the bed and forgot her questions. Nothing mattered except the feel of him against her, loving her over and over. The rhythm increasing in cadence, matching the thunder of her heartbeat.

She whispered his name without thinking, then got embarrassed. He paused long enough to tell her to say it again. So she did. She spoke his name aloud, gasped her pleasure, rotated her hips mindlessly and surrendered to his masterful touch. The fire grew, burning hot and brighter. The flames didn't frighten her—nothing frightened her. Travis was strong enough to save her. This night was a magical escape from her real world, from everything except the passion.

He moved faster against her, then shifted, slipping one finger into her woman's place, moving it slowly. Once again she was shocked, but this time there was no room for questions, no room for anything but the sudden tension that locked her muscles and the explosion that shattered her into a million tiny pieces of perfect pleasure.

He held her tightly in his embrace, comforting her as the aftershocks rippled through her. The dull ache in her side told her that she'd used her stomach muscles too much. Who cares, she thought sleepily, and sighed.

"That sounded very contented," he said, his voice rumbling against her hair.

"It is." She snuggled closer, rubbing her cheek against the soft flannel of his shirt. His shirt? She opened her eyes. "You're not even naked!"

"I know." His slow, lazy smile belied the erection she could see pressing against the fly of his jeans.

"Travis?"

"Hush." He brushed her hair out of her face and gently stroked her head. "Rest, darlin'. You've had a long and difficult day."

It didn't make any sense. If she'd taken too long with Sam, he had simply pleasured himself and left her unsatisfied. She'd always understood that a man's needs were more uncontrollable than a woman's, that a man had to find release or face a painful night. It had never been just for her.

"But you didn't . . . do anything."

"You're too sore," he said and reached down to touch her healing incision. "I saw you wince when you settled down. You can't even drive yet. There's no way your insides are ready for anything vigorous."

She drew her eyebrows together. She couldn't fault his argument. Just the thought of anything thrust inside of her was enough to make her side ache more. But this didn't *feel* right. It wasn't the way she'd planned it.

He moved his hand from her side to her breast and gently caressed the sensitized flesh. Her eyes drifted shut. It had felt so good when he'd loved her with his mouth. She couldn't remember ever experiencing such exquisite sensations. In fact—

The idea came to her full-blown. She rose up on one shoulder, then collapsed back on the bed.

"What?" he asked.

She didn't answer. Sam hadn't wanted her to do that. But Travis wasn't Sam, she reminded herself. Sam hadn't done what Travis had done to her, either.

"Elizabeth?"

She exhaled deeply. "I was just wishing I'd had more lovers."

"What?"

She laughed. "Just so I'd know how to handle this situation."

He shook his head. "You're handling it just fine. Trust me. Now lay down and relax."

She shimmied closer, so that she could rest her chin on his chest. "I don't think so."

"What does that mean?"

"Nothing," she said, innocently and sat up. She straddled his hips and leaned forward so she could start unbuttoning his shirt.

"What are you planning to do?" he asked.

"Just wait and see. If you don't like it, I promise to stop."

Chapter Ten

Travis warned himself not to blow it. Just because he was naked and she was sitting on his bare belly kissing his chest didn't mean she was going to reciprocate what he'd done to her. But he couldn't stop thinking about it. Couldn't stop imagining what it would be like to have her taste him, touch him in that most intimate way. He told himself just having her in his bed, trusting him with her body, was enough. The hardness between his legs throbbed in time with his heartbeat and told him he was a liar.

Her hands were everywhere. His shoulders, chest, neck, arms. Soft skin brushing, stroking. Her small hot mouth pressed against his flat nipples, teasing him to frenzied awareness.

She slipped back and down, settling between his legs. He thought about telling her she didn't have to do that. He could simply lie here a few minutes and explode from the need. He tried to think about other things, to get control, but every time he closed his eyes, he was back on top of her, touching and tasting *her,* loving her cries of pleasure, feeling her release against his lips. She'd been made to be pleasured by a man—by him.

Her hands rubbed up and down on his thighs. He looked at her. She nibbled on her lower lip as she studied him, obviously trying to figure something out.

"You don't have to do this," he said, cursing his mother for raising him right.

"Do what?"

Hell. "Whatever it is that has you confused."

She tossed her hair over her shoulders. The movement caused her breasts to sway slightly. The sight of her hard peach-colored nipples bouncing in the air made his erection surge toward her.

"I want to, but I'm afraid you won't like it."

He tried to laugh. It came out a little strangled.

"I've never done this before. I can't hurt you, can I? I don't want to, you know, do anything awful."

The muscles in his legs and arms started twitching. If it wasn't for the small red incision, bright and angry against her pale flat belly, he'd roll her on her back and bury himself deep inside of her. That would end the debate and the growing pressure.

"I doubt you'd do anything awful," he said, trying not to grit his teeth. "But we can stop now."

She smiled. "Did you know the veins on your forehead are sticking out?"

"I'm not surprised," he muttered, knowing he was being punished for some previous offense. It must have been pretty bad, whatever it was.

He couldn't stand it any longer. He started to sit up, determined to suffer the indignity of a cold shower when she reached forward and touched his arousal.

His groan sounded loud in the silent room. She bent over him, her brown hair falling like an erotic curtain, caressing the tops of his thighs. He sank back on the mattress and held his breath.

Her touch was sweet, wet and tentative. A delicate pressure, careful yet adventurous. He could have exploded then, but thought better of it. Her fingers traced small circles at the base of his desire, moving through the hair, slipping lower to cup his softer parts. Weighing them in her hands tentatively, then moving more boldly when he exhaled his pleasure.

It wouldn't take long, he knew. A few slow strokes, a flick or two with her tongue and he was ready.

"Elizabeth," he said, tensing his muscles, ready to stop and have her complete him just with her hands. "You can stop now."

She looked up and tossed her head. At that second their eyes locked. It was the most erotic sight of his life. Her heart-shaped face poised over his engorged maleness, her breasts swinging freely. Pale on tanned, he saw the lines of her bathing suit. She licked his sensitive tip once, then smiled.

"I don't want to stop," she whispered.

And she didn't.

It was nearly two in the morning when he woke up. He smiled in the darkness when he felt Elizabeth's warm body pressing against his side. One of her soft, delicate arms lay across his chest. Her face was buried against his arm. He could smell the scent of her body and the lingering aroma of sex.

In seconds he was hard. He didn't have to fully form the memory of what she'd done before he was ready to have her do it again and again. He figured he'd get tired of looking at her and making love with her in about fifty years. That thought scared the hell of out of him.

Slowly he slipped out of bed, being careful not to disturb her. He picked up his jeans and stepped into the hallway. After closing the door softly behind him, he pulled on his jeans and buttoned the fly.

He checked to make sure Mandy was sleeping soundly, then picked up her bear off the floor and set it on her pillow. Finally he made his way downstairs. Louise took care of the grocery shopping and kept him stocked with all the essentials. He reached in the back of the refrigerator for a bottle of beer and twisted off the top.

The cold liquid went down easily. Not bothering to turn on any lights, he walked into the family room and settled on the sofa. The leather was cool against his bare back. He shifted to get comfortable, then relaxed and closed his eyes.

A bigamist. He would never have guessed that one. It was hard to believe something like that had happened to someone as sweet as Elizabeth. It wasn't right. His hand tightened around the beer bottle as if the slick glass were Sam Proctor's neck.

She'd mentioned that her ex-husband—former husband, or whatever the hell he was to her—was still serving time in prison. Travis was glad. He hoped the bastard never got out. The anger inside of him simmered down to a slow burn, tempered by the question of what he was supposed to do now. Elizabeth had obviously been embarrassed when she'd told him the truth. He'd hated doing that to her. He'd tried to get her to stop talking, but she'd continued on as if finally telling someone about her past was the ultimate act of absolution.

He'd hated knowing she was uncomfortable around him. Had their lovemaking made it better or worse? He shook his head and took another swallow. The knot in his gut told him it was all about to get worse. Damn. He should have handled it better. He shouldn't have kissed her in the first place, or he should have tried harder to get out of making love with her.

He grinned mockingly. Oh, yeah, Haynes. Get out of it. As if making love with Elizabeth had been some irritating charity work instead of the most incredibly intimate, erotic act of his sorry life.

He rubbed his hand over his face, then scratched his chin. None of this was helping him answer the most important question. Now what? What did he do with the truth, and what about what happened between them last night?

Okay, knowing the truth. That was easy. Elizabeth would want it kept quiet. That wasn't hard to figure out. He just wouldn't tell a soul. He sat up straight and swore.

"Kyle." He'd asked his brother to run a check on Sam Proctor. Damn. He knew exactly what his deputy was going to find out. He would have to have a talk with Kyle and tell him to keep the information to himself.

The knot in his stomach tightened. He'd felt like slime when he'd asked his brother to run the check. He should have listened to that feeling.

A bigamist. It boggled his mind. He smiled suddenly, his mood lightening as he remembered what Mandy had said about her father. He'd had to leave because he was big. The kid almost had it right, he thought, draining the beer and setting the bottle on the coffee table in front of him.

His smile faded. Where did they go from here? Despite his stellar reputation, he wasn't the casual sex, one-night-stand kind of guy. He'd had enough of that at college. He generally held back physically until there was an emotional connection. He knew nothing was going to last forever, but he'd never played fast and loose with a woman before. Elizabeth didn't strike him as overly experienced. With his luck, she'd only ever been with one man—Sam. Which meant she was going to be hating life and him come morning. Would she expect something of him? A commitment of some kind?

It wasn't, he realized with bone-chilling shock, a horrible idea. He liked Elizabeth, he adored Mandy. They got along well and—

Slow down, boy, he told himself. Nothing was going to happen between him and Elizabeth. Last night was a…a… He hated to use the word *mistake*. It hadn't been a mistake for him. Last night had been an unusual circumstance. They'd both needed each other. But there wasn't going to be anything permanent between them. He didn't have what it took to make that kind of relationship work. Even if he did, Elizabeth had made it clear she wasn't interested in getting involved with him or any man. After what Sam had done, he almost couldn't blame her.

In a week her medical restrictions would lift. She would be driving, and leaving him for her own place. If they both tried, they could put last night in its proper place and stay friends. It's really all he wanted.

The sounds of the night crowded in around him. The cool air made him shiver. He told himself to go back to his bed, to snuggle against Elizabeth's warm naked body and savor the moments while he had them. But he couldn't. Not yet. Not when he'd finally realized how hard it was going to be to let her go.

"It's a fumble on the twenty-yard line. Dallas recovers and runs it in for a touchdown. San Francisco is now down by fourteen points."

Travis groaned and reached for the remote. He hit the mute button and sank back against the couch. Mandy looked up from her place on the floor where she was working on a jigsaw puzzle.

"Is your team doing bad, Travis?" she asked.

"They're getting their fannies kicked."

"Really?" She glanced toward the TV screen. "I don't see anyone kicking fannies."

He chuckled. "Hopefully it won't happen again."

She abandoned her puzzle and climbed into his lap. "I'll make you feel better," she said and gave him a hug. "They're magic, just like yours."

He hugged her back. "I do feel better. Thanks." He pointed at the puzzle. "What is it going to be?"

"A dog." She pursed her lips together. "Mommy says there's bunnies at our house and I can see them when we get there, but I was thinking maybe I could have a puppy instead. Do you think Mommy would like a puppy?"

"I don't know. You'll have to ask her."

She wrinkled her nose. "Maybe later. She's cooking, and if you ask her stuff now, she usually says no."

He'd heard the pots rattling in the kitchen and had decided to stay clear himself. He was giving Elizabeth time to recover from what happened between them last night. "You're a very smart girl."

"I know."

Her smile took a direct line to his heart. She wore sweatpants and a matching sweatshirt in bright pink with a redheaded mermaid on the front. Her pale blond hair was pulled back in a ponytail and her bangs hung almost to her eyebrows. She was going to be a heartbreaker in a few years; when she left with her mother at the end of the week, she was going to break *his* heart.

Elizabeth walked into the room. She stared at a point above and to the left of his head. "Mandy, there are still a few flowers left in the garden. Why don't you pick some for the table?"

"Okay." The little girl slid off his lap and grinned. "I get to pick flowers."

"I heard."

She practically quivered with excitement. "You can finish my puzzle if you want to," she told Travis.

"I'll pass and let you do it."

She nodded and ran out of the room, singing a song about flowers. Elizabeth turned to leave, then hesitated.

She wore her hair as she had the first time he'd seen her, in a ponytail on top of her head. The loose strands tumbled down to her shoulder. A light touch of makeup accentuated her chestnut-colored eyes. An oversize peach sweater hung midway down her thighs. Matching leggings outlined her curves, taunting him with what he'd seen and touched and tasted the previous night. Her flat loafers didn't give her any height, and she looked small and ill at ease.

"What's wrong?" he asked, rising to his feet.

"Nothing." Her voice was hoarse, as if she was having trouble speaking. "I was just wondering if you wanted to cancel the party."

"A couple of friends over for a late lunch and football is hardly a party."

"I know, but..." Her voice trailed off. She clasped her hands together in front of her waist and stared at the ground. "I thought you might prefer to keep me away from your friends because of last night."

That didn't make any sense. "Because we made love?"

She shook her head. "No, the other thing."

The spot of color on each cheek had nothing to do with cosmetics. She looked as if she were praying for the ground to open and swallow her whole. It was all his fault.

In an effort to be a gentleman, he had left their bed that morning to give her the privacy to wake up alone. If he was going to be completely honest with himself, he would have to admit there had been something other than altruism in the act. He hadn't wanted to wake up and see the regret in her eyes. Unfortunately, she thought *he* was the one having regrets. She might say she was worried about her confession, but her body language told him she was thinking about the sex.

He crossed the room and reached toward her. Before he could pull her close, she stepped back. "Don't," she murmured.

"I'm not sorry we made love," he said quietly, aware that Mandy could return at any moment. "I left you alone this morning to give you some privacy, not because I didn't want to be with you in bed. I wanted us to make love again, but I was worried about you being sore and Mandy waking up. It was wonderful, Elizabeth. At least it was for me. I guess I'll understand if you're having second thoughts."

"I'm not sorry, either."

She looked up at him and he saw the sadness in her eyes. It puzzled him. If she didn't have regrets, then why was she sad?

"It doesn't change anything, though," she said dropping her arms to her side.

Make that: it hadn't *meant* anything. He'd been so damned worried about what she would be thinking and feeling that he hadn't spared a thought for his own feelings. "So you're saying, 'Thanks for the good time, no regrets, but gee, let's never bother doing that again'?"

"Not exactly."

He would have laughed but there was this pain deep in his chest. He'd been a one-night stand. Women across the county would be crowing with delight if they ever learned a Haynes had finally had his comeuppance. He'd been looking for something more, and Elizabeth was the one backing off.

"Don't worry about me," he said. "As for the company. Hey, why would it matter that people came over? Don't worry, I won't talk about your secret or last night."

"Thank you," she said, looking at him oddly.

"So nothing's changed. We're exactly where we were yesterday. Friends. Great."

"Travis, are you okay?" Her brows drew together in confusion. "Have I said anything to—"

The sharp ringing of the phone cut her off. "Excuse me," he said, and reached for the phone on the end table. "Hello?"

"Hey, Travis, it's Kyle." His brother sounded wary. "I ran that guy you asked me to. Sam Proctor. You're not going to believe what I found."

"I already know."

"About the bigamy?"

"Yeah."

"Elizabeth Abbott is in the report. The second wife, or whatever you'd call her."

"I know that, too."

"You okay?"

Travis turned back toward Elizabeth, but she'd left the room. No, he wasn't okay; he was never going to be okay again. She'd touched him and loved him in his bed, and now she was going to shut him down. Part of him couldn't blame her. He was the last guy in the world she should get involved with. He would only screw up the whole thing. But his brief experience of paradise had left him hungry for more. He wanted to be different, he wanted to be the kind of man who could marry and have a family. He wanted—

"Travis, are you there?"

"Sorry. I'm fine. Look, Kyle, I want you to keep this information to yourself, okay?"

Kyle exhaled in disgust. "I might be the youngest, Travis, but I'm not a kid. I know this could hurt Elizabeth. I won't say anything."

"I know. I'm sorry. Look, could you just get your butt over here as quickly as possible?" He needed someone to run interference before he said or did something stupid. Worse, before he made a promise he knew he could never keep.

"I can't sit out there with those boys if I know you're in here doing all the work," Louise said walking into the kitchen. "What can I do to help?"

Elizabeth closed the oven door and smiled. For the first time that day, her sense of doom lifted a little. "Nothing. I've got everything under control."

"You make me feel guilty. I'm supposed to be looking after you."

Elizabeth laughed and moved to the kitchen table. "I'm feeling great. Doing more things every day." She bit down on her lower lip. She'd almost blurted out, "Last night Travis and I made love, and I felt wonderful afterward." That would have given Louise something to talk about. "My incision hardly gives me any trouble at all." Except for a slight tenderness after they'd— Stop thinking about it, she ordered herself. It only made everything more difficult.

"Do you want some coffee?" she asked, pointing to the full pot. "It's fresh."

"I'll get it," Louise said. "You sit down for a minute and rest yourself. There's no point in spending all this time getting better if you're just going to wear yourself out in one afternoon."

She poured herself a cup, then offered one to Elizabeth. She shook her head in refusal. Louise poured in milk and added a rounded teaspoon of sugar.

Today she was dressed all in purple. A frilly blouse that did nothing to hide her generous curves, a calf-length ruffled skirt and bright purple cowboy boots. Her short blond hair had been puffed and sprayed into little spikes. She wore saddle earrings and lots of black mascara. The kindness and concern in her blue eyes made her look beautiful.

"I'm doing great," Elizabeth said. It wasn't an actual lie. Physically she was doing well. Emotionally, she was hovering about a half inch off the ground. Last night had been perfect, but this morning, when she'd woken up alone in Travis's bed, all her doubts had crashed in around her. They'd made a terrible mistake. The lovemaking had been so right between them, but the memory was tainted by the reason he'd reached for her in the first place. Once Travis realized that, he wouldn't want to remember what had happened at all. He would put it and her out of his mind. She hated to think about that. She knew there was no hope for any kind of long-term relationship between them, but she'd counted on them staying friends.

"You want to talk about it?" Louise asked, then took a sip from her mug. She walked to the table and plopped into the seat next to Elizabeth.

"I—"

"Don't bother lying, honey. I can see the pain in your pretty eyes. Did something happen here, or is this about whatever made you come to town in the first place?"

Elizabeth stared at her. Had the other woman guessed or had Travis said something?

"Don't give me that look," Louise said. "It doesn't take a lot of brains to figure out something is wrong with you. When you first arrived you spent most of your time looking over your shoulder. Who are you afraid of?"

Elizabeth fought the urge to confide in Louise. She'd felt better after telling Travis the truth. Confession was good for the soul. But she was afraid. She hadn't even told her own parents. She couldn't face the disappointment and shame she would hear in their voices. Would Louise understand? She gathered her courage together.

"If it's about you and Travis being lovers, then you don't have anything to worry about."

Her courage fled and with it her composure. Her mouth dropped open. "He told you?"

Louise leaned forward and smiled. "No one had to tell me, honey. I could feel it the second I walked into this house." She patted her hand. "Don't worry. The boys are too dense to figure it out. Your secret is safe with me."

"It doesn't make any difference," Elizabeth said, staring at the water glass in front of her. She moved it back and forth over the bleached oak table. "Travis isn't the kind of man a woman settles down with, even if I was interested."

"You be careful about believing all of his press," Louise said. "He and his brothers paid a high price for their father's and uncles' ways. The boys have worked hard to be decent to the women in their lives. They mostly lack any kind of skills in relationships. No role models—at least that's what they usually say on those daytime talk shows." She smiled. "Maybe you should think about giving him a chance."

"I can't." She drew in a deep breath. The courage returned. "I came to Glenwood to get away from my life in L.A. Mandy's father was a bigamist, and I was his second wife."

She told the story quickly, even the embarrassing details about how stupid she'd been. She finished, then braced herself for Louise's well-intentioned scolding.

"That bastard," Louise said, glaring at her. "Excuse my French, but that's exactly what he is."

Elizabeth blinked. She couldn't have heard the other woman correctly. "No, you don't understand. It's my fault. I should have known."

"How were you supposed to know?"

"He was my husband."

"All the more reason to trust him. Oh, I just hate men like that."

"But, Louise—"

"Don't you 'but, Louise' me. You were a virgin when you met him, weren't you?"

Elizabeth was too surprised by her friend's anger to be embarrassed by the question. "Yes, but—"

"And you were faithful to him during your relationship."

"Of course, but—"

Louise rose to her feet and started pacing the kitchen. "I'd like to find him and give him a piece of my mind. No. I'd like him castrated."

Elizabeth giggled. "That sounds a little harsh, even for Sam."

Louise paused and leaned against the counter. "Okay, maybe we'll just threaten him with dismemberment. Just enough to put the fear of God into him."

Elizabeth's smile faded as she felt tears forming in her eyes. Louise wasn't judging her, she was defending her. It was a miracle.

"Does this means we can still be friends?" she asked tentatively.

"Why in the world wouldn't we be?" Louise hurried over to the table and bent down to give her a hug. Her spicy perfume comforted Elizabeth, reminding her of her own mother.

"Thank you," Elizabeth said. "Thanks for giving me a chance."

"I'm not giving you anything." Louise straightened and smiled. "But while we're on the subject, you might think about giving yourself a chance. Travis, too. I know that boy, and I think he's smitten."

It would never work, Elizabeth told herself. If she gave Travis a chance, he would break her already fragile heart. Leaving Sam had been hard enough. If she got much closer to Travis, leaving him would be the end of her world.

Chapter Eleven

They finished eating close to four. Despite Elizabeth's protests, everyone helped clear the table and set out dessert. Travis looked at the small group sitting around the dining room table. Jordan and Craig couldn't make it back for the game, so it was just him, Elizabeth, Louise, Austin and Kyle. Oh, and of course Mandy who had seated herself next to him. He was torn between wanting to ease her shyness with Kyle and Austin and being pleased that she sought him out for protection.

"Of course I specialize in stopping long-haired types like you," Kyle said to Austin.

The other man ignored the teasing and gave Mandy a wink. His charm even worked on six-year-olds. She dimpled delightfully, then buried her head in Travis's arm. Travis glanced over at Elizabeth and saw she had noticed the exchange. She gave him a little smile. Better, he thought, remembering how she'd avoided his gaze for the first part of the meal. Every time she looked at Austin, his gut clenched as he waited for her to figure out his friend was handsome as sin and richer than God. So far she seemed singularly unimpressed.

"Kyle is leading the pack this month," Travis said, stroking Mandy's hair. "Giving out the most tickets."

"That must make him popular with the locals," Elizabeth said.

Kyle shrugged. "At least I'm not like you, big brother. Always parking in the same place. He's got the worst record in tickets."

Elizabeth began cutting the cherry cheesecake in front of her and placing the slices on plates. "If you're the sheriff, why do you give out tickets at all? I wouldn't have thought that was part of your job."

He made the mistake of looking at Kyle, who was making cow eyes at him, mocking him before he'd even started to answer the questions.

He balled up his napkin and tossed it across the table. Kyle burst out laughing, Elizabeth remained calm, Louise muttered about boys being boys and Austin stayed out of it. As always, his friend was on the fringe of the group, watching but never actually belonging.

"I don't ask my men to do anything I wouldn't do."

"That's fair," Elizabeth said, as Kyle clutched his hands over his heart and pretended to swoon. "If you don't behave, Kyle," she said, her voice staying even and friendly, "I'm going to make you stand in the corner and not give you any dessert."

Travis burst out laughing. Kyle looked suitably chastised. Even Austin smiled.

"He also parks his car in one place," Austin said, taking the plate she offered. "By the main highway. Whenever he's out looking for speeders, we all know where to find him."

Elizabeth glanced at him. "I'm glad you were there," she said. "If you hadn't been, who knows what would have happened."

"Travis took Mommy to the hospital," Mandy said, taking her serving of cake and picking up her fork. "I was scared, but he used the siren and made sure Mommy was all better."

"Just doing my job," he said, slightly embarrassed.

Elizabeth saved him by changing the subject. She cut the last piece of cake and started to hand it to Kyle. His baby brother was her age, but she treated him as if he were several years younger. Travis couldn't help being pleased by that.

"Are you going to behave?" she asked, holding out the plate.

"Yes, ma'am."

"Good. No more trouble from you, young man." Her voice was stern, but her eyes danced.

Travis watched her tease Kyle and felt a warmth burning deep in his chest. He glanced around the table, at the people he loved most in the world. It felt right to have Elizabeth share in this part of his life. Louise chatted with Austin. Mandy scraped her plate clean. For the first time in years, he felt content.

Elizabeth looked up at him and their eyes met. The sadness and wariness from that morning was gone. In their place something soft and lovely flared to life. He wanted to make love to her. Instantly heat boiled through him, burning in his blood and engorging his groin. An answering passion made her lean forward slightly and lick her lower lip.

He wanted to feel her and taste her, loving her until she writhed with need. The room faded and all he saw was her. The V neck of her sweater had slipped slightly, allowing him to see the valley between her breasts and the hint of a curve. He wanted her naked, next to him. Under him. As much as he'd loved the feel of her mouth on him, this time he wanted to be inside, claiming her. He figured that line of thinking meant he was pretty primitive, but that didn't make his erection go away.

Louise stood up and asked if anyone would like coffee. Her prosaic question broke the spell between them, and Elizabeth looked away. After a few minutes, Travis managed to quench his desires. The conversation moved from speeding tickets to the local high school football team and the chance they had at the local championship.

Mandy climbed onto his lap. He put his arm around her back to support her. She leaned against his chest.

"You've got gravy on your shirt," he said, pointing to the spot on her sweatshirt.

She glanced down and held the shirt out so she could see it. "I always spill, huh?"

"Yeah, but I like it."

"You like it?" She grinned. "That's silly. You're not supposed to like it."

"Well, I do."

He bent over and tickled her under her arms. She squirmed and laughed. When he stopped, she sagged against him and sighed. "You're nice, Travis."

"You're not too bad yourself."

"There's a boy in my class. He said he lost his parents, but then he found new ones. I guess his mommy and daddy were too lost to ever find their way home."

He didn't know whether or not he should explain what the boy had meant by "lost." Before he could decide, she continued.

"He loves his new mommy and daddy, but he misses the old ones. He says new parents are fun. I lost my daddy. Mommy says he's not ever coming back. Could you be my new daddy?"

He felt as if he'd been hit by a speeding train. All the air rushed out of him and his chest ached. He tried to speak, but couldn't. His throat was too dry.

Mandy stared up at him, her wide blue eyes trusting him with her heart. He glanced around the table. Everyone else was busy with their own conversation. No one had overheard Mandy's question.

"I'm flattered you would ask me," he said at last, touching her soft cheek, then tucking a loose strand of hair behind her ear. "But I don't know how to be a daddy. I don't have any children of my own. Why don't I just be your friend instead?"

She frowned. "Do you have to learn how to be a daddy?"

"I think so."

She raised her shoulders and let out an exaggerated sigh. "Okay. You can be my friend, and then when you learn how to be my daddy, you can be that, too, okay?"

He hadn't cried in about twenty years, but suddenly he felt a burning behind his eyes. He pulled Mandy close and hugged her tight. "It's better than okay, Mandy. It'll be great."

The house was still. Elizabeth stood by the door and listened to the *creak creak* of the swing on the front porch. She balled her hands into fists, then consciously relaxed them. The company had gone home, Mandy was asleep in her bed. Elizabeth couldn't avoid Travis forever, even if she wanted to. But what was she going to say?

She shook her head. The problem wasn't what to say, it was where to start the conversation. They had many things to discuss, not the least of which was what had happened between them last night.

She walked toward the front door, placed her hand on the handle and paused. All of this would be a lot easier if she knew what she wanted. She knew what she didn't want.

She didn't want to make another mistake like the one she'd made with Sam. She didn't want to be a fool again for a man. The easiest and safest way to ensure that was to never get involved again. Especially with someone even worse than Sam. Travis was too good-looking by far. He was kind, tender, sweet with her daughter and hot in bed. By comparison, Sam was an amateur, his smooth-talking ways falling far short of Travis's charm. Logically, she had to steer clear of Travis Haynes. If not, she would be risking herself all over again, and she would have learned nothing from her false marriage.

False. Just the word was enough to send waves of shame surging over her. Her cheeks heated. She pressed her hands against her face and prayed that she would one day be able to look back on what had happened and not feel so disgusted with herself. Friends had told her she was overreacting. Even Travis had told her to stop beating herself up about it. They didn't understand, she told herself. They didn't know what it was like to have made that big a mistake in judging someone's character. *They* weren't going to have to explain it to Mandy when she was old enough to understand. They didn't have to spend the rest of their lives knowing they had been taken in by a con man. Elizabeth knew she had been so starved for love and affection, too eager to believe that someone—a man—finally loved her, that she hadn't wanted to see that Sam was using her.

She drew in a deep breath. One day she would be able to look back on this without wanting to crawl away and die. It had to get better; time was all she had. She grabbed the door handle and turned it, then pulled open the door and stepped out onto the porch.

The night was dark, the moon a faint sliver in the inky sky. Stars hung low, as if they wanted to eavesdrop on what she had to say. She knew Travis had seen her come outside, but the creaking of the swing continued in the same rhythm—slow, steady, seductive.

She told herself to go lean against the railing where it was safe. Better to keep her distance. But she was too tired and tense to be sensible. She moved over to the swing and sat next to him.

One long arm stretched along the back of the wooden seat. She relaxed and rested her head against the slats. He shifted, wrapping his arm around her shoulder and pulling her close against him. She told herself to resist, to stiffen and move away, but she couldn't. Her cheek rested against his hard chest. She could feel the muffled thudding of his heartbeat. The slow, steady sound reminded her of last night. She awakened several times to find herself in his arms. The warmth of his body, the scent of their lovemaking, and the sound of his heart had soothed her back to a restful sleep. For the first time in months, she'd felt safe.

"The meal was terrific," he said. His voice rumbled through his chest, vibrating against her skin. "Thanks for going to all that trouble. You've spoiled everyone. They're used to me cooking hot dogs or something out of a can."

"I enjoy cooking," she said, fighting the urge to look up at him. She wanted to see what he was thinking, she wanted to read the expression in his eyes. She was equally terrified of what she would see there. What if he didn't want her? Worse, what if he did?

"Do you cook a lot?" he asked.

"Some." She smiled and snuggled closer. "I used to think if I was a better wife, Sam would stay home more. So I took a couple of courses given by a restaurant and started really doing some exotic things. It didn't seem to help. For the longest time I assumed it was my cooking."

"It wasn't."

"Of course not. It was his wife and kids. The fanciest beef dish in the world can't compete with that."

"Elizabeth, Sam cared for you."

She grimaced. "Maybe. Sometimes, when I'm feeling rational, I believe that he did. In a sort of sick, twisted way.

If he'd really cared, he would have told me the truth about himself." She shook her head. "I don't want to talk about him anymore. Thanks for including me today. I enjoyed having your friends around. Sam never wanted— Damn. Now that I've spilled the beans about him, I can't seem to stop talking about what happened. Sorry."

"Don't be."

Travis slid his hand up her shoulder to her head. His long fingers slipped through her hair to the band that was holding her ponytail in place. He tugged gently, easing it down the strands until her hair was loose and falling over her shoulders. She should probably tell him not to touch her so intimately. She was giving him the wrong idea. But she couldn't help herself. She liked the feel of his hands on her. He made her feel safe and cherished. She hadn't felt any of those things in a very long time.

He bent down and kissed the top of her head. "You were saying Sam never wanted what?"

"Sam never wanted us to have friends over. He didn't want me to have friends at all. But the crowd today was nice."

He chuckled low in his chest. "If you think this was a crowd, you should wait until my other brothers join us. Between Craig's three boys and everybody's dates trying to figure out who belongs with whom, it's a madhouse. I'll give you plenty of warning before letting that group descend on you."

It sounded lovely, she thought wistfully, thinking of her own solitary childhood. She shifted on the swing. Her right breast pressed against his chest. Her nipples hardened in response to his body, but she ignored the tingling sensation.

"I wouldn't mind," she said, then realized she would be gone by the time Travis's family invaded. She would be driving at the end of the week and moving out to her own place next weekend.

A sharp stab of regret and disappointment startled her. She didn't want to think about what it meant, so she recalled what Travis had just told her.

"You mentioned dates," she said. "I thought the Haynes brothers didn't want to get involved with anybody."

"We all want it to work out, so we seem to keep trying. I guess each of us is praying for a miracle."

The bitterness in his voice surprised her. "You sound upset."

"It gets damned lonely," he admitted. "It's probably a matter of wanting what we can't have. Craig got burned big-time. His wife walked off with one of his closest friends, leaving him with a pile of bills and three little kids. Damn fool keeps looking for the right woman. Kyle dumps his girlfriends before they have a chance to dump him. I'm sure it has something to do with our mother abandoning him when he was fifteen and the string of women Dad brought into the house right after. We went through three stepmothers in three years. And then there's Jordan."

Travis paused. Elizabeth wished she could move closer to offer him comfort. She could feel his pain. It radiated out from him like the heat of a fever. In the past, he'd talked about his family and his resistance to believing relationships lasted, but this was the first time she'd really understood all that he and his brothers had been through. She was the last one to be giving him any kind of advice, though. Her own track record was pretty awful. So she didn't say anything. She reached up her hand to his face and stroked his cheek. His evening beard poked at her palm. He felt warm and alive. A quivering began low in her belly; she told herself this wasn't about sex.

"Jordan, hell, I don't know about him. He keeps everything inside. He was always the odd one out. The rebel." He grabbed her hand and brought it to his mouth. His kiss on her palm was sweet and damp, his tongue tracing an erotic line from the base of her thumb to her little finger. She shivered.

"After all," he continued, "look at what he does for a living. He's a fire fighter, the crazy fool."

He laughed and she joined him. It felt good to be with Travis like this. He turned toward her, angling one knee across the bench. His position moved them a little apart, but now she could see his face.

He looked good by porch light, she thought, studying the way stubble darkened the hollows of his cheeks and made his eyes more mysterious. She wanted to lean close and touch him all over, relearning the body she had caressed so intimately the night before. His pleasing scent made her remember other smells and tastes, his laughter made her think of other sounds. The way he'd called her name, his voice husky with disbelief and pleasure. Her breasts grew more sensitive inside her bra; her most secret place dampened in anticipation. Desire filled her, but she kept it firmly in check.

"I had an interesting conversation with Mandy at dinner," he said, resting his palm on her thigh.

"I thought I saw you two talking. What about?"

"Her father."

She started to fold her arms over her chest. He grabbed her hands, pulled them down on top of his knee and held her in place. "She was telling me that a boy at school lost his parents. She assumes that they're physically lost and won't be able to find their way back to him. She thinks Sam is lost to her, as well."

Elizabeth tried to ignore the soft denim of Travis's jeans, the heat of his leg below and the warmth of his hand above hers. She tried to ignore the feeling of panic boiling to life in her belly. She'd known it would come to this with Mandy, but not yet. She wasn't ready.

"I told her that Sam wouldn't be able to see her again," she said. "But I can't explain the rest of it to her. Not yet. She's too young."

She dropped her head so that she could stare at her lap. No doubt Travis would disagree with her decision. She didn't care. When she'd asked Sam to sign away the rights to see Mandy, he hadn't even bothered to protest. He'd never been much interested in the girl. Not having him visit every few months would make it less confusing for Mandy.

"I agree," he said, surprising her. "But I think you should be willing to let her talk about missing her father if she wants to."

"Thanks for the advice," she said, surprised she wasn't irritated with his interfering.

He turned her hand over and placed his on top, palm to palm. His skin was rough from his carpentry work—warm, yet dry. He had large hands, strong, capable fingers. She trusted his hands as much as she trusted the man. A big mistake, she warned herself, hoping it wasn't already too late.

"She asked if I could be her father instead of Sam."

Elizabeth's heart clenched. Fierce jealousy and possessiveness poured through her. She wanted to jerk her fingers free and use that hand to slap Travis away. How dare he try to worm his way into her daughter's affections?

She opened her mouth to speak, then closed it again. He hadn't done anything wrong, a small rational voice whispered. He had been nothing but sweet to her and her daughter. Of course Mandy would respond to that affection. She'd spent more time with Travis in the past few weeks than with Sam in the past year.

"What did you tell her?" she asked, daring to look at him.

His dark eyes met and held her own. He shrugged sheepishly. "I told her I didn't know how to be a dad, but that I was willing to be her friend. I hope that's okay."

He was obviously concerned about her feelings. She was grateful she hadn't given in to that moment of jealousy and destroyed the special friendship she and Travis had built. It made sense that she would be protective of Mandy. Look at all that had happened to them. But Travis wasn't the enemy. She would do well to remember that.

She smiled softly. "You shouldn't have lied to her, Travis."

He straightened, obviously startled. "I didn't lie to her."

"Of course you did." She leaned a little closer to him, allowing the night to shut out the rest of the world. "You know exactly how to be a father. It's something you do very well." She held up her hand when he started to protest. "Think about it. You took her to soccer so she could have fun and make friends. You eat raw French toast and tell her that her cooking is wonderful. You hold her tight and protect her from the world."

He dismissed her words with a shrug. "That's the easy part. Anyone could do that."

"Sam didn't. It's not what you do with her, it's taking the time to make the little things matter. I think you're a terrific father. Mandy does, too, or she wouldn't have asked."

"I— Thanks," he said, looking distinctly uncomfortable. His gaze darted around the porch, to the ground, the sky—anywhere but at her. "I hope I can still see her. You know, when you guys move."

"Sure. She'll love it."

"And I think you should talk to her about Sam."

"Travis, I know what's best for Mandy."

"You don't have to tell her about the bigamy, just let her talk about being without him. Glenwood is a small town. We don't have a lot of single parents around here. Mandy probably feels different from everyone else she knows."

"I hadn't thought of that," she admitted. "It makes sense. I'll talk to her." She drew in a deep breath. She should have seen that on her own. "See, you're not the only one who questions about parenting skills." Would she ever get it right? First she messed up completely by believing Sam. Now she was concerned about making a mistake with Mandy. When would the second-guessing end?

"You're going to make yourself crazy," he said, taking her in his arms and pulling her toward him. "Stop worrying. Everything is going to be fine."

"But—"

"No 'buts,' " he said, covering her mouth with his finger. "That's enough thinking for tonight. I don't want you to tax your brain with anything more complex than how wonderful this feels."

He lowered his mouth to hers. She told herself she should stop him. They couldn't do this again. But it felt too good. Too right. His lips were hot against hers. His arms felt strong and safe as he enfolded her against his broadness.

He shifted, pulling her onto his lap. Of their own accord, her arms reached around his neck. One of his hands slipped up from her thigh to her waist, then to her breast. He touched her curves, stroked the puckering nipple. Elizabeth gasped her pleasure and knew that she was seconds from losing control.

She pulled her mouth away from his drugging kisses, away from the pleasure and escape he promised.

"I can't," she whispered, fighting the tightness in her throat and the screams of protest from her aroused body. "Please don't make me do this again."

"Darlin', no one's going to *make* you do anything."

She risked looking up at him. He wasn't smiling, but he didn't look angry. "I didn't mean it like that. Oh, Travis, you are wonderful and there's nothing I'd like better than to make love with you tonight."

"But?"

"But I don't want to fall in love with you or care about you more than I do. If we make love again, I won't be able to be just friends." She pulled free of his gentle embrace and stepped onto the porch. It was tearing her up inside to leave him, but she knew she had to. For both their sakes.

"I'm doing you a favor," she said, looking down at him, hoping that wasn't hurt she was seeing in his eyes. "After all, aren't you the one claiming you don't want to make another mistake? Aren't you the one who doesn't want to get involved again?"

Chapter Twelve

The question hadn't left him alone in two days. Elizabeth was right—he *had* told her he didn't want to get involved again. It went against everything he believed. Trying for a long-term relationship was a sure guarantee of heartbreak. Not only for himself, but for the woman involved. It would be crazy to start something he didn't intend to finish. The easiest thing for both he and Elizabeth was to stop playing footsie under the table and get on with being friends. At the end of the week, when she was able to drive and her rental house was available to move into, she would go back to her life and he would get on with his. No big deal.

He moved closer to the edge of the soccer field and watched Mandy race across the grass as she chased the elusive ball. She and her new friends squealed with excitement when she connected with her toe. The ball landed far short of the goal, but no one cared, least of all Mandy. She raced over to him and grinned.

"Did you see me kick it?" she asked, panting.

"You bet." He ruffled her bangs, then gave her a little push. "Go back to the game, honey."

"Okay, Travis." She raced off.

He shoved his hands into his uniform trouser pockets. He was supposed to be taking care of paperwork back at the station. But this morning when Elizabeth had asked him if he could take Mandy to soccer practice, he hadn't been able to say no. Time was ticking by too quickly and he wanted be with the little girl as much as possible.

He wanted to spend time with her mother, as well, but that was dangerous. And confusing. What the hell was going on with him? He should be pleased that Elizabeth was well enough to spend the afternoon with Rebecca at the office learning about her new job. She was certainly excited enough to be out of the house. But he'd hated dropping her off at the child services center. It wasn't because he didn't want her to have a job or be independent, it was that he didn't like the reminder that she was leaving.

"You thinking about taking on a new coaching job?"

He turned and saw Austin walking toward him. As always, his friend was dressed in jeans and cowboy boots. A small gold hoop hung in one earlobe. He looked like a modern-day pirate.

"Just baby-sitting," Travis said, pointing to Mandy. "What about you?"

"One of the deputies told me you'd be out here," Austin said, stopping beside him. "I wanted to let you know I'm going to be out of town for a few days."

"Vacation?" Travis asked, then grinned. To the best of his knowledge Austin had never taken a vacation.

"Nope. I'm giving a paper at a conference in France. Technical stuff. I'll be gone about five days."

Travis nudged his friend with his elbow. "You know what they say about French women, buddy. Have a great time."

"Are you going to start living vicariously, now that you've got the hots for Elizabeth?"

Travis started to deny the statement, then figured, why bother? "You saw?"

"Sunday, at your place? Sure. The way you two were looking at each other, you about set the table on fire."

"It's more than sex."

"Then you've got a problem."

Travis looked at the field where Mandy was in the middle of the young crowd of soccer players. She darted left, the ball went right and she landed on her rump. He could hear her laughter from across the field. Involuntarily, he smiled.

"You know anything about being a father?" he asked.

"No."

"Me, neither. Except I wouldn't want to be like my old man. I'd want to be more interested in my kids than in other women."

"So *be* more interested in your kids."

"As simple as that?"

"Why make it hard?"

It made sense, Travis thought, in a twisted, Austin sort of way. "You have any kids?"

For the first time since they'd started talking Austin smiled. "I'm very careful."

"I just bet you are. You don't want any gold digger getting a part of your money."

Austin glanced at the playing field, then looked back at Travis. For once his guard wasn't up and Travis was able to see past the usual blankness in his cold gray eyes. Something ugly and painful flared there. Something that made Travis want to apologize for ever bringing up relationships, women or kids.

"It's not the money." The shutters went back down and Austin was once again in control. "It's about belonging."

Austin had never belonged. Travis remembered the first day his friend had shown up at the local junior high school. He'd been a skinny misfit of thirteen. Within two days he'd been in the middle of four fights and had a rainbow-colored black eye. He'd started an argument with Travis, not realizing that messing with one Haynes boy had meant getting involved with all four.

Travis looked over at the good-looking man next to him and wondered when he'd begun to change. He liked to think it had been at the moment Travis had stood with him, against his brothers. He always wondered why he'd done it. Maybe it had been the hopelessness he'd seen in Austin's expression, or the fear behind the bravado. Craig, down from the local high school had been willing to let Austin off the hook, but Kyle was too excited about his first fight with his older brothers. Jordan, more like Austin than any of them, had stood on the outside watching and waiting.

In the end no one could remember what the fight had been about. When the boys' vice principal had come to investigate, the Haynes brothers had closed ranks, including Austin as one of their own. He'd never forgotten, Travis knew. Austin hadn't said anything; he hadn't had to. Even after he'd run away from his foster home and gotten into trouble and been sent away, even when he turned up years later, never once saying where he'd been, even now that he was wealthy enough to live anywhere, he stayed close. Travis trusted him as much as he trusted any of his brothers. Maybe more. Austin stayed because he wanted to, rather than simply because of the loyalty of blood.

"You chose not to belong," Travis said.

"You chose not to get involved." Austin jerked his head toward Mandy. "Face it, Travis, you've got it bad for the lady and her little girl. You can run but you can't hide."

"No. It's not like that. I'll admit Mandy's got me by the short hairs. I would do just about anything for that kid. Her dad won't be showing up in her life anytime soon. I want to be there for her. Warn her away from guys like you."

Austin grinned. "Don't worry. I stay away from the innocents. Unlike you."

It was true. Austin only spent time with women who understood the rules of his game: no involvement. "Elizabeth's not an innocent."

"So you *are* involved."

Travis glared at his friend, then smiled sheepishly. "Okay, I'll admit I'm tempted."

Austin glanced at his watch. "I've got to get going if I want to make my flight." He turned to leave, then paused and looked back. The afternoon sun caught him full in the face, highlighting his strong features and boring into his gray eyes. For just a second, some emotion flickered there. Travis wasn't sure, but he thought it might be envy.

"You shouldn't believe it all, buddy," Austin said. "What people say about you. Sure you had some tough breaks with your dad and all. But it doesn't have to be like that again. You have a choice. Don't screw it up just because you think that's all you know."

With that he walked over to his car and climbed in. Travis was still staring after him long after he had disappeared down the road. He shook his head and turned his attention back to the game. Austin made it sound so damn easy. As if he'd *wanted* to mess up before, just because it was easier. It wasn't like that. He'd tried with Julie. They'd both tried. It hadn't worked out. Despite Austin's feelings to the contrary, Travis knew there was too much of his father in him to ever risk anything again.

"We make a sorry group," he muttered to himself. "Maybe men are just born stupid about women and love."

He watched Mandy sprint across the field and kick the soccer ball. It bounced off the goalie's shin, over his head and hit the net. There was a moment of stunned silence on the field, then the kids erupted into screams of delight.

Mandy caught his eye and grinned victoriously. Travis called out his approval.

The coached strolled past him. "Are you working with her between practices?" he asked.

"A little."

"It shows. Most parents don't take the time."

Travis started to remind the man that Mandy wasn't his child. He shrugged. It would take too long to explain. He worked with Mandy because they both enjoyed the time spent together. The fact that it improved her soccer game was just a by-product of the fun. Practicing football with his brothers had been one of the best parts of growing up in his family, he remembered. Not that their father had spent much time with them.

Travis frowned. Earl had been kept pretty busy. Between his job as sheriff of Glenwood, and his extracurricular activities, there hadn't been a lot of spare time leftover for four growing boys.

Without even trying, Travis found himself remembering the past. One day in particular, that day in the hardware store, came back to him. He'd seen his own father pick up a woman and take her with him. He'd heard most of their conversation, had winced at the practiced lines, had been shattered and embarrassed as his father had touched a woman who wasn't his wife. He'd seen the lust in Earl's eyes, watched as his father's big hands, hands too much like his own, had rested on that woman's back, then slid lower to her backside. He remembered the smiled promise, the way the woman had brushed her breasts against his father's arm. He'd seen her nipples hardening to tiny points through her thin tank top. At fourteen, what he'd seen had disgusted him, but the woman's body had also aroused him. The conflicting feelings had forced him to run away before he confronted his father.

Even now, Travis could feel the burning in his lungs as he'd run farther and faster than he ever had. Away from his father and that woman, away from what was happening to his family, away from his own adolescent desires. He remembered he'd cried that afternoon. Alone on the banks of the stream, hidden from everyone by a screen of bushes, he'd sobbed out his heart, crying for the pain of what he'd lost. Thinking then it had only been for the loss of his father, knowing now those tears had been for the end of his innocence. He'd never told anyone about that afternoon at the hardware store. His mother hadn't asked why he didn't return with the items she'd sent him for. He wondered now if she'd seen the truth in his eyes.

It had been nearly twenty years since that day, but he could still remember every moment. He'd clenched his fists, raising them high toward the heavens, and sworn he would never be like his father. He'd declared that he would never treat a woman like his father treated his mother. He'd sworn to be faithful, no matter what. He'd risked his soul in a pledge of honor to his yet unknown wife. At fourteen he'd assumed that all emotional problems could be solved if a man didn't cheat. With the hindsight of adulthood, he knew it wasn't that simple.

The soccer ball bounced past him, calling him back to the present. He reached over and grabbed it, then threw it back into the fray. The kids were tiring from their practice. A few wandered past the lines marking the playing field. Mandy was on the other side of the grass, kneeling on a stretch of dirt tying one of her shoelaces. Someone kicked the ball toward her.

Travis saw the bounce of the ball and in that moment, he knew what was going to happen. He started to call out her name, but it was too late. Before she'd even risen to her feet, he was partway across the field. She turned toward the ball, grinned and stepped after it. She hadn't finished tying her laces, though. When she took a step, she caught the loose lace, and tripped. She put out her arms to brace herself for the fall, but her forward momentum was too strong. She hit the dirt, hands and knees first, and went skidding.

The coach was closer and got there first. By the time Travis reached her side, she was crying hard enough to break his heart. The coach bent over to help her.

"No!" she screamed, pushing him away. "Travis! Travis!"

He was down beside her in an instant. "I'm here, honey." He gathered her close in his arms.

Her small body shook with sobs. He could feel her tears soaking his shirt, but he didn't care. The other children started to gather around, but the coach shooed them away.

"It's okay, Mandy." He bent over and looked at her knees. Dirt caked both of them and the right one was already bleeding.

"I have a first aid kit," the coach said. "Let me get it."

Mandy looked up at him. Her pretty round face was blotchy and damp. Her long lashes had spiked together and her blue eyes were filled with tears. Her breathing came in gasps, between the sobs.

"I—I h-hurt my h-hand," she said, as fresh tears rolled down her cheeks. He looked at her palms. They were scraped and bloody, with bits of dirt and small pebbles stuck to the skin.

"Oh, baby. I bet it stings, huh? I'm going to give you a magic hug to help, then we'll get you cleaned up."

"M-make it really b-big magic, okay?" she said, clinging to him.

As he hugged her for all he was worth, the pressure in his chest grew. Damn, he didn't want anything to hurt this little girl ever. Unfortunately, reality was going to get in the way of that desire. He couldn't control the future, but he could control keeping her a part of his life.

He picked her up in his arms and carried her over to the water fountain. There was a small hose attached to the middle of the pipe. He stood Mandy up and took off her shoes and socks; then he turned on the tap and grabbed the hose.

"This is going to be cold," he warned, hoping it was cold enough to numb some of the stinging.

She stood bravely as he hosed off her knees. The dirt came out easily. Her hands took a little more work, but he was able to get them clean without having to hurt her more. The coach handed him a towel to dry her off, some antiseptic and a few bandages. By the time Mandy had stopped crying, she was patched up and ready to go home.

He knelt before her on the muddy ground, not caring that he was ruining his uniform trousers. She sniffed, then wiped her eyes.

"I need another hug," she said, holding out her arms.

He pulled her close. The tears started up again, but he knew they were more from shock than from pain. "It'll be okay," he whispered. "I promise."

Her body was slight against his chest. Her little-girl scent—part dirt, part sunshine—made him want to smile. The trust implicit in her embrace twisted in his chest like a dagger. He was probably ten different kinds of fool, but he couldn't let her go.

He and his brothers had decided long ago that cops made lousy fathers. The hours were long, the interruptions unavoidable. For all his thirty-four years he'd believed that as much as he'd believed in the existence of gravity.

But as Mandy clung to him with her sobs breaking his heart, he knew he couldn't believe it any longer. Not when he remembered his own father. No one had forced his old man to pick up that woman in the hardware store. No crime, or criminal had been the reason he'd come home late every night smelling of sex and booze. Earl Haynes had decided early that his right in life was to have lots of women, his wife and family be damned. He had chosen.

Travis swallowed hard. It had been a decision on his father's part. Not genes, not an unavoidable family curse.

Earl had *chosen* his destiny. And he'd used his position as sheriff to hide away from his real responsibilities to his family.

Travis didn't want to risk hope and then have it blow up in his face, but Mandy wasn't leaving him a lot of options. In the past few weeks she'd stolen her way into his heart. He couldn't cut her out now. If it *was* a matter of choice, he could choose a different path from the old man's. After all, Craig was a great father. Travis could be one, too.

Mandy released him and stepped back. She smiled and wiped her face. "That *was* a magic hug," she said. "I feel better. Can we get ice cream before we pick up Mommy?"

"Sure," he said. He rose and held out his hand. Mandy slipped her smaller one trustingly in his and started walking toward the car.

He would talk to Elizabeth, he decided. Mandy needed a father and he needed the little girl. He would be there for her as much as Elizabeth would let him be. He'd made his decision and nothing was going to steer him off course.

Elizabeth stepped out into the bright sunshine and smiled. She felt wonderful being out of the house and back at work. If she had to be cooped up, then Travis's place was a wonderful home in which to recover, but after almost three weeks, she'd grown tired of staring at the same collection of walls.

She sat on the bottom step to wait for her ride. Late-September sunshine warmed her skin through the light cotton dress she wore. Beside her was a briefcase full of paperwork. Rebecca had teased her about not having to get it all done in one night. Elizabeth didn't mind the extra work. She had a lot of time to make up for. Besides, she liked feeling that she was actually accomplishing something.

A familiar black Bronco turned at the corner and pulled to a stop in front of her. She walked across the sidewalk as Travis leaned over and opened the passenger's door.

"Hi, guys," she said, slipping into her seat.

"We had ice cream," Mandy announced.

"Good for you." Elizabeth snapped her seat belt into place, then half turned to look at Mandy. Her breath caught in her throat. Mandy's face was tear-streaked and there were bandages on her hands and knees. "What happened?"

"I fell down, but Travis gave me a magic hug and now I'm almost all better." Mandy rubbed her left palm with her fingers. "But it still hurts a little."

"I'll bet." Elizabeth glanced at Travis.

He grimaced. "She tripped on her shoelace at practice. Unfortunately, she was outside of the grass playing field and on some dirt. I cleaned her up and patched the worst ones. I think she'll be okay."

"She looks fine. Thanks for taking such good care of her."

"No trouble."

They drew to a stop at a traffic light. He glanced at her. His normally open expression seemed slightly shuttered and cautious.

He faced front again. She took the opportunity to study his strong profile, the straight line of his nose, his trimmed mustache, the firm yet sensual curves of his mouth. How was she supposed to resist this man when even the faint scent of his body was enough to make her weak with longing?

Only a few more days, she told herself. She would already be driving her own car if the clutch wasn't so stiff. She'd tried it that morning, but shifting gears had caused a sharp pain in her side. Her gaze slipped over Travis again. Being chauffeured by him wasn't the worse punishment in the world.

"Would you mind if we went by my rental?" she asked. "The landlord dropped off the key at work. I'd like to take a look at what furniture is there and what I need to buy."

"Sure."

There was nothing in his voice to indicate that he was pleased or sorry to take her there. Did he think about her leaving as much as she did? Did he want his house back to himself or would he miss her? It wasn't fair, she told herself. She wanted Travis to miss her terribly, yet at the same time she knew she had no business staying involved in his life. She couldn't do anything but hurt both of them. She wasn't getting involved again. Ever. It was too dangerous. She didn't have the common sense to know when a man was right for her. Even if she did, everything about Travis warned her that he was all wrong. They were both relationship impaired, neither of them knowing how to make love work. It would be foolish to try.

So why was she thinking about it? She stared out the window and bit back a sigh. She had no answer. She was probably just tired from her first day back at work. Think about something else, she ordered herself.

As they drove through Glenwood, Elizabeth gave him directions to her rental house. The neighborhood wasn't anything like Travis's, she noted, eyeing the homes that hadn't seemed so small the last time she'd been here.

Mandy sat as far forward as her seat belt would let her. She peered out the window searching for the promised bunnies. "There were really three of them, Mommy?" she asked, her voice laced with pleasure.

"Yes, honey. I saw them from the kitchen window. They're probably hiding in the backyard. Maybe you could look for them."

Mandy bounced with excitement. "Okay."

Travis stopped in front of a small, tan-colored, one-story house. There were two windows facing the front, and a garage. She opened her door and slipped out. Mandy was already racing in circles on the lawn.

Elizabeth pulled the key from her dress pocket and led the way up the walk. She opened the door, then stepped inside. The house opened directly onto the living room. To her left was a small dining alcove, in front of her, the dark hallway. She could see the entrance to the kitchen beyond the dining room.

The carpeting was only a couple of years old. A muddy brown that would wear well and not show the dirt. Two gold patterned couches filled the living room. There were a couple of end tables and a big square wood-and-glass coffee table. The entertainment stand was empty. She would have to get a TV. She walked down the hallway. A green-tiled bathroom was flanked by two bedrooms, one slightly larger than the other. The master bedroom, if it could be called that, had a king-size bed and a single dresser. The other room was empty.

The kitchen hadn't been remodeled since the house was first built in the fifties, so the large tiles on the counter and up the wall were light and dark green. The refrigerator was newer, but the gas stove was large, with massive burners and curved edges. Over the kitchen sink, a window looked out onto a fenced backyard.

"There's no furniture in the other bedroom," Mandy said, bouncing into the kitchen. "Am I going to sleep on the floor?" She sounded slightly intrigued by the idea.

"No." Elizabeth brushed her bangs out of her eyes. "I'm going to buy you a new bedroom set."

"Golly!" Mandy's eyes got round. "Can I have a desk, too? So I can do my homework in my room like a big girl?"

"Sure." Elizabeth opened the back door. "Why don't you go see if you can find the bunnies?"

"Okay." Mandy raced outside. The screen door slammed shut behind her.

So far, Travis hadn't said a word about the house. She turned toward him. "What do you think?"

He stood in the doorway to the kitchen. With his arms folded over his chest, and his khaki shirt pulling across his broad shoulders, he looked like some kind of conquering warrior.

"It's very nice. I'm sure you'll be happy here."

There was something in his voice, something dark and broken. She wanted to ask what, but she was afraid. Instead, she dug in her purse and pulled out a small notebook. "I need tons of things. Do you have the time to wait while I make a quick list?"

"Sure." He stepped back to allow her to pass him.

But he hadn't moved back far enough, or the floor was uneven, or her feet unsteady because she managed to brush her arm against his chest as she went into the hallway. The heat from the brief contact sent a tremor up her arm and into her breasts. It was dark in the small house. Dark enough to make her forget it was still daytime outside and that her daughter was just a few feet away. Dark enough to give her the courage to look up at his face and meet his gaze. Dark enough to wonder if the fire would return to his irises and flicker there, matching the flames she felt burning inside.

The house smelled musty and unused. The furniture wasn't to her taste. After being in Travis's beautiful home, this place was a rude awakening. It could all be fixed, she told herself. A few throw pillows, some lacy curtains, a good scrubbing and airing out—then everything would be fine. But it wasn't the house at all. It was the man.

He tempted her. Even though she knew it was foolish and wrong and this time more than her pride would be at stake, she couldn't resist him. He made her care about him, even when she didn't want to. Even when it made her a fool twice in the same lifetime. Even when she knew they were doomed to heartbreak. Which is why she had to leave him as quickly as possible.

He reached out to hold her at the exact moment she stepped away. His arms hung there a moment, giving her time to step back into his embrace. He would kiss her. She could see the promise in his eyes. He would hold her and tonight he would make love to her. She turned her back on him and started down the hall.

Within twenty minutes she'd completed her list. Travis had followed her from room to room, offering suggestions. It was as if that moment in the hall had never happened. But it had. Her fingers trembled as she wrote out the items she would need. Her heart raced in her chest and her eyes burned with more than regret.

"I think that's it," she said. "The miniblinds will make a big difference at letting in light. Thanks for the suggestion."

"You're welcome."

She pocketed the small notebook and led the way back to the kitchen. "Is there some kind of mall around here? I need to buy Mandy furniture, as well as some other supplies for the house."

"There's a furniture warehouse store about forty miles away," he said as he followed her. "I have tomorrow off. I could drive you there if you'd like."

The screen door slammed open and Mandy ran into the kitchen. She glared at her mother. "I looked everywhere and I couldn't find even *one* bunny."

"I'm sorry, honey. Maybe they're hiding."

"But I looked!" Mandy's lower lip thrust out. "I don't care about any stupid bunnies. I want to stay with Travis and get a puppy."

Elizabeth drew in a deep breath. Of course, she thought, wondering why it hadn't occurred to her sooner. She wasn't the only one who was going to miss their host and his wonderful house. Mandy would, as well. She shook her head. She should have thought of that already.

"You'll like it here," Travis said, squatting down to the child's level. "There are lots of kids for you to play with right here on this street. You'll forget all about me, but no matter what, I'll still be around."

He paused, as if waiting for Elizabeth to disagree. She wasn't going to; she was pleased he wanted to stay in touch with Mandy. The little girl needed some continuity in her life.

"This house is dumb."

"It's not dumb," Elizabeth said, touching her daughter's hair. "I'm going to buy you a beautiful bedroom set and a real big-girl desk." She tried to ignore the flash of guilt. She didn't usually try to buy Mandy's cooperation, but desperate times called for desperate measures.

Despite the bribe, Mandy didn't look convinced. It was only after Travis tickled her into a giggling pile on the floor that her good humor returned.

While Mandy raced ahead to the car, Travis locked the front door.

"You should be able to get everything you need at the furniture store," he said. "The entire first floor is filled with household items. Linens, miniblinds...that sort of thing."

"Do you know if they deliver?" she asked, taking one last look at her new home.

"I think so. Are you thinking for the bedroom furniture?"

"Yes." She squared her shoulders. "Mandy is becoming too attached to you. I need to get us into our own place as quickly as possible."

Travis didn't answer. She wasn't sure if she was sorry or glad. Maybe a little of both. If he'd responded at all, she would have been forced to admit that Mandy wasn't the only one becoming too attached.

Chapter Thirteen

They took the elevator to the top of the giant furniture warehouse, then started the circular descent to the ground floor. Sample rooms had been set up, followed by rows of couches, entertainment centers and end tables.

"Oh, good. They *do* deliver," Elizabeth said, pulling her list out of her jeans pocket.

"Yeah, within forty-eight hours," Travis replied, pointing to a sign posted on the wall.

"Great. If we buy Mandy's bedroom set today, it can be delivered Saturday when we move in."

She'd been reading the sign, but she felt Travis stiffen at her side. She risked glancing at him. He stared down at her, his normally readable face expressionless.

"That's quick. When did you make that decision?"

Yesterday, when I figured out how much Mandy and I were going to miss you, she thought. "It makes sense, Travis. I'm completely back on my feet. I've arranged for

Mandy's afternoon daycare, although I'll be getting off work at three-thirty, so she'll need it for less than an hour. My car's clutch is still a little too stiff for me, but Rebecca is going to give me a ride to and from work for a couple of days.''

"I see.'' He turned toward a fabric-covered sofa next to them. "You've got everything figured out.''

"I guess I do. I'm sure you'll be pleased to see the last of us.''

"Sure.'' He looked back at her and smiled. "We both need our lives to get back to normal.''

If his smile didn't reach his eyes, she wasn't going to comment on the fact. If he noticed that she couldn't stop looking at him or brushing against him as they walked through the store, he didn't say anything, either.

The tension between them stretched until she could physically feel it tugging on her insides. She didn't want it to be like this. She wanted Travis to be her friend. She needed him to be there, to be strong. Was that wrong?

Before she could figure out the answer to the question, he darted across the aisle to a selection of leather furniture. There were three different rooms displayed, all in the same soft, buttery leather. He dropped down onto a black sofa and leaned back his head.

"This is wonderful,'' he said, closing his eyes. "I may do my entire house in leather.''

"Even the bathrooms?'' She bit back a giggle.

He opened one eye. "Laugh all you want, but this is *man* furniture.''

"Oh, I see. So you'll want a gun rack right next to the TV. And what about your famous knife collection? You know, the ones you used to hunt the woolly mammoth.''

She'd made the mistake of moving too close to him. He growled out a warning, but before she could jump back, he reached forward and tackled her legs, pulling her toward him. She landed in a heap on his lap. Their faces were inches apart; his breath fanned her cheek. It could have been a dangerous moment, but they were both laughing too hard.

His thighs were hard beneath her legs. Their jeans—hers blue, his black—rubbed together, generating an erotic heat. Low in her belly, wanting grew. She acknowledged the feeling, acknowledged that Travis's hands became less teasing and more caressing on her arms. But he didn't try to kiss her. In that moment of laughter, their friendship had been restored. Apparently neither of them wanted that threatened again.

The sound of someone clearing his throat broke through her musing. She looked up, then blushed like a high-schooler caught necking in the back seat of her father's car.

"May I help you?" the small, gray-haired man asked, his bushy white eyebrows raised above his wire-rimmed glasses.

Elizabeth tried to slide off Travis's lap, but his large hands held her in place.

"No, thanks," Travis drawled. "We were just testing the sofa."

"I see. Does it work to your satisfaction?" the man asked, glaring down at them.

"We're not sure yet." Travis winked. "I think it needs a little more testing."

The man turned on his heel and marched away. Elizabeth struggled to break free. "He's probably gone to get the manager."

"So what?" Travis leaned forward and kissed the tip of her nose. "The store is practically empty and we weren't doing anything wrong."

She couldn't help herself. She sagged against him and giggled. "Maybe you should have worn your uniform. At least then you could have threatened to arrest him."

"You just miss seeing me in my cowboy hat. If I'd known you were so attached, I would have worn it today."

"Oh, stop." She gave one last, hard push on his chest and broke free. She scrambled to her feet and smoothed the front of her shirt. Her fingers caught on an open button right above her bra. "I was flashing him," she said, horrified.

Travis chuckled. "He was getting a bit of an eyeful, but I doubt it's anything he hasn't seen before." He stood up and stretched. "Need some help?" he asked, approaching her.

"Don't even think about it." She slapped his hands away. "No more pit stops. We have a list." She waved the piece of paper in front of him. "I want you to behave for the rest of the day. Do you promise?"

He put his arm around her shoulders and pulled her close. She knew she should resist, but it was just for one day, she told herself. They were in a public store. What's the worst that could happen?

"I'll behave," he said, whispering in her ear. "But I just might want to test-drive a mattress or two."

She managed to steer him clear of the adult bedroom section, but they spent almost an hour picking out Mandy's furniture. She stood between a bedroom done in white, with a canopy bed and delicate furniture, and one done in light pine. That bed was a four-poster design with a raised mattress.

"She'd practically need a step stool to get on it," Elizabeth said, gauging the distance.

"But it comes in a double. The canopy doesn't. If you get the bigger bed, she can have a friend over to sleep with her. Even if they use sleeping bags on top of the covers it'll be more fun than one of them on the floor."

She eyed him warily. "How do you know what little girls want?"

"Mandy tells me things."

"What kind of things?"

"Things like how she'd enjoy having a friend spend the night occasionally, and how much she wants a puppy."

"A puppy?" Elizabeth looked at the bed. "It would be a lot less messy to get the larger mattress. What do you think of the desk?"

It matched the pine dresser. There were two small and one large drawer on either side. A bookcase sat next to it.

Travis knelt down and ran his hands over all the edges of the desk. He checked the workmanship, then tested the drawers and the sturdiness of the shelves.

"I like it," he said. He glanced up at her. "If it's about money—"

"It's not," she said, cutting him off. She perched on the edge of the four-poster bed. "You might not understand my logic, but running off and leaving everything Sam had bought us wasn't something I did lightly. I know it wasn't the most sensible thing I've ever done, but it was a symbolic act for me. One that really proved to me I wasn't kidding about completely cutting him out of our lives. I think doing that is what has allowed me to heal as much as I have." She held up her hand. "I know what you're going to say. I haven't healed completely. I know there are a few things I'm working through, but I'll get there." She paused and drew in a breath. "Why are you grinning at me?"

He stood up and pulled out the desk chair. After turning it around, he sat down, straddling it, resting his arms along the slatted back. "You seem to know everything, so you figure out why I'm grinning."

"Travis!"

"I was just thinking about how strong you are. I believe that you will put this behind you and get on with your life. I admire that."

She ducked her head. "Thanks," she said softly. "Your support means a lot to me."

A different sales clerk approached. This one was a young woman in a navy suit. "May I write up an order for you?" she asked, her gaze locking on Travis's.

Elizabeth was too contented to care. "Yes, for me."

The young woman forced her eyes away from Travis. "What can I do for you?"

Elizabeth hesitated, then pointed at the pine set. "I'd like this bedroom set. All the pieces, please. Can you have it delivered on Saturday?"

They made the rest of her purchases quickly. They had one argument in the linen section, picking out sheets for Mandy. Elizabeth wanted something floral while Travis voted for the redheaded cartoon mermaid. In the end she bought them both.

"You're worse than Mandy," Elizabeth grumbled as she tossed the sheets into her cart.

"You love it," he said, coming up behind her and planting a quick kiss just below her left ear. Instantly a shiver raced through her body. She did love it. That was the problem.

They went through the kitchen accessories. She picked out some dinnerware and glasses. She started to hold up the box for his approval, then stared at him.

"What?" he asked, standing at the end of her cart. "Have I grown horns?"

"I don't care if you like these," she said.

"Thanks so much."

"No." She smiled. "I didn't mean it in a bad way. I meant, I don't have to get your approval on anything. I don't have to get anyone's approval ever again."

Travis frowned and planted his hands on his hips. "I have a lot of flaws, Elizabeth, but I'm *not* an ogre."

"Oh, I know." She put the dinnerware in her cart. "I suddenly realized that I don't have to get Sam's approval. Even though he was gone so much, I thought he should be a part of the decision making. I waited to get his opinion on drapes, dishes, what time Mandy should go to bed. I don't have to anymore. I can do what I want."

"It sounds like you're over him."

She glanced up at him. He held himself stiffly, as if regretting making the observation. Around them, shoppers chattered about their purchases. She could hear the faint electronic beeping of the cash registers. They stood alone in the middle of housewares discussing the state of her heart. Why did she feel her answer was so important? It couldn't be. Not now, not after she was just getting over what had happened.

"I am. The relationship had been in trouble for a long time. I was ready to ask for a divorce, and then it turned out I didn't need one. I know what he did to me has made me wary of trusting anyone again. But that's about pride, not about my heart. I've been over Sam Proctor for years."

"Soon you'll be over me, too," he said, his voice teasing.

But she didn't smile back. "Travis, I'll never get over what you did for me and Mandy. You came to my rescue when I was in dire straits, and I'll never forget that. You gave me more than a roof over my head. You were good to Mandy and a great friend to me."

You showed me how it's supposed to be between a man and a woman.

But she didn't say her last thought aloud. Better for both of them if they simply put it out of their minds. If only it were that easy. If it had just been sex, she would have been able to forget. Being with him had been more than that. It had been warm and tender, loving and caring. He'd made love to her slowly and easily as if he'd been waiting for her all his life, as if he'd had all the time in the world.

He'd made her feel cherished.

"I'll never forget what you did," she repeated. "I'm going to miss you when I move out."

She waited, but he didn't answer in kind. And suddenly the warmth in her belly turned very, very cold.

Travis checked the rearview mirror for traffic, but the main highway was empty on a weekday afternoon. He looked in the mirror again, this time glancing at the boxes and bags stuffed in the back of his Bronco. They'd managed to fit everything in except for Mandy's bedroom set. That would be delivered to Elizabeth's new house in time for her to move in on Saturday. She was really leaving.

He didn't want to think about that, or how it made him feel. He tried to come up with some topic of conversation. The cab had been quiet for too long. Elizabeth sat in her seat, with her hands folded on her lap. She never once glanced at him.

He knew why. He hadn't said he would miss her, as well. He cursed under his breath. Those words were inadequate to describe what he was feeling. Hell, he didn't even know what he was feeling. Everything was confused. It had happened so fast. One minute he was living his life, with no concerns and no questions. A few short weeks later he was deeply involved with a woman and her daughter. He didn't know what he was supposed to do. Should he ask her not to leave, or just forget about her? Could he risk another relationship? Would she be willing to take that chance? Was it genetics or bad luck that kept the four Haynes brothers single? Was he or was he not a duck?

The last question made him smile. He saw Elizabeth glance at him out of the corner of her eye. He drew in a deep breath to plunge into an emotional discussion, but at the last second chose something more safe.

"Mandy's going to love everything you bought her," he said.

"I hope so." She brushed her hair off her shoulders. "Everything cost enough. If she doesn't like it, I think I'll make her get a job to pay me back for everything."

He grinned. "We can always use another deputy."

For the first time in almost an hour, Elizabeth grinned back. She looked at him, some of the concern leaving her eyes. "She'd love that. I suspect she'd spend her day running the siren."

"That would be a problem." His smile faded. "Look, I've been thinking about this whole money thing. I don't want you to pay me for the rooms. You're going to need it to get on your feet, financially."

She turned until she was facing him. He gave her a quick glance. Her mouth pulled into a straight line and her jaw was clenched.

"I insist," she said forcefully. "We made a deal, Travis. The money was the only thing that allowed me to accept your hospitality. It was too little to begin with, it probably didn't even cover food. If I can't pay you, it's too much like lying about everything."

He should have known she would make this more difficult than it had to be. He grabbed the steering wheel tightly, then moved into the right lane for the turnoff to Glenwood. "I don't need the money and you do. As for covering the food bill, give me a break. You two hardly eat anything. I want to do this for you. I want to help."

She rested her hand on his forearm. He liked the feel of her fingers brushing against his skin. It was hard not to get distracted.

"I don't need your help anymore," she said. "Even if I did, I can't accept it. This isn't about you, it's about Sam.

He paid for everything. He didn't want me to work. When I did, after Mandy started school, he was very unhappy. He insisted that I keep my money for myself. I have almost a year's salary saved up. It might sound silly to you. You've always been responsible for yourself. But for six years a man controlled my life. I don't want that to happen again. Please don't start changing the rules on me now."

He drove past the sheriff's station and the small park with the duck pond. At the corner he turned left and entered the residential section where Elizabeth was going to live. He made a right on her street, then pulled into the driveway and turned off the engine.

He understood what she was saying, but he didn't have to like it. So much of her life was still tied up with Sam Proctor. He rubbed the bridge of his nose. Who was he to talk? So much of his life was tied up with his past and reputation.

"I don't care about the money," he said at last. "If you insist on paying me, at least let me use the money to buy Mandy something. A bike, maybe. Is that against the rules?"

Elizabeth shook her head. "No. That would be wonderful. I appreciate all you've done with her. She really cares about you."

"I care about her. I know you don't want the rules changed, but I don't have a lot of choice about this one. I can't let go of Mandy. I don't want to lose her. I'm not saying I'm a great father figure, but I'm not as bad as I thought. I want to stay involved with her." He shifted in his seat, turning to face her. "Can we make that work?"

He hadn't expected tears. Her big brown eyes glistened as she blinked frantically. One tear slipped onto her cheek. She brushed it away impatiently. "You're a damn fine man, Travis Haynes. Don't you dare let anyone tell you otherwise."

He could feel something uncomfortably like a blush heating his cheeks. He cleared his throat. "Yeah, well, don't let it get around, okay? I have this reputation."

She leaned forward and touched her hand to his cheek. "I'm beginning to think your reputation is all talk. You're far too decent to be any kind of a heartbreaker. I would like it very much if you would continue to see Mandy. I'll work around your schedule or whatever it takes. She adores you."

In the close confines of the Bronco, the scent of her body—the sweetness of her woman's fragrance and the spicy temptation of her perfume—mingled together in a seductive aroma designed to drive him crazy. Her face was so near his, he could see the individual lashes framing her dark brown eyes. A few curling hairs drifted onto her cheek. The red lipstick she'd put on that morning had long since worn away, leaving her mouth soft and rose-colored.

This conversation was supposed to be about Mandy, but all he could think about was Elizabeth. Even as his mind screamed at him to just let her go, his heart protested the parting. He was torn between what he believed and what he wanted. Could he fight the legacy of his father? He and his brothers were so terrified of falling in love, of failing. Was it circumstance or destiny? He'd chosen to become involved with Mandy. Could he choose to become involved with Elizabeth? Could he choose to love her? Could he make it work?

He'd tried once, and failed. Julie had been his wife. But he'd never felt these powerful emotions before. He'd never needed her the way he needed Elizabeth. Was it enough?

"Travis?"

He had to let her go. It was the only sensible decision to make. Everything in his past warned him that he would fail if he tried again. Yet his heart begged for one more chance. What if everyone was wrong? What if he *could* do it?

Making it work with Elizabeth would be worth anything. What did he have without her?

He took her hands in his. Her fingers were small and delicate, yet capable. She stared at him, her eyes concerned yet trusting.

They hadn't been together long enough.

She was moving out; he didn't have any more time.

"Don't go," he said.

Chapter Fourteen

"What did you say?" Elizabeth asked, sure she must have heard him incorrectly.

"Don't go. I want you and Mandy to stay with me."

"Are you crazy?"

"Maybe. But stay anyway."

"No," she said loudly. "No, I can't. I won't. Don't ask me. Dammit, Travis. What are you doing?"

She didn't wait to hear the answer. After undoing her seat belt, she opened the truck door and jumped down to the ground. She moved to the back of the Bronco and started grabbing her packages. He stood and watched her.

"I care about you. I don't want to lose you."

Each word was a blow to her heart. Her chest tightened and her breathing became labored. "I asked you not to change the rules. Why are you doing this?"

"Why are you angry?" His voice was low and quiet. She could hear the pain in each word.

The anger would keep her strong, but she couldn't tell him that. When she'd collected as much as she could carry, she walked past him to the front door. After fumbling with the key, she stepped inside and dropped her bags on the ugly gold sofa.

The house still smelled musty. The small dark rooms would never be more than what they already were: a temporary escape from her life, from her past and the shame that haunted her.

She stood in the center of the living room and fought the tears. Pain clawed at her stomach. She folded her arms over her belly and tried to hold it all inside. Not now, she prayed. Not like this. Not Travis. Didn't he know how much she'd grown to need and trust him? He couldn't change now. It wasn't right. It wasn't fair.

She heard him behind her. He set several boxes on the floor.

"Elizabeth."

"Don't say anything." She turned to face him. "I don't want to hear it. We had everything planned. We were going to be friends. Travis, I desperately need you in my life, but only as my friend. I can't do more. It's too dangerous. I've made that mistake before and I'm never going to do it again."

He was tall and powerful standing there in the darkened room. His white, long-sleeved shirt emphasized his strength and good looks. She studied the lines of his face, the sadness in his dark eyes. His arms hung loose at his side, but his hands were clenched into fists.

"You don't understand," he said.

He was right, she thought. She didn't understand and she didn't want to.

"I love you."

His words hit her with the force of a lightning bolt, and she nearly went down. Her legs trembled and her breathing stopped. She stared at him, then gasped in a breath. He loved her?

"You can't," she said.

He shrugged. "All my life I've been told I couldn't be a good husband or father. My dad made a mess of both. My uncles are all failures in that department, as well. Every time I tried to make it work, I couldn't. After a while I gave up trying. If it looks like a duck and walks like a duck and sounds like a duck, it's probably a duck."

She remembered the small stuffed yellow duck he'd brought her when he'd gone shopping with Mandy. Even then he'd been wrestling with his feelings for her. She should have known. But what difference would it have made? Would she have left him? She wanted to say yes, of course she would have, but she wasn't sure it was true. Her time with Travis had been magical. Would she have willingly cut it short?

"What I have figured out," he said, continuing, "is that everyone has choices. Earl and his brothers didn't try hard enough. They could have made it work if they wanted to. I could have made it work with Julie. I cared about her. The marriage failed because of a lack of chemistry or each of us being lazy, not because I'm incapable of making a relationship last."

"I don't want to hear this." She started toward the hallway.

He grabbed her arm as she passed him. "You have to listen. It's important. This thing between us isn't going to go away. I'm willing to take a chance, Elizabeth. I know you've been burned. I have, too. I know it's frightening. It's too soon, we don't know each other well enough. But I can't risk losing you and Mandy. I love you both. I never thought I'd ever say those words again, but I believe them to be true with all my being. Trust me. Trust *us*."

She tried to pull away, but he wouldn't let her go. She was forced to look up at him, at the fire flaring in his eyes. These flames frightened her more than the fire of desire. His gaze burned with the heat of conviction. He did believe what he told her, that he loved her. That they had a chance. She wanted to weep from the sadness of it all. Couldn't he see that this was all a cruel joke? It would never work out; she wouldn't let it.

Oh, but she wanted to believe. Her heart had leapt when he'd said he loved her. For a single heartbeat, joy had filled her. Reality was too powerful, though, and couldn't be ignored.

"I don't want to hear this," she said and looked away from him. "I don't believe you. Even if I did, it doesn't change anything."

He was stunned. She could tell by the way he stiffened. He released her instantly and stepped back. "Why?"

She closed her eyes against his suffering and against the temptation he offered. If only she had never met Sam, she might have been able to respond to the gift Travis offered. But she had met Sam and he had changed her.

"Love isn't enough. I loved Sam and look what happened. In his own twisted way, he might have even loved me."

"I don't appreciate the comparison. I'm not a bigamist. I don't have a secret past. I'm not going to destroy your life, I'm going to make it better."

"I like my life just the way it is. Mandy and I don't need anyone. Sam disappeared, never bothering to say why he'd done it. He barely apologized. He signed over custody of his daughter as if she meant less to him than a car. I'm never going to risk that again. Never." She knew she was practically shouting, but she couldn't help herself. He wanted too much. She wouldn't take a chance, she couldn't. "I know. The loving doesn't keep you safe."

Travis moved close and placed his hands on her shoulders. "I am not Sam," he said, speaking slowly as if she couldn't make out the words clearly. "I would never do that to you. What I do is a part of who I am. The ideals of my job are here—" He touched his chest, then brushed hers, just above her left breast. "And here. You know that, Elizabeth. You've always known you could trust me. That's why you came home with me. That's why you're afraid now. You don't want to believe, but I'm not going to give you another choice in the matter. I'm not Sam Proctor. I won't leave you or lie to you. I'll take care of you and Mandy. I'll be here every night to protect you."

His words were like quicksand. The more she struggled, the deeper she sank. Soon she would be swallowed whole into his world. She fought against his spell. "I don't need rescuing. I'm fine on my own. Why won't you believe that?"

Suddenly she was free. He jerked away from her and the quicksand disappeared into nothing. His emotional bonds had snapped. She was alone, as she had requested.

He walked to the window and stared out at her front yard. The pain radiated out from him. Waves and waves crashed over her, making her want to weep for both of them.

"Why?" he asked, without looking at her.

She had no answer because she didn't understand the question. Did he ask why she couldn't love him back, or why he had loved her at all? She didn't want to know which. He had come to the end of his journey, had shed the false covering learned from his family and had finally seen the true man inside. To what end? She was the last woman in the world to be able to give him what he needed. She would carry that guilt with her forever.

"I'm sorry," she whispered. "So very sorry. I want to be what you need, what you want, but I can't be. If it was just me, I might take the chance again. But I have to think about Mandy. I won't risk either of our hearts."

"Why won't you listen?" he asked, still staring out the window. "I'm not Sam."

"I know. I just wish it was enough."

He turned then. Anguish filled his face, drawing his mouth straight and tightening his jaw. "Have you considered the fact that it might be too late?"

She fought the urge to step back. Too late? Too late because *she* had already fallen in love with him? "It's not." It couldn't be.

He smiled then, a cold smile without humor. "You'd better pray that you're right."

"Please don't be angry with me. I wish I could explain."

"No!" He crossed the room in two strides and grabbed her. This time his grip was hard and bruising. Before she could start to fight, he pulled her up against him. "I'm the one who has to explain. Why can't I find the words?"

"Because there's nothing you can say."

"You're wrong."

She expected a verbal assault. Instead he began another campaign, one much more deadly to her peace of mind.

He kissed her. Not the hot ravishing kiss she might have expected. Despite his firm hold on her shoulders, his mouth was tender against hers. Familiar warmth curled through her, starting at her toes and working its way up to her breasts. The fingers on her shoulders began to knead her tense muscles, soothing them, relaxing her to the point of weakness.

He used his body to speak for him. His chest pressed against hers, offering strength and a place to rest. Long, powerful legs brushed her own. His arousal spoke of passion and perhaps even love if she was foolish enough to believe.

She told herself to push him away, to be cruel to be kind. Better for both of them. She raised her hands to his arms to give herself the leverage necessary to walk away; then she felt the sweet brush of his tongue on her lips.

Instantly her body responded to the caress. Her breasts swelled. Already puckered nipples sought the relief of his touch. Between her thighs the ache deepened as moisture dampened her panties. One last time. One last moment of passion. One last embrace. One last chance to lean on him, to accept his strength and his comfort. While his love frightened her, she could understand and accept the solace of his body. When he knew what she had done—willingly come to him, knowing it was never going to be more than this moment—he wouldn't forgive her. She wouldn't have to bother with sending him away. He would go on his own, hating her.

He was her weakness and her greatest strength. She would be with him, fully knowing that each moment of pleasure would cause her to die a little.

She opened her mouth to him, accepting him inside. He swept over and around, touching, tasting. She stroked his shoulders and back, then moved up to slip her fingers through his curly hair. When he stepped away from her, she murmured a protest. He picked her up in his arms and carried her toward her bedroom. She clung to him, kissing his neck, tracing the line where his afternoon stubble met smooth skin, wrinkling her nose at the slightly bitter taste of his after-shave.

The king-size bed had no sheets or covers. He placed her in the center, then bent over her. Before he could touch her, she began to unbutton his shirt. She worked quickly, while she was able, then pulled the loose ends free of his jeans. She crushed the still-warm fabric in her hands, savoring the feel of his body heat. He sat up and shrugged out of the shirt.

His chest was broad and tanned, with a faint sprinkling of dark hair between his flat nipples. Slipping free of his long legs, she, too, sat up, mimicking his position and pulled her own shirt over her head. Their eyes locked. A smile tugged at the corner of his mouth. She caught the spirit of their game and reached for her shoes and socks.

Her athletic shoes hit the floor the same time as his boots. She settled back on the bed, kneeling in front of him. He reached for the first button on his fly. She did the same. As he unbuttoned, she unzipped.

The air around them grew thick with tension and the heady smell of desire. Her heart pounded harder and her fingers trembled. His hands moved to the waistband of his now-open jeans. She shook her head.

He raised his eyebrows questioningly. She touched his bare chest, then fingered the strap of her bra. They weren't starting from the same place. He sat back on his heels and watched.

She wanted to unfasten her bra and pull it off quickly. Instead she drew her fingers up from her belly, along her ribs to her breasts. Travis swallowed. She locked her gaze on his face, watching him watch her. His breathing increased.

He rested his hands on his thighs, motionless, and she could see his hardness straining against his white briefs. He was already large and swollen with desire.

Slowly, very slowly, she reached for the front fastener. It released and slid open across her pale breasts. The lace cups caught on her nipples. His breathing increased. She tossed her head, sending her hair back over her shoulders and freeing the bra. It drifted down her shoulders and she tossed it to the floor.

Travis returned his hands to the waistband of his jeans. She matched the movement. They pulled them off together. Clad only in briefs and panties, they stared at each other. She was already weak with desire. Every inch of her body was ready for him. Her breasts ached, her thighs trembled. She drew down her panties. His briefs followed, freeing his engorged maleness to view.

The silence in the room was broken by the faint sound of cars passing on the street and the occasional call of a bird. Their breathing blocked out all other noises. She would have thought she would find this dance unnerving, but it aroused her. She liked knowing what she could do to him without saying a word or even touching him. She liked that his skin gleamed with perspiration and his hands shook as they hung at his sides.

Their eyes met.

She raised her hand to his neck. He matched the motion. She wanted to see more of him, she wanted to know what pleased him. She needed these memories to carry her through the long winter of her life.

He took her breasts in his hands. She covered his flat male chest. When he tweaked her nipples, she did the same. The rate of their breathing increased.

She moved her hands lower, across his belly. His hands followed. Her gaze dropped to his hardened length. How powerful and male he looked.

Her eyes burned as tears threatened. He moved closer, at last drawing her down on the bare mattress. He kissed her face and neck and chest, then suckled her nipples into taut points of need. She felt his hardness probing her thigh. When he would have pulled back, she reached for him drawing him closer to her waiting moisture.

He hesitated before entering. She knew he worried about her healing muscles. She didn't care about any of that. She needed him to be inside of her. She arched her hips toward him, enveloping him in her heated dampness. He groaned once and thrust forward.

The feelings were too perfect, too intense. She clutched at his back, then lower at his buttocks, urging him deeper. Her breath came in pants. He'd barely begun to move when her muscles began to convulse around him. He stared at her, obviously surprised by the suddenness of her release. Fighting against her instinct to hide, she kept her eyes open, letting him see her wonder, her pleasure, her sorrow as her body spent itself. He moved back and forth, giving her all the time she needed to quiver against him, reveling in her soft cries of ecstasy. When the tension in her body had become a satisfied hum, he moved again, quickly bringing himself to the same place.

The game played on as he met her gaze, leaving his own emotions bare as his body shook with release. She saw the muscles in his chest and neck tighten, then relax. His eyes flashed with pleasure and promise, then flared with love.

As he held her close and she listened to the pounding of his heart, she at last gave in to the tears. She believed he loved her. Knowing that truth, she would still leave him. The tears fell silently in mourning for all she had lost.

Travis turned left onto his street and did his best not to speed. He'd left the station early, even though Kyle had been giving him trouble most of the day. His brother knew him too well not to notice his sudden lack of concentration. Thank God nothing out of the ordinary had happened that day in Glenwood. Of course any kind of serious crime was pretty unusual in the small community. Even so, Kyle had been on him from early that morning, making comments about his big brother being at the mercy of a woman. Travis had taken the teasing good-naturedly for two reasons. First, because there had been a note of envy in his brother's voice, and secondly because it was true.

He hadn't been able to think about anything but his night of making love with Elizabeth. After they'd gathered themselves together yesterday afternoon, they'd left her place to pick up Mandy, then had spent the evening together. He grinned as he pulled into the driveway. Elizabeth's car was gone, but he wasn't concerned. She'd taken it to work that morning. As she'd lain in his bed with him that morning, watching the sunrise, she'd said she felt better than she had in days. He knew the feeling. Being with her, holding her, telling her he loved her, had changed him, as well.

It had been a night without sleep, but he didn't care. The promises her body had whispered had been enough for him.

He stopped in front of the house and got out of the car. After reaching in the back seat, he pulled out the bottle of chilled champagne he'd picked up on his way home, and a bouquet of lilies and exotic orchids. He was bearing more than gifts. In his back pocket was a list of arguments to convince Elizabeth that they belonged together. He understood her concerns. Hell, he even shared some of them. They had both been burned in a big way. She with Sam, and him with his whole damn family. But that didn't mean they were destined to fail at love. It just meant they had to try a little harder to make it work. He took the porch stairs two at a time. The victory would be that much sweeter for their effort. She was right for him. She needed him, Mandy needed him. And more important, he needed *them*. But he only had tonight to convince her.

He opened the front door and stepped inside. The quiet of the house was unsettling. He frowned and tried to figure out why. His brow cleared. He was used to coming home to Elizabeth and Mandy, but neither of them was there. Even Louise was off today.

He walked into the kitchen and stuck the champagne in the refrigerator. They would be back shortly. He would start talking to Elizabeth then. He had to convince her. If he didn't, she would leave him in the morning. He didn't doubt that he could eventually show her that they belonged together, but he knew it would be a lot easier when they were still living in the same house. If he had to, he would resort to guerilla tactics and seduce her.

He knew she cared about him. Last night her body had spoken the words for her. He'd told her over and over that he loved her and would never hurt her. She'd heard him. He liked to think she'd believed him. He shut the refrigerator door and leaned against it. He was in love.

He shut his eyes and smiled. Who would have thought it would happen to him? He'd given up hoping. All his brothers had. If he'd known what being in love was really like, he wouldn't have made the mistake of marrying Julie. He knew now that had been about pride and a desire to prove everyone wrong. Not the greatest basis for a marriage. This time he was getting involved for all the right reasons.

He laughed out loud for the sheer joy of it, then pushed away from the refrigerator. A piece of paper caught his eye. He turned to look and saw that Mandy had left him a new picture. He picked it up, staring at the three figures shown standing in front of a large white house. There was a brown blob in front of the three figures.

"It's us," he said aloud, his throat suddenly thick with emotion. Mandy had drawn a family scene with him—he recognized his khaki uniform and Stetson—Elizabeth, and Mandy herself. The brown blob was probably the puppy she wanted so much.

He put the picture back on the door, anchoring it with magnets. He would thank her when she got home. He started to walk out of the room, then paused. Slowly, very slowly, he turned back and stared at the sketch. It hadn't been there that morning. He would have noticed it. Which meant she'd done it that day at school. So Elizabeth had picked her up, brought her home and then . . .

And then what? And then she'd left? For where?

A cold feeling swept over him. Without thinking, he raced toward Elizabeth's room. The door was partway closed. He flung it open and stared at the perfectly made double bed. The dresser was clean, the end table bare of anything save a white envelope addressed to him. He didn't have to look at the signature to know who had written the note. He recognized Elizabeth's handwriting. There were no personal effects in the room, no half-packed suitcase, no nightgown hanging by the bathroom door. No smell of perfume or makeup.

He grabbèd the note without reading it, then climbed the stairs and entered Mandy's room. His chest ached as if someone had wrapped a band around his ribs and was slowly tightening it. Her room was the same as Elizabeth's: clean and impersonal, as if no one of importance had ever lived there.

He couldn't breathe, he couldn't see. He couldn't do anything except feel the pain. It surrounded him, filling every pore of his being until it darkened to black and he fought against drowning in the hopelessness. She was gone.

She'd left without giving him a chance to convince her to stay. She'd left after they'd made love throughout the night. She'd left after he'd told her how much he loved her. None of that had mattered to her. *He* hadn't mattered to her.

When the honed edges of the razor-sharp emotion had faded to a mind-numbing ache, he opened the envelope. Several fifty-dollar bills floated to the floor. He held the single sheet of paper and read it.

Thanks for your warm hospitality, Travis. I don't know what we would have done without you. I hope you understand that I think it's time for Mandy and me to make our own home. We were both becoming too attached to you.

It wouldn't work, you know. No matter how much we wanted it to. I wish it could have been different. I wish *I* could have been different. But it wasn't meant to be. I hope you find someone as wonderful as you deserve, and that we can still be friends. I need a friend like you in my life, but I'll understand if that's asking too much.

He stared at the words, studying the shape of her letters and the way her signature scrawled across the page. He thought about the champagne and the flowers, the list of arguments and how he'd assumed loving her would be enough. He crumpled the note and let it fall to the ground, then walked down the stairs and out into the coming night.

Chapter Fifteen

"How drunk are you going to get?" Rebecca asked as she stretched across the leather couch in Travis's family room.

Travis stared at the half-empty glass in his hand, then glanced at the bottle sitting on the coffee table. There were about three more inches of Scotch waiting for him. Through his slightly drunken fog, he wondered how much longer it was going to take for the alcohol to allow him to forget. The liquor was dulling his senses enough for him to breathe without feeling that his chest was going to cave in, but he could still sense the broken edges of his exposed heart. He could still remember everything. Damn Elizabeth Abbott and damn his own sorry hide for ever being stupid enough to care.

He drained the glass in his hand, then rose from the leather wing chair sitting at right angles to the sofa. It was exactly three steps to the coffee table. He kept the bottle that far away deliberately. As soon as he wasn't able to navigate those three steps, he would know it was time to stop drinking.

"A lot more drunk," he said carefully, conscious of the effort it took to form words correctly.

Rebecca stared at him. Her dark hair was held away from her face by a headband. Even though it was Saturday afternoon and most people were dressed in jeans and casual shirts, she wore a floral print jumper over a white silk short-sleeved shirt. He knew it was silk because she'd explained it to him once. He'd actually figured out the difference between it and cotton. That's how he'd known Elizabeth's skin had felt like silk against his body.

He stared at her white shirt and wondered if it would feel like Elizabeth's skin. Or would it feel differently because Rebecca wore it? Or if he was still sober enough to grab the Scotch bottle. Maybe if he asked politely, Rebecca would pour for him. He frowned. Judging from the way she was glaring at him, he didn't think she would be willing to cooperate.

As if she'd read his mind, she grabbed the bottle. He held out his glass hopefully. She shook her head and set the bottle on the far side of the couch. He sighed and sagged back in his chair. He didn't have a prayer of getting that far. Not with the buzz filling his head or the weakness in his legs. His coordination was shot. He just wished a benefit of his condition included a lapse in memory.

"I want to talk to you while you're still reasonably sober," Rebecca said, settling down on the edge of the sofa closest to him.

"Terrific. Pour me another drink—then I'll listen."

"I'm your friend, so no, I'm not going to pour you anything else. You're drunk enough. In the morning, you're going to wish you were never born."

He set the glass on the floor next to him. "I already wish I hadn't been born. Nothing's going to change that."

"Elizabeth needs time."

"What the hell are you talking about?"

"This isn't about you, Travis. This leaving. She needs some time to find her way. You've got to give her that." She spoke slowly and patiently, as if dealing with a slow-witted child. He thought about protesting, but he didn't think he could get the words out. His tongue was getting thicker by the minute, and who had started spinning the room?

He leaned back in the chair and closed his eyes. That was better. "Of course it's about me," he said carefully. "I'm the one she left."

"Fool." She said the word affectionately. He thought about taking offense, but he didn't have the energy. "You're her knight in shining armor. Unfortunately, your timing couldn't have been worse."

That comment was almost worth opening his eyes for— almost. "That's me. A knight. Show me the dragon. I'll slay it. Maybe it'll slay me instead. That would be better."

"Travis."

He held up his hand, then let it drop to his side. When had his arm gotten so heavy? "Sorry. Didn't mean to get maud . . . maud . . ." What was that word?

"Maudlin?" she offered.

"Yeah. That. So my timing stinks. Nah. It's not that. It's me. I tried. Not supposed to try. Forgot who I was." He rubbed his hand over his face, then grimaced as he felt two days' worth of stubble. He hadn't shaved that morning. Hadn't done anything except drink more Scotch and try to forget. He couldn't forget; he made a lousy drunk.

"You've got it all wrong," Rebecca said, sounding slightly impatient.

"I know." He risked opening his eyes. Rebecca was glaring at him. He closed his lids again to shut her out. "It was all pretty pointless from the beginning. Who was I trying to kid? She figured it out. That I couldn't do it. Not the right type. Who'd want me for her kid's father?"

"I would."

Travis looked at her. "You're just saying that because I'm your friend and you have to be nice to me." He got so caught up in being pleased that he'd completed such a long sentence that he almost forgot what they were talking about.

Rebecca stood up and moved over until she was standing in front of him, looking down. Fire flashed in her eyes. She planted her hands on her hips, her chest heaved. She wasn't built like Elizabeth. Rebecca's curves were subtle. He'd never cared one way or the other because he'd never really been attracted to her. It didn't mean anything. But he still admired her.

"You are so beautiful," he said wistfully, wishing that staring at her got him aroused. He only had to think about Elizabeth and he was ready to make love, but Rebecca left him with a warm fuzzy feeling and zero passion. The great cosmic joke.

Rebecca drew in a deep breath, then let out a laugh and sank to the floor. She knelt between his legs and rested her hands on his thighs. "You need your butt kicked."

"That's pretty harsh." He raised his eyebrows, or thought he did. His face was getting numb.

"You're thinking about yourself, Travis, and none of this is about you at all. It's about Elizabeth. She's got the problem, not you. Finally you've figured out that you can make a relationship work. I think that's terrific. You're right, you do love her, and she left you." Her big eyes grew sad as they met his own. "Find it in your heart to forgive her. She's running because she's afraid. That's good. That means she cares back."

He covered Rebecca's hands and squeezed tight. "If it's so good, why does it feel so bad?"

"Because she hurt you. But hang in there. Give her time to understand what she's given up. She'll come around. I promise."

His face was completely numb, his tongue thick, his legs heavy beyond movement. None of it helped. He could still feel the sharp stabs of pain in his chest and gut.

"I told her I loved her," he said, softly. He had to look away from his friend's compassionate gaze. "I promised her the world, and she left anyway."

"Give her time."

"Why? Nothing will change." He forced his thick lips into a smile. "I can't blame her for leaving me. Look at what Sam did to her. Look at who I am. There's no way she's going to get past my reputation. I'm the last man on earth she'd ever want. That's why I'm drinking, Rebecca. So I can forget the truth."

She touched her cool hand to his cheek. "Is it helping?"

"No. I played the game and I lost." He shrugged. "I gave her everything I had and it wasn't enough. Let it go, honey. I'm going to try my damnedest to do just that."

Seven days later it didn't hurt any less and he still hadn't learned to forget. He'd given up the alcohol by Sunday morning. Mostly because he had a job to do and responsibilities he couldn't hide from. Also, because he was a lousy drunk. Even Rebecca had told him that when he'd awakened with the mother of all hangovers. He knew he had to get on with his life. Elizabeth had chosen not to be a part of that. Fine. He didn't understand her reasoning, but he respected her right to make that choice. But there was still the matter of a six-year-old girl.

He stood in front of Elizabeth's front door for several minutes before gathering the courage to knock. He heard voices from inside, then the sound of little footsteps hurrying down the hall.

"I want to get it," Mandy said. She opened the door and stared at him. "Travis!"

She flung herself at him. He caught her in his arms and pulled her hard against his chest. Her thin legs came up around his waist.

"Hi, Mandy," he said, and was surprised his voice sounded so gruff.

She buried her face in his neck and sniffed, then glared up at him. "You've been gone, Travis. You said you'd come to my soccer game, but you didn't. Mommy said you were working." Her pale blond eyebrows drew together mutinously. "You promised me you'd come. Why weren't you there?"

Because I couldn't face seeing your mother, he thought, then kissed her forehead and set her on the ground. His relationship with Mandy was important to both of them, regardless of what was going on between him and Elizabeth. He squatted down beside the little girl. "I'm sorry," he said, holding her shoulders. "You're right. I *did* promise. I'll be there for the next one, and all the ones after that. I might have to leave early if I'm working, but nothing else will keep me away. Okay?"

Mandy thought for a moment, then grinned. "Okay. I'm going to get a goal next time. You watch!"

Something small and brown scurried out the front door. Mandy shrieked. Travis leaned down and grabbed the fur ball by the scruff of its neck and raised the animal up to eye level. It was a small dog of undetermined breed. Big brown eyes stared into his face; then the puppy barked excitedly and licked his nose.

Mandy laughed. "That's Buster. He's our new dog. We got him at the pound. He sleeps in my bed and everything."

Travis smiled and handed her the puppy. Mandy held him carefully. Buster wiggled in her embrace, quivering with excitement. Apparently the dog had already figured out where his loyalties lay.

Travis heard a soft sound and looked up. Elizabeth stood in the center of her small living room. The band around his chest tightened as he looked at her familiar heart-shaped face.

Her mouth was pulled straight, as if she were in pain, and her eyes were dark with emotion. Her pale color, the shadows and lines of exhaustion, told him that she'd been suffering as much as he. Because he was a fool where she was concerned, he was pleased with the obvious signs of her distress. He had meant something to her.

His happiness faded as quickly as it had arrived. The operative word about her feelings was *had*. Whatever affection she'd maintained for him hadn't been enough to keep her in his house or his bed. It hadn't been enough to allow her to believe in him.

"Hello, Travis," she said, her voice soft and husky.

He rose to his feet. God, he loved how she sounded. Even now, just looking at her and hearing her, his whole body went on alert. From the ten or so feet that separated them, he could smell the scent of her perfume. She wore a cream sweater over jeans. Her hair was pulled back in a braid. He supposed there were men who wouldn't think her beautiful, but to him she was perfection itself.

"Elizabeth."

He was afraid she would see how she affected him so he stuck his hands into his leather jacket pockets. The business-size envelope there crackled as he touched it. His ace in the hole. Later, he told himself. Patience was the key.

Elizabeth studied him, her gaze drifting over his face, to his chest and lower. He saw the slight blush that appeared on her cheeks. He got to her. Good. Please God, let it be enough.

"Mandy, why don't you take Buster into the backyard and play?"

Mandy nuzzled her pet and giggled. "Okay." She turned away, then spun back. "Travis, there's a play at my school. I'm going to be broccoli and an Indian. Please come."

He tore his gaze away from her mother. "I wouldn't miss it for anything. Give me a kiss before you go."

She raised her face. Her lips were pursed. He bent down and brushed them with his own. She gave him a sweet smile that warmed him to the bottom of his soul, then ran through the living room and into the hall.

"Would you like to come in?" Elizabeth asked, moving to the door and drawing it back.

"Sure. For a minute. I still have some things to take care of today." He stepped inside and glanced around the small living room. She'd hung the miniblinds at the front windows. A lace shawl was draped over one of the ugly gold couches. "This is nice."

She closed the door and wrinkled her nose. "No. It's still small and dark, but it's ours. We're making it a home." She cleared her throat. "How have you been?"

He could have made it easy for her, but he was hurting too much inside. She'd gone and left him, and then had made a home for herself and her daughter. He'd been abandoned, cast aside without a second thought. "How do you think?"

She folded her arms over her chest, then straightened them. "I'm sorry," she said.

His hands closed into fists, but his jacket hid his reaction from view. "Are you? Why don't I think so? If you were sorry, you wouldn't have walked out of my life."

"I meant to call." She stared at the carpet.

"So you're a liar as well as a coward."

Her head shot up. Anger burned in her eyes. "How dare you say that to me?"

"If the shoe fits, lady. You're the one who snuck out of my house like some damn thief. You didn't even have the courage to say goodbye in person. I thought that we meant something to each other. I guess I was wrong." He stopped talking because it was starting to hurt too much. The act of breathing caused his chest to ache. Deep inside, around his heart, the hole deepened as pieces of his soul slipped away.

"You have no right to judge me," she said, leaning forward toward him. "No right at all."

"The hell I don't. What about all your concerns about Mandy? I'm more than willing to have her in my life. *You're* the one keeping her away from me."

"I—" Her anger fled as quickly as it had flared. Her shoulders slumped. "You're right. About everything. I'm sorry, Travis."

He wanted to go to her and hold her tight. He wanted to fight her battles and conquer her demons. The only flaw with the plan was the fact that he was her biggest problem.

"I didn't want to make love to you that day, but I couldn't help myself. You make me feel . . ." She shook her head sadly. "I can't explain it. You make me want things that I know I can't have. I can't do what you need me to do. I can't be that woman. I can't trust again."

"You mean you won't."

Their eyes met. Her pure brown irises shone with tears. "I won't," she agreed. "I wish I was stronger. You are a wonderful man. Strong, sensitive, caring, funny. Far too good-looking for your own good, or my peace of mind."

She was ripping him apart inside. He didn't know how much longer he could stand this. "You forgot about being dynamite in bed," he said, hoping the joke would make them both feel better. It didn't help him, and judging by the tears on Elizabeth's cheeks, she didn't find it all that funny.

"That, too," she whispered. She reached up and brushed away the tears. "That's why I ran. Because it was too wonderful. I couldn't bear to believe and then have it turn out to be another mistake."

He'd expected to be sad, even disappointed. He hadn't thought he would feel the cold ice of rage. He pulled his hands out of his jacket pockets and clenched them into tight fists. He'd lost it all—they'd both lost everything—because she was afraid.

"I thought you were stronger," he said, fighting the urge to roar with anger. "My mistake."

She flinched as if he'd slapped her.

Before she could say anything he spoke again. "I don't claim to understand what you're thinking. But there are more than two people involved here. I have a commitment to Mandy, and I intend to honor it. Are you going to give me trouble with that?"

She mutely shook her head.

"Good. Then I'll be at her school play and her soccer games and anything else she wants me at."

"Thank you."

"Don't thank me. I'm not doing it for you. I'm doing it for Mandy and for myself."

There was a loose strand of hair floating around her face. He wanted to touch that strand, to brush it back and tuck it behind her ear. His rage disappeared as quickly as it had come. He wanted to stroke the smooth skin of her face and neck. His fingers ached to touch her. His body rebelled at being left unsatisfied. If it wasn't for Mandy, he would gladly go the rest of his life and never see Elizabeth Abbott again. She was going to be the death of him.

He reached in his jacket pocket for his keys. His fingers touched the envelope again. He pulled it out and looked at it.

"I thought there might still be a chance," he said. "But I see Rebecca was right."

"What did she say?"

"That this wasn't about me at all. This is your problem and there's nothing I can do to help you get over it." He looked at her then, studying the shape of her face, the smooth skin, the tears. He'd finally fallen in love. Unfortunately it was with the one woman who would never trust him enough to love him back. A perfect ending to a Haynes family story.

He handed her the envelope. "It's not worth the paper it's printed on, but what the hell. It'll give you a laugh. Years from now you can use it to remember me by. That crazy Haynes brother who was stupid enough to fall in love."

"Travis!"

She raised her hand toward him. He gave her the envelope, being careful not to touch her. It would be too easy to get lost in her for the night. Just one last time. However he knew if he did it again, he would never find his way back. This time he would stay lost.

She opened the envelope. He told himself to leave, but he couldn't help standing there watching. Just in case it got ugly, he reached back and gripped the door handle.

She pulled out the three sheets of paper and studied them. A slight frown drew her delicate eyebrows together. "I don't understand."

He opened the door and stepped onto the porch. "It's a report from a private investigator," he said and shrugged. "I paid to have myself investigated. Just so you'd know I have nothing to hide. His number is in there, along with his license information. The guy's legitimate. Check it out if you don't believe me."

"But why would you do this?"

"I wanted you to know I wasn't like Sam. I didn't realize it was already too late to change your mind."

The harvest play was held in the school auditorium. The seats weren't all that comfortable, but Elizabeth knew her restlessness was due to more than the hard wooden chair. Travis had promised to come and see Mandy in her acting debut. She, along with the other first-graders, had small parts in the school production.

Elizabeth had draped a sweater over the seat next to her on the outside left aisle. Her heart thundered in her chest. She prayed Travis would show up and not disappoint her daughter. With equal fervency, she prayed he *did* forget the date, time or location of the play. She couldn't face him again. Nothing made sense anymore, but she was getting used to living in a state of confusion.

Leaving Travis had felt horrible, but she'd known it was the right thing to do. What choice did she have? It was either leave with some small portion of her heart intact, or risk making the same mistake again. She'd judged so badly with Sam, how could she risk doing it all over again? It wasn't just about her, either. What about Mandy's feelings? She'd already lost one father. She would really be hurt to lose Travis.

But he was still seeing her daughter, a little voice in her head whispered. She tried to ignore the sound, much as she ignored her sweating palms and trembling legs. Good thing she was sitting down, she thought, trying to find the humor in the situation and failing badly.

She shifted on the hard seat, and smoothed her narrow wool skirt. The autumn weather had taken a cool turn. She'd bought several sweaters and a few skirts and trousers in a nearby town. Rebecca had accompanied her on the shopping trip. Try as she might, Elizabeth hadn't been able to gather the courage to ask her friend about Travis. She supposed her reticence was part embarrassment, part shame. If Rebecca had given Travis advice, then she knew the entire story. Elizabeth had wanted to say that it wasn't her fault, but she knew it was. She was the one who didn't have the courage to try. She sighed. No one understood what it was like to wake up one morning and find out her entire life was a lie. Okay, she should get over it, but not just yet.

The crowd of excited parents continued to file into the rapidly filling auditorium. Elizabeth looked over her shoulder, scanning for a familiar face. She nibbled on her bottom lip. What if he showed up? What if he didn't?

At last she spotted Travis threading his way through the other adults. She stood up so that he could see where she was sitting, then quickly sat back down. What if he didn't want to sit next to her?

She hunched down and stared fixedly at the stage. He'd already told her it was a lost cause. She still remembered the words as clearly as if he'd just spoken them. He'd been standing in her living room, handing her the detective's report.

Why had he done it? Why had he paid to have himself investigated? She'd called the man, then the state licensing board. Everything had checked out. Travis had no secrets in his past. She appreciated the gesture, but it didn't change anything.

"Are you saving that seat for someone?" a man asked.

She recognized the voice before she looked up and met his gaze. He wore his khaki uniform, with the Stetson she loved so much. The brim hid his eyes from view, but she could see his trimmed mustache, and the straight line of his mouth. He wasn't smiling. Why was she surprised?

"For you," she said, and moved the sweater.

He settled next to her. His arm brushed hers on the armrest. She started to move, then left her arm in place. If he didn't like them touching then he could be the one to shift in his seat.

Brave words, she told herself. They were in the middle of a crowd. Nothing was going to happen.

"You look very nice today," he said.

She glanced down at her new skirt and sweater, then smiled and looked at him. "Thank you."

Her smile faded when he removed his hat and she saw his eyes. Nothing flared to life in his brown irises. No emotion darkened the volatile color, no quick grin curved his lips. She was looking into the face of a stranger.

And then she knew the truth. He hadn't been lying when he'd said it was all a lost cause. Whatever feelings he'd felt for her had been locked away in a place she could never reach.

The room darkened and the first students appeared on the stage. There was no time for conversation. Elizabeth blinked several times and knew that it didn't matter. She'd turned her back on his offer of love, she'd taken the detective's report and had never called to discuss it with Travis. He'd gotten her message loud and clear. He knew she wasn't interested, so he was shutting her out. She'd gotten exactly what she'd asked for. Everything was working out perfectly.

Chapter Sixteen

"What on earth did you expect?" Rebecca asked that night after dinner at Elizabeth's house.

Elizabeth shrugged. She cocked her head toward the living room. Mandy was watching one of her favorite cartoon videos. "I didn't expect him to ignore me like that."

"You tell the guy to take a flying leap, and now you're surprised that he's not all over you?"

Elizabeth took the chair opposite her friend. She placed her coffee mug in front of her. "No one ever mentioned the words *flying leap.*"

Rebecca sighed. "I saw him the next day, Elizabeth. He was in bad shape. You walked out on him without a word. In my book, that qualified as pretty cruel behavior."

Elizabeth stared at the table. She could feel the heated blush on her cheeks. "It was awful. I'm so sorry I did that. Travis is a great guy and he deserves better."

"I'm not the one you should be telling this to."

"I know that, too." She risked glancing up. "What am I going to do?"

"What do you want from all this?"

That was easy. She wanted him to sweep her off her feet and make mad, passionate love to her. She wanted to spend the night lost in his arms. She wanted him to promise to love her forever, then hold her tight and never let her go.

Her eyes began to burn. He'd already done that and more. She'd rewarded him by throwing it all in his face. But she couldn't risk another mistake.

"I don't know." She saw Rebecca's wide mouth twist with impatience. "Go ahead and yell at me, but you don't know what it's like. You haven't made the same mistakes I have."

"I've made others." Rebecca leaned back in her chair and tucked her long curling black hair behind her ears. "I've made plenty of mistakes. One thing they've all taught me is that the way to learn from them is to get on with your life. Hiding out accomplishes nothing."

"Is that what you think I'm doing?" Elizabeth demanded.

Her friend looked at her steadily. "Yes, I do."

"You don't know what it was like."

"You're right. I don't. So what? It's over, Elizabeth. Travis isn't Sam. You're losing a good man because you're terrified of making the same mistake again. Here's a news flash. Everyone makes mistakes. And everyone gets to deal with making at least one huge one. Forgive yourself and get on with your life."

"You make it sound so easy."

"You make it sound so hard. It doesn't have to be."

Elizabeth sipped from her coffee. After the play Travis had stayed long enough to congratulate Mandy and to warn the girl he wouldn't be able to stay for the entire soccer game the following Saturday. Elizabeth had offered to bring her home instead. They'd made the arrangements, then had parted. It had been so civilized, she'd wanted to scream. She didn't want calm, rational conversation with Travis. She wanted the passion.

"It's difficult to give up hiding once you've learned how," she said quietly.

"I know. But you have to try." Rebecca leaned across the table and squeezed her hand. "If you don't forgive yourself and get on with what's important, you'll have paid the highest price of all."

Elizabeth sighed. "I'll have lost Travis."

"Worse. You'll have lost yourself."

Elizabeth stood in the silence of her small house. It was lunchtime and Mandy was still at school. Buster was asleep on his bed in the corner of her daughter's room.

Normally, being alone was a pleasure. She reveled in the quiet, knowing it would soon explode into childish laughter, the sounds of the television and Buster's high-pitched barking. Today she found no peace.

The pain in her heart hadn't gone away. If anything, it had grown, along with her sense of failure. She gripped her purse tightly in her hands and stared at the living room. When she'd left Sam, she'd been so sure she'd made the right decision. She'd protected herself and her child and had sworn to never make that kind of mistake again. She'd promised herself never to be emotionally vulnerable to love.

Had that been the lesson Sam's deception should have taught her?

She walked into the kitchen and studied the calendar pinned to the wall. Mandy had marked all her soccer games. Tomorrow Travis would arrive early and take the girl to breakfast. They would leave, laughing with each other. Elizabeth knew she would stand at the window and watch Travis smile at her daughter. She would feel the loss when he touched her easily, perhaps even carrying her piggyback-style to the car. She envied her daughter's relationship with Travis. Elizabeth shook her head and wondered when she'd become a fool.

Next to the calendar was a bulletin board. Several of Mandy's class projects had been pinned up, as had a postcard from Elizabeth's parents. They were back from their trip. They'd called a couple of weeks ago to tell her all about the Orient. Elizabeth had listened politely and had avoided questions about her personal life. She'd never had the courage to tell them the truth about Sam. Her parents sensed something was wrong, but they wouldn't ask.

She couldn't tell them the truth. They wouldn't understand how she could have been so stupid. Elizabeth tossed her purse on the small table and balled up her fists. Damn him. She was tired of living only half her life.

It wasn't an emotional connection that kept her tied to the past. She knew that much. Her feelings for Sam had faded over the years. Looking back with the perfect vision of hindsight, she could see that she'd never loved him. He'd charmed her, showing up in her life just as she was ready to spread her wings.

So why couldn't she let go? She glanced down at her hands and slowly straightened them. Her fingers were bare. For over six years she'd worn a wedding band. She'd thought she was married. Mrs. Sam Proctor. It had all been a lie. That's what she couldn't let go. Being married had been part of her identity. It's as if she'd lost part of herself when she'd learned the truth. Her world had exploded, nothing had been as it seemed. She'd been left empty and broken, feeling as if she'd spent her whole life being a fool.

And lonely, she thought suddenly. Very, very lonely. Sam had kept her isolated from the world. He hadn't wanted her to work or have friends. Now she knew it was his way of making sure he controlled the game. She'd finally defied him and started working. That had given her a measure of independence, but hadn't taken away the feelings of isolation. She'd spent her entire marriage being on her own.

She stepped closer to the bulletin board and touched one of Mandy's drawings. It was a duplicate of the one she'd done for Travis. Three stick figures stood in front of a white house. Her daughter had even drawn in a puppy. The sight of the brightly colored picture made her smile. Mandy was going to be all right. Even as her world had been falling apart, Elizabeth had made sure she'd been there for her daughter. Her smile turned wry. Of course she'd had six years practice of being a single parent. With Sam gone so much, most of the responsibility had fallen on her shoulders. She knew she was capable of making it all work out.

So what was she trying to prove?

The thought came out of nowhere and stunned her. What *was* she trying to prove? That she was strong enough to make it on her own? She knew that already. That she had to punish herself for making a mistake? Maybe. She should have known. She should have seen the clues. She should—

"Stop!" she said out loud. "Just stop."

She hadn't known. She hadn't thought to look for clues. Did that make her a bad person? Was Rebecca right? Did everyone get one free big mistake? Was it time to let the whole thing go?

Her gaze drifted from Mandy's picture to the postcard her parents had sent. The feeling of loneliness swept over her again. She realized how much she hated hiding from them, hiding from the world. She'd been so worried about what everyone would think that she'd allowed the fear to rule her life. She'd left herself with no support to get her through the rough times.

Without giving herself time to talk herself out of it, she walked to the phone and picked up the receiver. She dialed from memory.

"Hello?"

"Hi, Mom. It's me."

Her mother laughed with delight. "Your father and I have missed you, honey," the older woman said. "How have you been?"

Elizabeth felt the hot tears flood her eyes and flow down her cheeks. She leaned against the wall and twisted the cord in her fingers. "Not that great, Mom. I have some things to tell you. About Sam. I don't know how to say this. I'm so sorry. I never meant to disappoint you. It turns out—"

"Just a minute, dear. Before you say another word, you don't have to apologize for anything to either me or your father. We love you, no matter what. Do you want us to fly out and be with you? We could get a flight today."

Elizabeth sank into a kitchen chair and smiled through her tears. "No. You don't have to. Mandy and I are okay. But thanks for offering." She drew in a deep breath to tell the rest of her story and realized she'd spoken the truth. She was okay. Probably for the first time in years.

"You're not eating," Mandy said, waving her fork at Travis's full plate. "Don't you like the pancakes?"

"I'm just not hungry." He winked at the little girl. "You sure wanted your breakfast, though."

Mandy looked down at her half-eaten meal. A thin pancake wrapped around a sausage was all that was left of everything she'd ordered. "I was hungry. I went to bed early, so I could sleep a lot. Mommy says I need to be rested to do good at my game. I'm going to score a goal."

"I bet you are."

She chatted about school and all her friends. He studied her small face, loving the way her eyes lighted up with her stories. Her hair was pulled into two pigtails. A red ribbon, matching her red-and-white soccer uniform, had been tied on each end. Her fresh-scrubbed face looked innocent and trusting.

He sipped from his coffee cup and tried to control the emotions swelling up inside of him. He adored this little girl. He missed the sound of her laughter and her cartoons, the endless questions, the way she crawled into his lap and demanded a story. He missed being loved by her.

He knew she still cared about him. They had planned several activities together over the next few weeks, but it wasn't the same as living with her. Or her mother.

Damn, he didn't want to think about Elizabeth. But he couldn't help himself. Staring at Mandy, knowing most of her features came from her father, he still saw traces of the woman he loved in her face. Loving and losing Mandy had broken his heart. Loving and losing Elizabeth was killing him.

The hell of it was he didn't know what to do. He couldn't think of any more words to convince her. He knew Rebecca had been right in telling him this was Elizabeth's problem and not his. Knowing the truth didn't stop him from wanting to fix everything. He couldn't, though. No one would tell him exactly what to fix. Louise preached patience and cooked his favorite meals. Neither made him forget. He'd tried words, he'd tried making love, he'd even tried giving Elizabeth that damned detective's report. Nothing had worked, and he'd run out of ideas.

"Mommy called Grandma yesterday," Mandy said, then nibbled on her sausage. "She told me."

"That's nice," he said, then frowned. Hadn't Elizabeth mentioned she didn't talk to her parents much because she was ashamed? She hadn't even told them the truth about Sam. A flicker of hope sparked in his chest, but he doused it with cold, wet reality. Calling her parents didn't mean anything.

"They're coming to visit us at the end of the month. Grandma's going to take me out for Halloween."

"Are you sure?" he asked.

Mandy nodded vigorously, her blond pigtails bouncing against her shoulders. "I talked to her last night. I'm going to be a fairy princess."

A phone call was one thing, a visit quite another. If they were coming out, Elizabeth would have to tell them the truth. Maybe she already had.

Hope threatened again. Travis did his best to ignore it. So what? They were her parents. She still hadn't contacted him in any way. This morning, when he'd driven up to get Mandy, she'd sent the girl outside without giving him more than a brief, impersonal wave.

Mandy put her fork down and looked at him. Something in her big blue eyes made him give her his full attention. "What's wrong?" he asked.

"Are you and Mommy fighting?"

He didn't have an answer for that one. They weren't angry at each other, but they sure weren't getting along. "Why do you ask?"

Mandy shrugged. "Mommy was crying last night. I heard her after I went to bed."

His gut clenched into a hard knot. Rather than give in to the impulse to jump up and find Elizabeth, he gripped the table. It wasn't his fault she was crying. If she wanted his comfort, she knew where to find him. He'd already told her he loved her. What else was there to say?

"We're not fighting," he told the little girl. Although he wasn't sure he hadn't made her cry.

Mandy seemed relieved. He changed the subject. "I told you I can't stay for the whole game," he reminded her. "I have to work this afternoon."

"I know," she said, nodding. "I'll score my goal early, okay?"

He leaned across the table and ruffled her bangs. "You do that, kid."

They left the restaurant and he drove them to the park. Most of the parents and children were already there. Mandy ran off to join her team. Travis walked to the edge of the field and stared at the players. He didn't want to look around and see Elizabeth. If there was any lingering trace of her tears, he would feel obligated to ask what was wrong. Maybe it was weak of him, but he couldn't face her shutting him down again. He needed a little time to let the wounds heal.

Apparently she didn't share his feelings. He'd barely been there a minute when he inhaled the soft scent of a familiar perfume. His body reacted instantly. His groin flooded with heat and his chest tightened.

"Hi, Travis."

"Elizabeth." He forced himself to look at her. She wore an oversize blue sweater over jeans. Her hair was loose and shiny in the autumn morning. All traces of tears were long gone. Her brown eyes glowed with something, but it wasn't pain or unhappiness. He wanted to believe it had something to do with him, or at the very least, was the result of talking to her parents, but his luck wasn't that good. He glanced around the field. There were several single men here. Any one of them could have put that special light in her eyes.

He wanted to ask about her parents and what had prompted her to call. He wanted to tell her how much he loved her and beg her to come back to him. He wanted to hold her in his arms until he convinced her that they belonged together. He did none of those things. He couldn't move, couldn't breathe, couldn't do anything but endure the heartache of knowing what could have been.

"Mandy mentioned you'll be leaving early," she said.

"Yes. Can you take her home?"

"Of course." Her gaze met and held his own. He tried to read her emotions, but he couldn't. Just as well, he thought, turning away. What was there to see?

"I've got to go," he said abruptly and walked away.

"Travis?"

He kept on going. If he moved fast enough, maybe the pain wouldn't be able to catch up with him.

Elizabeth stared at Travis's retreating back. The hurt and hunger in his eyes had left her with tangible wounds. She could feel the ache pouring through her body. Every part of her screamed at her to take a chance. One small risk. He wasn't Sam. He wasn't lying about anything in his life. He'd told her the unvarnished truth about himself, his past and his family. She'd seen his shame when he'd talked about his father. Travis had even risked telling her he loved her. He had no secrets left.

She took a step after him, then paused. Could she risk it? What about the mistakes she'd made?

"Take a chance."

Elizabeth spun on her heel and found Rebecca standing behind her. "What are you doing here?" she asked.

"One of the kids from the children's home is playing. I thought I'd come watch and show support." Rebecca stared at her. "Elizabeth, this may be your last opportunity. Don't be a fool."

"I can't." Elizabeth closed her eyes. "I can't risk—" Her eyes flew open. She clasped her hand over her mouth, then dropped her arm to her side. "I can't risk losing him, can I? What have I been thinking? Travis Haynes is the best thing that ever happened to me."

Rebecca grinned. "Finally. He went that away." She raised one finger and pointed.

Elizabeth hurried off in that direction. She scanned the growing crowd but there was no tall man in a Stetson anywhere. She stopped and looked toward the parking lot. Her heart sank. The sheriff's car was gone. Travis had left.

Disappointment dragged at her. Now what? Should she wait until he came off his shift? She shook her head. No, she couldn't wait another minute. They'd both suffered for too long.

She ran to a phone on the edge of the park. Dialing quickly, she shifted her weight from foot to foot. Finally the phone rang.

"Sheriff's Office."

It wasn't Travis, but the voice was familiar. "Kyle?"

"Yes."

"Hi, it's Elizabeth Abbott. I'm looking for Travis. Is he around?"

There was a pause. She bit her lower lip. Maybe Travis had told his brother about her behavior. If so, Kyle might not want to help her. Oh, but he had to.

"He's subbing for one of the deputies. He's out on patrol, giving out tickets."

"Oh, then I'll never find him."

"I don't know about that. Is this good news?"

She clutched the metal cord. "Very good news, Kyle. The best news."

"He's been walking around here like a kicked dog."

"I know. I'm sorry about that."

"He deserves something wonderful, Elizabeth." Kyle's voice got husky. "He's a good man."

"I know. Believe me, I know. I need to find him before it's too late."

There was a pause; then Kyle said, "Do you remember where he stopped you that first day?"

"Yes."

"He always parks in the same place. The locals know to avoid him. If you go now you'll be able to find him."

She thought for a second. "I have to wait until the soccer game is over. I can't leave Mandy alone."

"I'll be by in five minutes to get her."

"You'd do that for me?"

"I'm doing it for Travis."

She had to fight against the tears burning in her eyes. To think she might have lost the man she loved because of her own fears. "Thank you, Kyle. I really appreciate this."

"Yeah, well, don't make me regret it."

"I won't. I just hope it's not too late. By."

"Elizabeth?"

"Yes?"

"It's not too late."

She hung up and prayed he was right. She started toward the parking lot. At the sight of her car, she paused. Travis knew her car. She didn't want to give him time to get away from her or start to think up reasons why it wouldn't work. Not now. She glanced around the playing field and saw one of the coach's wives standing close to her. She rushed over.

"Mary, can I borrow your car for a few minutes?"

The young woman looked startled. "Didn't you bring your car?"

"Yes, but—oh, it's difficult to explain. I need to find someone and I don't want him to know it's me until it's too late and please, I promise I'll be careful."

Mary looked at her for several seconds, then grinned. "Sounds like man trouble to me."

"It is."

The blonde reached into her jeans pocket and pulled out a set of keys. "It's the red station wagon right there."

Impulsively, Elizabeth gave the other woman a hug. "Thanks. I'll be right back."

"Take your time."

She ran to the car, slid inside, fastened her seat belt, then started the engine. After drawing in a deep breath for courage, she pulled out of the parking lot and turned onto the main road.

Travis stared morosely down the highway. Even for a Saturday morning, the traffic was light. He'd only seen half a dozen cars and all of them had been going the speed limit. Not that he was in the mood to stop anyone.

He leaned his head back and groaned. Mandy was going to be upset that he'd left before her game had started. There was no way he could explain to the little girl that he hadn't had a choice in the matter. It had been too hard to stand there staring at Elizabeth and knowing he could never be a part of her life. Just seeing her had been difficult. How was he supposed to get through the torture of being her friend?

Friends. He swore. She might as well just shoot him in the back and get it over with.

He heard a car engine and straightened. A red station wagon barreled around the curve behind him and zoomed past onto the straightaway. Travis checked his radar and raised his eyebrows. Someone was going somewhere in a hurry.

He pulled out onto the highway and hit the gas. His patrol car was gaining, but slowly. He flipped on his blue light and accelerated, then frowned when he realized the driver in the red car was going faster than he'd thought. He stared ahead, but all he could see was the person wore a baseball cap. At last the driver glanced in the rearview mirror, saw him and turned off onto the shoulder of the road.

Travis parked behind the car and collected his ticket book and Stetson. He stepped out and walked over to the car. The window was already rolled down.

"You were going pretty fast there." He flipped open his ticket book, then glanced up at the driver. And about dropped his pen. "Elizabeth?"

"Hi." She jerked off the baseball cap and her brown hair tumbled over her shoulders. "I wondered if you'd see me."

"You were hard to miss, especially when you hit the straightaway doing eighty." He glanced at the unfamiliar car and frowned. "Why are you driving this?"

"That's not important." She opened the car door and got out. "I was speeding. Are you going to give me a ticket?"

He frowned. What kind of game was she playing? There was an odd flickering in her eyes, some suppressed emotion. Her mouth quivered, but he couldn't tell if she was upset or trying not to smile. None of this made sense.

"You *were* over the speed limit," he said.

"I know. Ask me for my story."

"What?"

"Travis." She planted her hands on her hips. "Isn't it a tradition here in Glenwood? If I tell you a story you haven't heard before, don't you have to let me go?"

He shoved the ticket book and pen into his back pocket, then folded his arms over his chest. He could feel his heart thumping. That damn hope flared to life again. This time he let it burn hot and bright. This time he dared to believe. But he wasn't going to ask. She was going to have to tell him.

"What's the story?" he asked cautiously, wondering if she was about to say something he wanted to hear, or if she would deliver the death blow.

The odd flickering in her beautiful brown eyes turned into something he could have sworn was caring. Her mouth curved up in a smile. When she leaned forward and placed her hands on his chest, it was all he could do not to pull her close.

"I love you," she said, then touched her lips to his.

Fire exploded through him. His mind echoed with the wonder of her words. He grabbed her arms and held her away from him. "What did you say?"

"Oh, Travis, I've been a fool. I was wrong to judge you by Sam's actions, and wrong to let the past destroy my future." She shook her head. "Our future. I could have lost you forever."

"Elizabeth." He breathed her name. "You would never have lost me. I have nowhere else to go. No one else to love."

"I love you."

He wrapped his arms around her waist and pulled her hard against his chest. He kissed her once, softly, savoring the reality of knowing they were at last together. Then he angled his head and thrust his tongue into her mouth. They met in a conflagration of sensation. When they came up for air, they were both breathing heavily.

"Does this mean I don't get a ticket?" she asked, and smiled.

He grinned in return. "It's a story I haven't heard before, so I guess not."

"Good. I would have been a little cranky on our wedding day if you had given me a ticket."

He stared at her.

Her smile faltered. "You do want to marry me, don't you? I mean I assumed that was the next logical step." She bit her lower lip and blushed. "Oh, Travis, we don't have to if you don't—"

He grabbed her hands and pulled them to his mouth. After kissing each palm, he stared into her eyes. "I love you, Elizabeth Abbott. Will you marry me?"

A single tear slipped down her cheek. "Yes."

"We can get married when your parents are here if you'd like." When he saw her confused frown, he kissed the tip of her nose. "Mandy told me. You'll be a beautiful bride, darlin'."

He bent his head toward her mouth again. The kiss quickly heated them both. He was thinking about which of their houses was closer when a burst from a siren made them jump apart.

Travis turned and glared at the patrol car rolling toward them. Kyle was driving, with a young girl bouncing at his side. When the car came to a stop, Mandy opened the front door and jumped out. Her smile about split her face in two and her blue eyes were shining.

"Mommy, Mommy, Uncle Kyle says you and Travis are getting married, and we're going to live happily ever after. Is that true?"

Elizabeth laughed and pulled her daughter close. "Uncle Kyle has a big mouth, but yes, it's true."

Kyle got out more slowly. "Sorry, Trav. I just thought the kid might want to know."

Travis pulled Elizabeth and Mandy into his embrace. "No problem, little brother. We are going to live happily ever after."

Mandy looked up at her mother. "Are you going to have a baby now?"

Elizabeth glanced at him. He swallowed hard. "Maybe," he said, not wanting to hope for too much.

"Yes," Elizabeth said firmly.

The joy in his heart doubled.

Kyle came forward and slapped him on the back. "Another Haynes son. You can name this one after me."

"Why a son?" Elizabeth asked.

Travis touched her cheek. "There hasn't been a daughter born to the family in four generations."

"I'd forgotten about that." Elizabeth looped her arm around his waist. "I just might surprise you all."

He held her close and felt the loving warmth of her body. "You already did, Elizabeth. You already did." She had been, he knew then, the best surprise of all.

*   *   *   *   *

Get Ready to be Swept Away by
Silhouette's Spring Collection

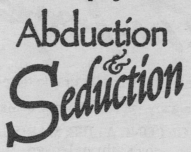

Abduction
&
Seduction

These passion-filled stories explore both the dangerous
desires of men and the seductive powers of women.
Written by three of our most celebrated authors, they are
sure to capture your hearts.

Diana Palmer
Brings us a spin-off of her Long, Tall Texans series

Joan Johnston
Crafts a beguiling Western romance

Rebecca Brandewyne
New York Times bestselling author
makes a smashing contemporary debut

Available in March at your favorite retail outlet.

Silhouette®

MONTANA™
Mavericks

Stories that capture living and loving beneath the Big Sky, where legends live on...and mystery lingers.

This January, the intrigue continues with

OUTLAW LOVERS
by Pat Warren

He was a wanted man. She was the beckoning angel who offered him a hideout. Now their budding passion has put them both in danger. And he'd do anything to protect her.

Don't miss a minute of the loving as the passion continues with:

WAY OF THE WOLF
by Rebecca Daniels (February)

THE LAW IS NO LADY
by Helen R. Myers (March)

FATHER FOUND
by Laurie Paige (April)
and many more!

Only from ▼ *Silhouette*® where passion lives.
™

MAV6

The new year brings readers a powerful new trilogy—

This Time Forever

by Andrea Edwards

In January, don't miss A RING AND A PROMISE (SE #932).

Just one look at feisty Chicago caterer Kate Mallory made rancher Jake MacNeill forget all about Montana. Could his lonesome-cowboy soul rest as love overcomes unfulfilled promises of the past?

THIS TIME, FOREVER—sometimes a love is so strong, nothing can stand in its way...not even time.

Look for the next installment, A ROSE AND A WEDDING VOW (SE #944), in March 1995. Read along as two *old* friends learn that love is worth taking a chance.

AEMINI-1

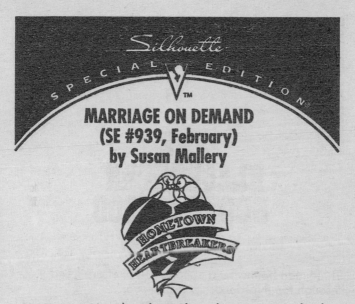

Silhouette
SPECIAL EDITION ™

MARRIAGE ON DEMAND
(SE #939, February)
by Susan Mallery

Hometown Heartbreakers: Those heart-stoppin' hunks
are rugged, ready and able to steal your heart....

Austin Lucas was as delicious as forbidden sin—that's
what the Glenwood womenfolk were saying. And
Rebecca Chambers couldn't deny how sexy he looked
in worn, tight jeans. But when their impulsive
encounter obliged them to get married, could their
passion lead to everlasting love?

Find out in *MARRIAGE ON DEMAND*, the next story
in Susan Mallery's *Hometown Heartbreakers* series,
coming to you in February...only from
Silhouette Special Edition.

Silhouette

SPECIAL EDITION™

THE BLACKTHORN BROTHERHOOD

by Diana Whitney

Three men bound by a childhood secret are freed through family, friendship...and love.

Watch for the first book in Diana's Whitney's compelling new miniseries:

THE ADVENTURER
Special Edition #934, January 1995

Devon Monroe had finally come home, home to a haunting memory that made him want to keep running. Home to a woman who made him want to stand still and stare into her eyes. For there was something about Jessica Newcomb that made him forget about his own past and wonder long and hard about hers....

Look for THE AVENGER coming in the fall of 1995.